TOO CLOSE TO CALL

TOO CLOSE TO CALL

Michael Kelsay

UNIVERSITY PRESS OF MISSISSIPPI / JACKSON

Too Close to Call is a work of fiction. Names, characters, incidents, and places are fictitious or are used fictitiously. The characters are products of the author's imagination and do not represent any actual persons.

"These Foolish Things." Words by Holt Marvell, music by Jack Strachey. © Copyright 1936 by Boosey & Co. Ltd. Copyright renewed. All rights for USA, Canada, and Newfoundland assigned to Bourne Co. New York. All rights reserved. International copyright secured.

A version of Chapter 1 appeared as a short story in the *Virginia Quarterly Review*.

www.upress.state.ms.us
Copyright © 2001 by Michael Kelsay
All rights reserved

Manufactured in the United States of America

03   02   01   4   3   2   1

Library of Congress Cataloging-in-Publication Data

Kelsay, Michael.
   Too close to call / Michael Kelsay.
      p. cm.
ISBN 1-57806-369-8 (alk. paper)
   1. Mayors—Election—Fiction. 2. Medical wastes—Incineration—Fiction. 3.
Inheritance and succession—Fiction. 4. Marijuana industry—Fiction. 5.
Politicians—Fiction. 6. Kentucky—Fiction. I. Title.
PS3611.E47 T6 2001
813'.6—dc21 2001022617

British Library Cataloging-in-Publication Data available

This book is for Mary,
lovely Lake Charles girl

For a gentleman, only lost causes should be attractive.
—Jorge Luis Borges

TOO CLOSE TO CALL

CHAPTER ONE

The images came, once again, unbidden and unwelcome, and for the umpteenth time I was treated to a preview of my own damn funeral—but by now I'd had just about enough of it. So I rolled over in bed and punched the pillow up under my chin, cleared my throat and coughed, hoping that bona fide movement and sound might interrupt the ghostly montage: the red hymnals, the threadbare Sunday suits, the long faces filing past. Since I'd seen it all before, and had even grown used to it over the last eight nights, it was now simply annoying, like a toilet running after everybody's gone to bed. You know? There's that endless commotion and you think, Christ!—too cozy under your own quilt—why doesn't *somebody* jiggle the handle?

I knew the church well. Dry Branch Baptist, just down KY 651, about four miles from our place. It stood like a keep at the mouth of Cane Valley, a deep and sudden hollow. Three generations of my family had been baptized, wed, and eulogized on its grounds. Baptisms were performed in the waist-deep water of the Left Fork and weddings beneath a crown of coffee trees by Swift Camp Creek. But funerals were indoors. There was a cemetery beyond the grove of coffee trees, but there weren't any Spooners buried there. We always took ours away with us.

My folks, Savannah and Virgil Spooner, had of course been resurrected for this, my final milestone. Mama gnashed her bridgework and made lurching, hysterical attempts to fling herself across

3

my blanched corpse. To no avail. But she did succeed in exploding flower arrangements and rending the dark, heavy bunting about my bier. Deddy, off to the side a bit and well beyond Mama's field of force, fidgeted with a toothpick and off and on worked it around a nettlesome crevice in the back of his mouth. Several times he wondered out loud if folks didn't usually have a snort or two at an event such as this. Being bereaved and all, and in need of comfort.

My little sister Drema, abandoned once again and robustly unforgiving of it, paced ferociously at the rear of the chapel, kicking at the worn floorboards with her heavy, scuffed motorcycle boots and cursing me under her breath. A damp V spread across her back. Her eyes were full of firecrackers and marching men, and I knew she'd swallowed a handful of pills. As she liked to say—and who was I to argue?—she *had* her reasons.

Willie, sweet and tolerant Wilhelmina Rains, my girl, was seated next to her mother, Juanita, and was folded in on herself like a morning glory at noon as she wept there in the first pew. Perhaps not quite aggrievedly enough to suit me, but really, how much would ever have been enough? Should she have chewed her fists and railed against God? I don't know that that would've helped at all. But her eyes, her neck, her short dark hair—she looked good in black, and I wanted to be there with her. *There* there.

On the periphery, a loose confederacy of well-meaning but generally worthless cousins and such moiled and roiled and here and there burst into stagey fits of stomping and keening. But that's just how my people are. It's honest, and they're born to it.

And me? I was nestled into the blindingly white, satiny folds of the coffin's padded lining, like a fat letter from home, full of bad news. I wore my only suit and a stranger's bow tie. And either somebody close smelt of lime and tannin, or I did. I was certainly deceased as far as the others were concerned, my body having finally succumbed to disuse and abuse, but my mind was alive and firing on all cylinders, racing headlong toward the solution to a problem all but unsolvable—namely, *How do I turn this thing around?*

Then the preacher Pons, redolent of brimstone and rosewater and soured milk, took the dais. He removed his dusty fedora and slowly ran his finger around the inside band, over and over. He surely didn't look happy about what he'd come to say. Finally, he set the hat aside and squared himself to his audience.

"Son of the Living God, eternally and mercifully shining forth in all Your majesty and grace," he began, voice all aquiver with the Spirit and his face tilted toward Heaven itself, "we are confabulated here this sweltry noon to bid fond farewell, Toomey Spooner. We ask You for Your guidance. We want to comfort the family and friends of the so presently departed, for they are in their time of need. We're here to worship in perfect, holy communion with You, our Lord and Savior, Jesus Christ the Nazarene, and to stand in utter awe of the vast Unknown Unknowable." A long silence ensued, deep and still as an abandoned mine, while the preacher Pons poured his awful gaze out across my unblinking mourners. "Not a thing we'll encounter in this vale of tears is vivider than death. Nothing. Ol' Death walks with us every day, silent, waiting, and near invisible. But when he comes—whoa, boy!—he swoops down on us in Technicolor. Brighter'n the noon sun, bigger'n the night sky, pricklier'n a bed of nails!" Preacher Pons let his audience absorb this. "And we've got some death here among us today, folks. Right here! And I suggest"—his voice dropped low, and he seemed to lock eyes with each and every worshipper as he hissed, "*you get on down here and take a damn look!*" Then he leveled his long, bony finger at me and it trembled in midair. The sickening aroma of carnations and roses and lilies roared up around me. "Now, what kind of man was Toomey? We can only guess, really, because we can never know what is truly in another man's heart. But we know he was decent enough after his own fashion. Isn't that right?" Murmurs of assent. "For instance, even though he never got around to it, we all know he intended to one day adopt a little muchacho through that Save the Children bunch. Isn't that right? I mean, we've all heard him *talk* about it, haven't we?" More assent, some chuckling. "Lessee," he said, finger to his temple, eyes to the floor, "well, as far as we know, he paid his taxes on time and obeyed the traffic laws, and I suppose that's worth something. What else?" Here Pons seemed to be calling for help, but there was none forthcoming. The old preacher stretched his arms across the lectern and his chin dropped to his chest while he pondered this question. Finally, he looked up. "Only other thing I can think of is the time he drove the school bus for three days when Rod Burnham was out with that attack of diverticulitis. *But*"—the preacher Pons ground his jaw now as if he were chewing on a strap of leather; he was ready to make a hard point, and we all knew his voice would now soar—"none of that's enough." More chewing. "What's our *most* precious gift?" Life! "And to what end do we *live* that life?" Life everlasting! "And what's required of you to enter the *King*dom of Heaven?" Faith! "And faith *leads* us unto what?" Good works! "That's right." And here Pons resumed a conversational tone. "But Toomey had no faith in anything, and was, *there*fore, incapable of good works. Can't have one without the other. Nossir, it can't be done." Pons paused to consult his notes before continuing, then pushed them aside. "Thus," he said, "Toomey Spooner misspent his life. Thus, he squandered his most precious gift—that which we give to others. Thus"—and the preacher Pons arched his spider-like eyebrows and hunched his shoulders, as if he couldn't help what had to be said. Or done. He whispered, "Thus," again, hoarsely, almost inaudibly, and bent to me on one knee, as if to pray. I heard what sounded like a match struck on its box, and then the preacher Pons stood up and back. In a minute, orange flickered over Willie's face, and heat and smoke were all I knew.

My thoughts had galloped away from me, it was true, but I wasn't dreaming. Not exactly, anyway. I couldn't have been, because I wasn't asleep. Oh, my bedroom lights were out and had been for an hour or more, but I was wide awake, the clock humming, the house settling, the oddly familiar tableau unfurling like a bad film, but jumpy and noisy, too, because of loose sprockets and ruined stock.

The fact was, control had by then been slipping from me for a while, maybe even a little at a time ever since I found Deddy, dead as driftwood, in the hoof-pocked paddock. I'd walked out back to throw scraps to the chickens and there he was, sprawled in the mud and manure, the left side of his face resting in the warm muck. I knew he was gone. Two roosters were having at one another in the knee-high corn, unaware of my father and me, frozen there in the midmorning sun. I don't know how long I stood there before I bent to him. When I put my hand to his cheek, I could feel that he was already cooling off. The coroner said he'd had a severe drug interaction and ruled the death accidental. Later, going over the coroner's report, I discovered that the drugs were opioids and alcohol. Or, more specifically—and I was working from personal knowledge here—Percodan and Maker's Mark. My old man had ODed. (As to the "accidental" aspect of the coroner's report, yes, I think that it was technically true. But at the same time meaningless. Virgil took Percodan. He drank Maker's Mark. On purpose.)

But back to that long, seminal night, and what all followed my ragtag funeral review:

Fully awake now, and feeling a little fatigued by it all, I rolled over onto my back, onto a cool spot under the covers. From there I could see lemony slices of moon through the Levolors, and maybe I did and maybe I didn't glimpse a shooting star out over Johnson Knob, a mountain, a shadowy pyramid against the night sky. But just in case I had seen a shooting star, I made a selfish wish. And for the next five or six minutes, with the otherworldly focus of the tightrope walker, I was fully conscious of every breath I drew. I lay so very still I might actually have been mistaken for dead had there been anyone about to peek in and check on my slumbers.

But it was no use.

I couldn't sleep for love nor money because the last eight nights had sorely tested my mettle, by which I mean my capacity for doing without. Sobriety had just wrecked what little peace of mind I had coming into the thing, and I hadn't of late felt much like me. Willie said it was the same thing as when she gave up chocolate—which she did about once a week—but I'd seen her slip instantly into sleep without so much as a Hershey's Kiss.

But, like one of those Russian dolls, there were reasons nested within reasons, and the thing was, I couldn't sleep because I'd been a little rash and perhaps overeager to please Willie Rains. And because I'd made a pair of promises to her which I later had bountiful occasion to rue and rue.

So, what poleaxing trauma had so staggered me eight nights prior? It won't sound like much, I know. But here it is: I decided that I probably ought to get a job. And, toward that end, that I probably ought to quit drinking, too.

The evening of all this big decision making began like any other, with no hint at all of life-changing events. Willie and I had driven over to Belfast for steaks at the Ponderosa. As always, the place was preposterously neat but nonetheless somehow unhygienic. Filmy. A pimply boy looming over a stack of coffee cups took our orders for medium-rare T-bones. He had bloodshot eyes that crackled and fizzed, and I sized him up quick as a young man who would one day do grievous harm to the people he loved. I mentioned it to Willie.

"How can Toomey Spooner just decide something like that? Huh? That's like framing the poor boy." She had a point, but so did I.

She led the way to a booth between an elderly farm couple and four richly scented Mann County matriarchs. I recognized them. Probably everybody did. One of them was a Missus Fitzgerald, from whose son Dickie I'd once taken—no, not taken, *saved*—a goat. It's enough to say he—Dickie—had mistreated her. The goat, that is. The Missus didn't let on she'd seen me and that was fine. She was at least vaguely aware of an animus between me and her boy. The farm couple was getting up to go.

From behind expansive dark sunglasses, Willie said, "God. Look at that, would you?" and tipped her pretty chin. I cut my eyes across the aisle to a very sorry family of five. Nope. I wasn't interested, not right then.

"What about them?" I asked. You see that sort of thing all the time and I wasn't real inclined to think about it. But something was up.

"Nothing." Willie pushed a frozen pat of oleo back and forth across a piece of melba toast with the tip of her butter knife, and I tipped an inch of bourbon from my dead brother Sewell's flask into my Coke. Willie casually scanned the tabletop—salt shaker, pepper mill, Lea & Perrins, Heinz 57—and then locked her eyes on mine.

"Guess what?" she said. She glanced at something over my shoulder before bringing her full attention to bear. "Drema called last night. This morning, really. Believe it must've been about four in the a.m."

I bit into a radish and considered this news. I felt tired and slack and—well, a little bored and flocked around. I sighed and said, "Oh no."

I had asked my little sister Drema, as if that would do any good, to please not bother Willie, especially not at all hours. Willie, for her part, was fond of Drema and had even encouraged the friendship, but Drema had never developed a sense of Willie and her rhythms. Drema's middle of the night distress calls Willie found intolerable.

"Oh yes. Quite drunk, of course, or something, and sounding a little bit lethal. Said she believed she was going to have to waste Odel. Her word, 'waste.' Wondered what *I* thought of the idea. She was actually calling to get my blessing."

Drema lived in Lexington with her girlfriend, Lorraine Dent, who also just happened to be Odel Dent's estranged wife. A calamitous role, at best. I'd checked into it, and Odel was a sincere and violent man with a string of arrests—passionate and effective battery seemed to be the theme—and at least one two-year stint in Eddyville to prove it. Lorraine's recent lesbianism didn't suit Odel even a little, and he was fixated on Lorraine's return to the Dent home and her *natural* role as object of his dull desire. Incredibly, Drema's attitude toward the situation was somewhat sporting, and she saw herself as at least Odel's equal in apocalyptic potential.

"Shit, Willie. I'm sorry." And I was. Plus pissed with my baby sister.

"Well, don't be. Drema's life is fascinating, really. I mean, how in the name of God does a girl get there is what I want to know." A teenager in a cowboy hat and plastic palomino skirt served our steaks and potatoes. My attention wandered back across the aisle.

Mom, Dad, a boy and a girl, maybe five and six, and Granny. Not a word passed among them, and the boy had his fat pink tongue pressed to the black Naugahyde bench. The old woman gazed fixedly at something half a continent away. Desert islands. My first instinct—not to look—had been correct.

"Y'all enjoy sour cream or chives with your baked potatoes?"

"Please."

"Besides," Willie went on, "it presents an opportunity to discuss something I've been a little shy of." My guts sprang to life and shot me a warning signal. Our waitress, all smiles, reappeared with a stainless steel carousel brimming with sour cream, bacon bits, and finely chopped green onions. This time I noticed she wore an impressive diamond engagement ring. Willie smiled and thanked her.

"Willie," I set my knife and fork down, "listen: it's not that I can't take it, 'cause you know as well as anybody, I can. But let's just enjoy these T-bones and take it up on the way home. Would that suit you?"

"We'll talk, though?"

"I can't hardly wait. Just not right now. OK?"

We finished our steaks and had coffee with our pie. Then we had cigarettes with our coffee. I tipped a little more bourbon into mine and blew big convoluting smoke rings that skimmed the Formica table. Willie slipped her ring finger through two or three. Then a little more bourbon with a second cup. We talked about the weather, the day's and week's events, and speculated on the lives of our fellow diners, what sorry defeats they must've endured. The usual. On the way out, I paid the bill and ferried a ten back to the table. Something about that big diamond ring, I don't know. It just didn't seem like enough of something. That, or too much of the wrong thing.

Out on the Foothills Parkway, I lit a fat joint and passed it over to Willie. I held the smoke deep until that sweet fog flooded my brain, just the way I knew it would. Boy. We had the wings pushed back wide and the cool October air whistled in and swirled about, lifting leaves and hay and paper from the floorboard. I noticed the pinpoints of Orion burning clearly out over Fox Den Mission, throbbing like pulsars. Willie passed the joint back and exhaled. Smoke billowed in the cab for a moment before it was sucked suddenly and with a swoosh through the vents and into the night.

"Now, Toom?"

"Now." I looked over at Willie, but she was bent to the passenger window. We passed beneath a streetlight and it flashed across her face, neck, bosom, lap, and legs, and each sang to me in its turn. "I always want to know what's on your mind. Otherwise, the two of us together wouldn't be worth Jerry Toller's sworn testimony."

Willie laughed about that before she continued. Jerry was my second cousin, a salesman whose mendacity was well known. "Well, all I'm saying is this is just something to think about. Considering your history." She waited until I said OK. "Now, consider your family for just a minute."

I said, "Drema and Hunt." Hunt is my father's half-brother who lives in a bombed-out hovel on the back side of my property. He's also lunatic, though somewhat outside the Spooner tradition of passive self-ruination.

"Yes, Drema and Hunt, but I'm taking the long view, too." Willie took a long drag, the coal flickering orange across her face, and spoke while she held it deep. "Uncle Teddy and Bobby Ray and Virgil," she exhaled, "the General and O Boy and—"

"You know what, Willie? This isn't a criticism, but if you don't come at this thing a little straighter, I might never get it." I flicked the nub of the joint at the vent, but it blew back in and showered us with tiny coals. We howled and slapped at each other, and Willie daubed spit on her really minor wounds. I flipped the dial to a staticky C&W station out of Winchester.

> *In one of our weaker moments,*
> *We posed as man and wife,*
> *Stole time, parole time,*
> *And called that thing a life.*
> *Let's raise a toast*
> *To one of our weaker moments.*

Willie wanted to know what we had been talking about.

"My fallen kinsmen, and how, I assume, they somehow or the other relate to me or us."

"Oh yeah." Looking out the passenger window, Willie picked at her jeans. "It seems to me we have a future together, Toomey. I think you know you're the only cracker alive whose babies I want. But." Willie scooted in close and slipped her hand over my thigh. "But your gene pool frankly does not inspire my optimism. By way of this very casual alcoholism, and what seems to me to be a hereditary inertia—punctuated by these sudden and alarming outbursts of just compulsively antic behavior—you Spooners have one by one driven yourselves to the brink of extinction. You do nothing, do nothing, do nothing, and then do something wild and extravagant—and that's no way to live. Honey," she said earnestly, "you're an endangered species." She was right and I knew there was nothing to be said about it. "Drema's next, I don't think there's any question about that. She's on her way out, Toomey, and you can't help her." Right again, and I registered these facts as they flew: check, check, and check. I slipped my arm over Willie's shoulder and drew her in. "I just wish you'd slow down is all, before there are consequences. And get busy with something for chrissakes. Anything! I can't bear to think of you headed nowhere, too." We were by then deep in the Slashes Tunnel, approaching the dark patch of Kentucky night at the other end. And I thought: she *is* right. I *don't* have to do this. And I *do* need to get busy. With something. *Any*thing.

"The thing is, and this is the hard part, Toomey, I'm afraid I won't be able to keep loving you—and that kills me. I'm afraid if you don't accomplish something, I'll lose respect for you. And if I lose respect for you . . . I just can't stand thinking too closely about that."

For a few minutes we were silent.

"Is that it," I asked, "is that everything you wanted to say?"

"My God, Toomey, isn't it enough?"

"It's a lot. But I just want to make sure: is that really the whole thing?"

"Yes, my love. It is."

The Bible tells us there are ten irreducible commandments carved in stone. Well, that strikes me as being a little inflexible. I've cooked all those *commandments* down to one general *suggestion*: Beware Reckless Whimsy. And that's all the advice I have for anybody ever.

I cranked my window down and the cold air surprised me a little. The temperature had to have dropped fifteen degrees in as many minutes. I used to watch the Weather Channel about as much as I watched CNN, and I knew the massive cold front that stretched from Canada into the Gulf of Mexico was sweeping through. The moon squatted on the horizon behind a web of branches whipped by the wind. I pulled Sewell's silver flask out of my jacket. "For us," I said, "and the fruit of our peculiar union, *los bambinos*." Getting rid of booze seemed like a good starting point, at least. And Willie knew what that flask meant to me.

By now, the moment had acquired a life of its own, and some vital connection between thought and action had snapped. I was just going. So, I kissed the flask—for Sewell's sake, I think: I *do*—and hurled it end over end, silver flashing in an arc, over the cab and deep into the brush beyond the shoulder of the parkway, where I would never be tempted to return and comb the weeds and bushes. I was stoned and it was the easiest thing in the world.

Altogether too easy, in fact.

"Geez, Toom." At least Willie was pleased. It was not exactly what she'd asked for. But the implications were obvious(!): we were entering a new epoch.

I gunned the engine of my monster Dodge Ram and shifted into overdrive, convinced I'd done the right thing.

Well, that's not entirely true. Even then I wondered. At least a little.

But back at Willie's peeling clapboard house on Stanton Street, just inside the front door, she turned on me with a wicked smile and an irrefutable *thereness* and crooked her finger right under my nose. "Come here, you." We made long and messy love right there, on through the kitchen, and finally all over her cozy bedroom, where we slept until noon.

So that's how it started—just these little things adding up. A misthought bit of bravado. Willie there to witness it and mistake it for the real thing. And, as if on cue, yours truly punctuating the proceedings with a sudden and alarming outburst of compulsively antic behavior.

I had four years of college just like everybody else—matriculating at the University of Kentucky in Lexington—but I took a degree in English literature, and so was wholly unprepared for anything resembling gainful employment. Oddly, this didn't concern me. I would figure something out. However, that harebrained bit with Sewell's flask, and the unmistakable implication that it carried, that I would quit drinking, did concern me. Increasingly. Because what I discovered is that it's very hard to sleep without a drink, with nothing much to slow you down. I couldn't understand how everybody did it. I mean, *all those thoughts!*

But on that crucial eighth night, I crossed some Rubicon, some point of no return.

Following that dreadful funeral business, and curled into a comfy ball there on my bed, with the lights out and my eyes shut, I tried doing some simple math. I thought it might bore me enough to put me to sleep. For a while it was strictly abstract, but then, and without warning, it took an unwelcome turn towards home. *I am thirty-nine. Thirty-nine is nineteen years from twenty. So I am as close to twenty as I am to . . . shit!* Needless to say, that wasn't any help at all.

Jesus.

Exhausted in every way, I slipped from between flannel sheets and into my ancient brocade robe, one of the few luxuries my father had ever allowed himself. Deddy wasn't cheap, not by a long shot, he simply preferred throwing his easy money at women and whiskey and didn't concern himself with much else. Especially after our mother died. Yet . . . yet nothing. No more excuses.

I sat up on the edge of the bed, yanked the chain on my bedside lamp, and pulled on a bulky pair of red rag socks—I take comfort in certain socks, and these were a pair of my favorites. I wiggled my toes inside the socks and watched them. A moth was bouncing around inside the cylinder of the lampshade. Pop . . . pop, pop. Et cetera. I didn't have a thing in mind, except that soft, silvery moth and the odd fact that every fiber of its being was rather directly engaged with seventy-five watts of GE firepower. The clock on the nightstand said 3:42. Holy cow. Maybe a little CNN.

But then, as it had Buddha unawares beneath the bo tree, it hit me whole and all at once, complete and fully formed, a big idea. Willie had nailed it. I understood it was indeed time for me to stake a claim of some sort, to winnow and expand, to account for myself. To assert the actuality of me! Yes. I insist on the right of the individual to defy time, history, and his or her own blood.

Or at least the right to try.

But like Deddy used to say, you had to have the proper tools for any job. For instance, as he also used to say, even Jesse James would've floundered and been taken for a fool—and shot dead on the spot—had he found himself wagging a pop gun at Allan Pinkerton's earnest boys.

Case in point: By five o'clock my rigid resolve had given way to pretty extreme intemperance—it had started as a celebration, of course—and I was down at the edge of the pond, still swaddled in Deddy's burgundy robe, blazing away at the water with a big .38, and muttering, "She loves me," p-pow!, "she loves me not," p-pow!, and in any six-shot configuration, that's bound to end in "not." At risk of obviousness, I know, I'll point out there was an empty seven-fifty of Jim Beam bourbon whiskey perched on the foot of the dock, and—or so it seemed to me then—it was just begging for what for. So I atomized it. The moon was low and luminous, and I cast a razor-sharp shadow across the water and onto the opposite bank. Then, and without prior warning, there in the moonlight, aspects of the night conspired to inform me: We're all drowning in shit. My eyes stung and leaked a little, and I had to sit in the mud and algae and wrestle with a simply worded question.

Now what?

Well, not waking up next to a middle-aged woman, who is childless, divorced, and vexed by life, and who was once a girl in my graduating class of twenty years before, a woman to whom I have hardly spoken in all those intervening years, but who, one night, when through some circumstance (a birthday party, a barbecue, etc.) we are thrown together, and for mildly diabolical reasons—which are always, and I mean *always*, related to alcohol—I decide I have just got to have, and to whom, once I've effected an escape from her dire little home, I am reasonably confident I will hardly speak again for another twenty years, if we should both be lucky enough—or cussed enough—to last so long. Not that.

And: I'd never again hold a woman in my arms, smelling her warm hair, feeling her love for me—full and perhaps forever—in her voice, her skin, her motion beneath or above me, not selfish but eager, and think even then: no, you're not the one, you will *never* be the one; but let her continue to think she is for weeks, or months, or even a year, and then, at the moment when she's most vulnerable—which will coincide exactly with that moment when I finally know I just can't take it anymore—have a few drinks, six, say, or nine, or fourteen, and tell her the truth in every ugly and highly exaggerated particular.

On the other side of it, no more false, but poetic, drunken declarations of love. Because that's where all the trouble starts.

No. I loved Willie. None of that would do.

I made a list like that and it filled a lot of negative space there in the night. I will not, not, not—and that's half a program. But I felt like the me I knew was disappearing, and so I fired off a few more rounds just to hear the report with my own ears.

And I sat there for a long time, trying to finish this simple sentence: I will _____.

I will what?

Several hours later, about the time the first wedge of blue edged in over the treeline, I faced some pretty dreadful facts dead on. One, I was my Deddy's boy. Virgil Spooner was no doubt the ghost in the machine, the man behind the curtain. The nexus upon which my inner life turned and turned. Inward and downward.

Two, the money had clearly ruined them all. Ridiculous sums for nothing but the great dumb luck to have plopped their hardscrabble Scots-Irish asses square on a massive seam of coal—at that time, one of the largest ever discovered around here. My great-great-grandfather, who bought this land in an Irish mail order transaction, distilled corn all his days, for fun and profit, and took the coal more or less for granted, firing his still with it and burning it for heat in the winter. But his grandson Agee, my grandfather, who had an altogether keener sense of commerce than either his father or his soon-to-be-swindled neighbors, hit it big with the mines and never looked back. And so on down to me. I didn't have much, but I knew if I was prudent and penny-wise I could make it last. After Agee, it was like we were all just sitting on our hands, waiting for it to be over. And it very nearly was.

And three, I wasn't a boy any more. At thirty-nine I was missing all my molars and I had, thanks to cigarettes and an inherited disinclination to productive activity—as highlighted by Willie—the lung capacity of a rat. My knees ached nearly full-time by then, and I had to wear my glasses to watch TV. On the other side of it, my hairline was intact, and my musculature was still sleek. Without exercise. But I'd seen age sneak up and pound the soup out of the men in my family. For instance, one day Uncle Teddy's spearfishing in the rapids of the North Fork, laughing and telling lies and gulping Weidemann's, and the next he lay near death in Eugene Clay Memorial, gray and emptied out, full of tubes shooting vital fluids to and fro. From the pink of health to the morgue, in thirty-six hours.

I finally rose from the muddy bank, my joints popping, and clambered across the dock, woozy but there. *There* there. Indubitably. Shards of glass glinted across the foot of it in the morning's first low light. Used to be a whiskey bottle. Watching milky clouds glide across the surface of the pond, I let my father's old robe slip from my shoulders, stepped ever so carefully amongst the slivered and shattered bottle, and dove into the cool black pond.

I felt the water close over my feet.

Treading water, my hair slick on my head and water running down across my neck and eyes, and blinking it away, I wondered what it all added up to. All the perfectly grilled steaks and tall cool whiskeys and really good movies. Even all the times you made love to the only one you want, or the morning you watched the sun come up over Lake Cumberland, bobbing with your old man in that dented, leaky canoe. Work, I knew. That's all there is in the end. Accomplishments. Something the survivors could chisel into a tombstone. I quailed at the thought of exiting the world exactly as I'd entered: fat and bald and blank.

It wouldn't do.

And I knew then what the preacher Pons had all but spelled out for me. That mine was a sin of omission. That there are things you don't do that are every bit as bad as the bad things you do do.

Not only had I never worked, not really, not counting those two summers my father made me dig postholes and muck stalls out at the Herrick place, but I had never contributed anything, really, to anybody, ever. The earth was not a better place for my having trod upon it. No career, obviously. But no nothing. Excepting Drema and Hunt, no lasting relationships. No wife. No children to succeed me on this planet and carry us Spooners into the unknowable future, remember to others our triumphs, our failures, our tall tales, our small travails. No great work of art, no curious but fascinating journal of life as it was being lived at the tail end of the twentieth century, no document whatsoever. A cipher. And I knew that it was all true, that I was indeed in grave danger of wasting my life, of leaving a vacuum, that thing that nature abhors.

I floated there quietly on my back and sneezed when the sunlight fell across my face. I dove deep into the cold water and felt my penis shrivel to nothing. Mockingbirds swooped through the tall pines, singing everybody's songs but their own. My dog, Zero, stood on the dock, back from the broken glass, and watched, his head cocked at an angle. Here, boy. His ear twitched, but he stayed put. Nothing abstract in that—no, Zero was in and *of* this material world through which we merely pass.

But before I climbed out of that pond, up the rope ladder and onto the dock, wrinkled and waterlogged, naked, dripping, and blinking, I'd somehow or the other decided it was absolutely necessary that I become the next mayor of Oceana, Kentucky.

Somehow or the other? Well, strictly speaking, that's probably not true. Because I was, once again, just following in the footsteps of Virgil before me.

Which is not to suggest that my father was ever actually elected to any office at all—only that upon occasion (and briefly but intensely) he burned for the favor of the electorate, but only because he'd glimpsed in whatever office he sought an awesome instrument of revenge. And the old man could be downright biblical in matters of retribution.

So, from time to time, and always hard upon the heels of some personal setback—brought about by the decision of some local officeholder or another—Virgil swore vengeance was his and declared himself a candidate for whatever office he deemed best suited to serve his interests. Mayor (twice). Judge-executive (once). Property valuation assessor (once). Sheriff (once). And always with the intention of unsheathing the terrible swift sword of elective dominion and smiting, once and for all, his puny antagonist.

For example, when I was ten or eleven and Deddy decided to run for the office of property valuation assessor, the then-PVA of Mann County, Richard Fitzgerald, had not long before set in motion the fantastically laborious process of reassessing all the properties in the county. This for the purpose of updating and enlarging Mann County's property-tax base. That it was right, courageous, and long overdue was recognized by politicians and pundits from abroad—in places like Frankfort, Louisville, and Lexington. But locally, such cool objectivity did not prevail. No, his brave decision amounted to something like political hara-kiri for the "arrogant" (Deddy's word) Mr. Fitzgerald.

But Deddy managed to remain more or less indifferent to the whole thing—right up until the moment he received *his* reassessment. Then, of course, he grew quarrelsome and vituperative, damning that Fitzgerald fellow to hell. Because the assessed value on our place had more than doubled—though, in fact, its true value had probably trebled or quadrupled in the years since its last assessment.

Anyway, he jumped into the upcoming race for PVA and displayed a shocking overall energy as well as a rather oversized genius for vicious, swelling invective. But several other men entered the race, too, with basically the same agenda as my father. So Deddy set the tone and then withdrew to the sidelines to let the other combatants take care of that bastard Fitzgerald. As he saw it, my father's work was done.

(A footnote: Only days after the conclusion of that famous campaign—and it has remained well known, right up to the present day—poor Richard Fitzgerald, who had fought quixotically to retain his office, died of a massive coronary, making a widow of his young but tough-as-hobnails wife, the aforementioned Missus Fitzgerald, and an orphan of his only child, a boy my age.)

And that was a pattern that obtained time and again. Sooner or later (and usually sooner), an air of reality would prevail and Virgil would realize he was constitutionally incapable of sustaining any interest at all in coalition-building, fund-raising, baby-kissing, handshaking, or backscratching—or, in short, public service. At this point, Virgil would simply drop out of sight. By the time election day rolled around, most folks had forgotten that he'd ever even been a candidate and were mildly surprised to find his name still on the ballot. This was a conspicuously ill-conceived formula for electoral success.

In time, Virgil's serial candidacy became something of a joke, locally. And only because he was otherwise well liked and taken more or less seriously, Virgil himself just narrowly avoided becoming a laughingstock, which, in any handbook of politics, ought to be rule #1.

But I didn't have any ax to grind—not yet, I didn't—and my candidacy was conceived as an offering, a contribution, an oblation: to

Spooners past and Spooners yet to come, and to Oceana, too, but, most of all—despite that I knew she'd take some convincing and that I'd take some not-inconsiderable heat, never mind that she had practically come up with the idea—to Wilhelmina Rains herself.

And if there were some hereditary component in any of this delirious decision making that long, long night, it was at that time wholly lost on me.

CHAPTER TWO

I met the new day with an industry and vigor and optimism I'd not known for a while. Because, goddamnit, I had a plan. And this was an entirely new feeling.

By nine I'd showered and shaved and downed half a pot of blackest El Pico ("Fresco y Aromatico!"). It was crisp but comfortable out, the sun barreling in low over treetops about half yellow, orange, and red with autumn. Flocks of swallows and martins—and I don't know what all—winged their way toward Africa and the Amazon basin. Through the kitchen window I enjoyed their random, shifting patterns against the bright sky and feathery, layered clouds. Or perhaps they weren't random at all. I'd read somewhere that chaos theorists were plotting the dispersal of stars in the universe and the growth of crystals. Maybe one day a belief in anything random or chaotic will seem as quaint as the simple faith of cargo cultists. I don't know. I lit a cigarette, shot a thick plume of smoke through a shaft of sunlight, and thought, unplottable. Fucking A. By ninethirty I was racing in the Ram toward Oceana. Zero sat in the cab next to me, hunkered low and seeming to evince a quiet concern for his old master's new countenance.

I drove straight to the post office to register for the May election.

"Complete boxes A, B, C, skip D—see, 'for office use only'—then do E and F. And skip G. 'Office use' again. Sign and date it here, here, aaaand . . . here." Mrs. Stamper leaned across the counter, drawing her dress together at the top button with one hand and pointing to the three places on the form with a pen she held in the other. "Then there's another form for the commonwealth and the matter of registration fees." Peering at me over darkened bifocals, she said, "I've always been fond of you, Toomey. I sure have. But honestly, sweetness, I believe you're wasting your time."

"Well, Mrs. Stamper, I sure hope you're wrong there."

"Well, OK, then that's two of us." She smiled from behind the counter, fiddling with a wad of Kleenex tucked in her sleeve.

"Besides, I've been feckless for a while now." I looked up from the personal data form I was filling in. "And what have I got to show?" Box E concerned itself with felonies. I checked no, no, no, and no.

"What I meant," she said, "is that those other boys play rough. Despite appearances, they're pretty professional, pretty tough, you know? They generally grind each other up pretty fine, and I don't want to see anything happen to you."

"I appreciate it." I shrugged. Mrs. Stamper went back to rubber-stamping a pile of something. I knew she was right. And she knew I knew she was right. But that was part of it, wasn't it? To finally do something and, in doing something, to cut against the grain, too.

I finished up the forms, paid my fees, and thanked Mrs. Stamper for everything. She wished me good luck, and I told her I expected I'd need it. As well as her vote. I thanked her and left.

Leaving the post office, I turned right on Boone Avenue and then left onto Main Street. A coal truck rumbled by and small chunks of coal bounced and rolled through the street in its wake, ricocheting off the curb and the tires of parked cars. The poorest families in town helped heat their homes in winter with coal scooped from the gutters. And some of that coal had started out on my place, had been mine, out there beneath the soil and shale and limestone.

It occurred to me then that those coal scraps might be about all I'd ever given of myself. And even that was nothing but an accident.

But I was now registered to run for mayor.

I was a candidate.

I dropped in on Willie over at the Stonecastle River Detention Center where, as a social worker, she counseled overanxious or otherwise agitated detainees. Her office was in the basement, at the end of a long, damp hall. I walked in without knocking.

"Whoa there, cocksucker! You best be—"

"Stop that, Randall! Hi, Toomey." Willie smiled and stood up behind her desk. "Randall, Toomey's a friend of mine." Randall wore an orange jumpsuit with SRDC stitched on its chest. He was shackled in cuffs and leg irons and was seated across the desk from Willie. One of his upper teeth was far too long and rested on his lower lip.

"Sorry, man." Randall tried to cross his legs, but the irons pulled him up short. "Shit." He glanced down at his ankles. "Pardon my French. But you know how it is," he said to me. "I thought you was one of them other cocksuckers."

"But I'm not?"

"Nossir. You're not."

"Willie?" She closed a manila folder spread over her lap. Probably Randall's lurid bio. "Can you make it out to my place for lunch? I'll have something special."

"Sure. Twelve-fifteen, twelve-thirty good?"

"Yeah, perfect. Randall, I'm just curious, you know—what are you here for?"

"I'd rather not say."

"Why?"

"Puts people off's why. Which plays hell with my self-esteem. And Miss Rains, I'd appreciate if you didn't discuss my crimes with this gentleman over lunch."

After lunch—a clear mushroom soup and Cornish hens stuffed with wild rice, garlic, and mint, all from scratch—I cornered Willie by the microwave with silly speeches and wet kisses and hands riding up under her mohair sweater. Shoes and cabinets clattered. She was moaning a little and moving with me and arching her back like Miss Wong when suddenly she froze. Silence. She drew her face away, a blank, eyes locked onto mine. "Bourbon. I can smell it."

"Yes."

"Yes? When, Toomey? And why, and what does it foretell?"

"Well. Last night, all night. Because I had a burst of clarity, which is harder to take than you might imagine. And all it means is, I think, is that I went for a while without, and then I didn't, and now I will again." I was pretty sure this didn't add up to a satisfactory response. But I still had my trump card, my ace in the hole.

"Eight days," Willie said, referring to my brief (extended) dry spell. I was a little surprised that it seemed to have become this important to Willie. But I also knew I'd violated some basic trust. She was framed in the window, her back to me, watching Meshach, Shadrach, and Abednego, my goats, denude a sprawl of withering wild roses spread along the back fence.

"I know. I *know.*" I wished she'd look at me.

Then Uncle Hunt pushed open the back door and froze, hand on the knob, one foot in, one foot out. He was carrying a big carp, his fingers hooked in one of its gills. He looked at me and he looked at Willie. Back at me. Then he withdrew, quietly pulling the door to.

"Should I be alarmed?" She asked this without inflection, her back still turned to me. Zero sat in the corner, his big head going back and forth like he was following our exchange. Now he, along with Willie, awaited my response. A couple of cleanly picked Cornish hen skeletons lay unhappily piled together on the table.

"I don't think so." I *didn't* think so. "Willie?"

"Hm?"

"You're looking at your next mayor. I'm all signed up." Finally, Willie turned to me from the window, but remained a silhouette backlit against it. "And that's what I finally decided last night."

"You did, huh? But I thought you said you had a 'burst of *clarity*.'"

Oceana lies at almost the exact interface of the eastern mountains and the Bluegrass, Kentucky's rolling horse country, but, somewhat counterintuitively, it is in no sense an admixture of the two. Oceana is a mountain community, period, with the dangerous roads, high unemployment, wretched schools, chronic poverty, and depraved politics to prove it. (Which is not to say that these conditions do not obtain elsewhere in the state, but simply that they are *all* present in the immediate vicinity of greater Oceana.)

Around here, good fortune results not from who you know—since everybody knows everybody, more or less—but from whose favor you have managed to curry and on whose shitlist your name has failed to appear. And a second cousin on my father's side, Jerry Toller, as deeply Machiavellian as any man I ever hope to know, had, for almost seventy years, remained a moving target and master of appeasement. He was, therefore, a good man to know.

So, driving into Oceana from my place, you're forced to slow down as you round a steeply banked curve, but then you pick up speed again as you start down a long straight grade. Soon Oceana comes into view in the valley below, at first impressionistically. But then, halfway down the long grade, and still well above the town, Oceana comes into *focus*, and what commands your attention is not the Greek Revival county courthouse, nor the Bourbon & Letcher Academy, an institution responsible for three former governors' secondary educations, but a shimmering glass structure jutting at odd angles like a vast wing, rising higher at one end than the other, and surrounded on all sides by factory-fresh cars and trucks in all the colors of the visible spectrum. And this anomaly on the landscape is owned and operated by my cousin Jerry.

"Toomey! Been a month of Sundays, boy, and then some." Jerry crossed the showroom, smiling as he surveyed his inventory, and slapped me on the shoulder with his right hand. Clouds passed high over the tinted glass above us, and shadows slipped through the showroom. "Got-damn!" he said in a lowered voice, conspiratorially, closing in, "good timing. I'm overstocked up to here and in a real good position to *deal*!" My eyes, as they had been since I was a child, were drawn to his empty left sleeve, folded in half, cuff tucked into his armpit. (A boating accident on the river, that's all I know. Oh, and that my father had been present. And escaped without injury. And that the two men had been drinking, immoderately, all day. And that really is all I know.)

Jerry is of that breed of men who are in it—business, that is— not for the money per se, but because it is a safe and socially acceptable outlet for the compulsion to bushwhack innocents. Jerry's an ebullient and charming redneck, whose company I've always enjoyed, but whose peculiar skills lay not in simply swindling others, but in a mildly perverse capacity for making the swindlee a full and eager participant in the misdeed committed upon him. I guess you could say Jerry's specialty is in creating an *impression*.

"Sorry, Jerry, I'm not looking to upgrade. But do you have a few minutes?"

"Course I do, Toom. Course." Back across the showroom, Jerry barking good-naturedly to sales staff and potential buyers, urging everybody *on*, me trailing in his wake. "I *have* heard the news, Toomey," he spoke across his desk, "and I assume this visit one way or another concerns your candidacy. Hm?"

"Yessir, it does." There was a faint, high buzzing, perhaps in my head, perhaps external. "I'm serious about this thing, and I expect I'll need some help along the way. Specifically, in the area of introductions to people who can help me . . . with my candidacy?" I couldn't bring myself to mention money out loud.

"And you think that I could maybe be some help." Jerry rearranged himself behind his desk. "Toomey, let me ask you a question. Do you realize that the political arena hereabouts is a fucking miasma of graft and incest? And further, that you nor anybody else can tread shit for very long without swallowing a couple mouthfuls? Now, given your old man's experiences on the field of battle, I expect you're aware of all this."

"I am, yessir. More or less. In fact, it's all I can do to bottle up concerns Willie has along those very lines."

For a moment Jerry looked as if he were trying to force a bowel movement, or perhaps suppress a hot belch, but then he relaxed. "Well, OK then. That said, I'll do what I can." He slipped two Camels between his teeth, lit them, and passed me one. "I've recently made the acquaintance of a group of civic-minded fellows from out of state. Businessmen like myself. They're looking to invest a bundle in the area, maybe right here in Oceana if the climate's right. If you're interested, and your interests coincide, I'll wager they'd see fit to advance your campaign any way they could."

"Invest in what?"

"They're in waste management. Clean and safe disposal of environmentally noxious industrial by-products." Jerry shot a thick plume of smoke at the ceiling. "Deer season opens Saturday, and these old boys live for large game. Why don't you join us? Hm? Discover for yourself what they're all about."

"Waste management?"

"'At's right, son, but don't let it put you off, just like that," Jerry said, snapping his fingers. "They're the good guys. 'Panthrex: Managing with care the world's waste resources today, that we may waller in a cleaner, less awful tomorrow.' Something like that."

CHAPTER THREE

Having finally made camp on a darkening Virginia plain at the end of a long and unsettling day, General Truman Spooner—my great-great-grandfather's brother, contemporary and confrere of Robert Hunt Morgan, and the Confederate renegade who was by now operating quite beyond any mandate at all, save his own—was for the first time feeling the rather immoderate ballast of his own history. Second in his class at West Point. Landed with Scott at Veracruz in '47. Military advisor for a time to the confoundedly ambivalent abolitionist—aka, the Great Compromiser—Henry Clay. Elected to Congress in '52.

But now . . . now there had descended upon the general, most unexpectedly, a vast black emptiness. It filled his heart and his head. And because of his former trajectory, because of his nearly unparalleled record of achievement, he felt this emptiness very keenly indeed.

Spooner told his biographer, who was almost always at the great man's side, that he had resigned himself to the situation—to the loss, that is, of whatever it was that accounted for the successes he had managed to pile up—for he believed that the good Lord giveth, but that He did indeed taketh away, too. And that now, unhappily, He was evidently in an Indian-giving phase. "I'm all out of tricks. I'm exhausted. I'm sick and tired of all this death. And of my joyless life. Now, if you'll excuse me, sir, I'd like to be alone with this bottle of bourbon." The biographer said good night and took his leave.

But with the first paling of the new day, General Truman Spooner emerged from his ragged tent with a restored confidence and an elaborate plan for engaging the Yankee bastards on the very shores of the Potomac. He told the biographer to credit the Kentucky whiskey, for it had helped him to "think anew." Those were his very words, dutifully recorded for posterity. And three days hence, on the very banks of the Potomac—just as he had declaimed— Union forces dispatched General Truman Spooner and the boys in gray so mercilessly, and with such a malignant ferocity, that even the big northern newspapers excoriated the massacre, one of them calling it "a gratuitous obscenity."

That story has lived for 135 years because my family has delighted in its telling. But why? What does that say about us? That a glorious failure is our highest aspiration? Or that the only things worth trying are so grand, so downright hubristic, that the attempt all but guarantees our failure? That seems likely to me, but I don't really know.

But what I do know with utter certainty is that, like the general, I too had often asked special favor of Kentucky whiskey—and with the same decidedly mixed results. And, having for now disavowed the known cure, I was having a new dream, serially, night after fucking night: it was a very lurid rendering indeed of that old holocaust on the Potomac—except, of course, I am now present and taking the awfullest of it: a mortar scoops away a divot of my hair; a saber lays me open and my warm, wet viscera uncoil down the bank and into the dark river. But I do not die. Thus I'm available to have endless indignities visited upon me.

Speaking of which—

It was now the middle of November, a little more than a month since my fateful decision to seek the mayoralty, and almost exactly six months until election day. And I was now ready to test the waters—or to at least dip in my big toe, wiggle it in the current, and make sure it would not be bitten off by the horny creatures of fable lurking below.

The National Guard Armory, Oceana Auxiliary Unit, a frequent stop on the pro wrestling circuit, sat above and at a little remove from Oceana proper, though still within sight. It perched on an artificial plateau against an otherwise steep hillside, where the dirt had been scooped away to accommodate it. Its long gravel drive topped out onto an asphalt parking lot, crowded with cars and pick-ups and all manner of four-wheel drives, some foreign and powerful and sleek, some domestic and muddy and rusted. Inside the armory's long Special Events Hall—its gym—plank bleachers were collapsed accordion-like against the concrete walls, and red and green crepe paper, arranged something like an inverted blossom, twirled gaily just higher than the piled-up hairdos and tall cowboy hats of couples chatting and two-stepping and lining up for refreshments. An electrified country band commanded the stage, anonymous behind long, squared-off beards and silver glasses, a la ZZ Top.

We were there at Willie's insistence. She was sure that this event, the annual Stocking Stuffers' Ball, would be an unparalleled opportunity to officially launch the Citizens (so far, me and Willie) for Spooner dreadnought with maximum impact. A charitable forum at which I ought to be seen. Involved in the community. Concerned. No fuckup, I. Etc., etc. Not Willie's words exactly. But despite her initial incredulity, her really alarming disbelief (and I mean, if she didn't believe it, who would?), she had then embraced my campaign with such enthusiasm, such an abundance of sincere *joie de politique*, as to emerge as my de facto campaign manager.

The Stocking Stuffers' Ball is always held the Friday night following Thanksgiving, which is often the eve of the second and final Saturday of deer season. Consequently, the males in attendance are somewhat distracted, what with visions of twelve-point bucks splayed at unhappy angles over the forest floor. But the females, contrarily, the wives and sisters and daughters and mothers of the hunters, bring with them to the ball sheer and maximum focus, and they conduct—or rather *execute*—the real business at hand: cajoling one another in the severest possible terms to pony up for the Stocking Stuffers' Fund, a sort of community chest insuring Christmas bounty for our area's less fortunate. White trash every other night of the year.

(To my knowledge, no money at all had ever been directed toward Oceanans of African-American descent, who mostly congregated in and around Davies' Bottom—which was at least technically within the confines of Oceana—and, to this day, it remains unclear to me whether they had been rudely excluded or had sometime long ago consulted their dignity, found it firm and intact, and simply refused to participate.)

The objects of this outpouring, pretty much unfortunately for everyone, also attended the ball—were, in fact, required to if they expected their cut of the bonanza—where they skulked dismally at one end of the hall, frequented the open bar, and, with lowered gaze, scowled hatefully at the Capezio pumps and the Tony Lama lizard skins of their benefactors.

Dickie Fitzgerald and his arch, white-haired mother, the Missus—yes, the same Fitzgerald matron from that night at the Ponderosa—banged through the fire exit. They seemed to be in costume, she in long white gloves and a crazy welter of beads and sequins, he swaddled in cranberry tux and wide silky cummerbund.

She veered badly, high heels clattering on the gym floor, and very nearly spilled her drink. Dickie, with the unerring instincts of a border collie, caught her elbow and herded her along toward the bar.

"Toomey." Willie poked at me and nodded in the direction of mother and son. A little dread welled up inside me. A lifetime of antagonisms springing to life. "It is now time to let bygones be bygones. Do you understand? I mean, who knows? For reasons of their own, maybe *they'll* rally round your cause. You know, politics and strange bedfellows." I understood. And Willie had been right to figure in the Fitzgeralds, one of many unknowns, yet another whopping x factor. The Fitzgeralds had money and a certain extreme visibility—actually pretty unattractive up close—which those with neither respected. The upshot of which was that the Fitzgeralds swung local opinion considerably, for good or ill, and they weren't to be ignored. So, yes, I understood: it was necessary that I at least attempt greasing this particular chute. Come what may.

"Now why don't you run on over there and say something nice."

Oh, Willie, so sincere, that face, those eyes, how on earth could I say no?

"Well . . . *OK*." I forced a smile.

Willie smiled, too, but genuinely, and, with her healing hands arranged over my shoulder and back, gently set me in motion, her slight pressure barely perceptible. The band, Carry Me Home, was working its way through a weirdly polka-like rendition of "Free Bird." I sailed across the crowded floor. And this bird, oom-pa-pa, you cannot chay-yay-yange. Dickie saw me coming and tried to skirt away past his mother.

"Whoa there, Dickie. Been awhile."

"Spooner." Dickie pulled up, composing his face, tugging at his cuffs. "No scenes tonight. That's strict orders." He nodded in the direction of his mother, now looming unsteadily over the donations table. We had a history of calamity between us. I suppressed an urge to explain that all that was now behind us, a-way back in the bad old days.

"Well then"—I tugged at my cuffs, too: two can play at this game—"I can respect that." Looking past Dickie, I saw Willie dancing with Jerry, his empty half-sleeve flapping up and down, his bulk nearly elegant in motion. "So. How's life out to the big house?"

"You don't get out much do you?" Dickie looked away, lifted a plastic cup to his lips. "It sucks, actually. Inky has evicted me on grounds of I don't know what. She and Dickie Junior have staked out the house, so I'm over at Mom's. For the time being, at least. I suspect we'll iron this thing out, though."

"Maybe. *But.*" I cocked an eyebrow and looked away from Dickie, across at the two-steppers and the band. I felt his eyes on me.

"OK, damnit. Meaning what?"

"Mm, I don't know, Dickie. Just that Inky's always been a pretty single-minded gal." I lit a cigarette. "I know I don't have to remind *you* of the time she collected up and disposed of all your—"

"Hell no, goddamnit, you don't have to remind me of *that*, Spooner, you sumbitch, goddamn you." Dickie's scalp contracted, his ears flashed red and slid back on his head a half inch. He craned his neck as if to loosen his collar. "Do you know you've got a tone problem? I swear to God, you can't say 'hi' without making it sound a little ugly."

"All I meant is that maybe Inky's prepared to winnow again, you know, simplify."

"See, now that's exactly what I'm talking about. And to think I was confiding." Dickie strode away toward the crowded dance floor, a little bent at the waist, his head tilted at an odd angle.

And I can't say what it was that goaded me to treat Dickie that way. Ever. From the beginning, from when we knew each other as schoolboys, well before any strong evidence of his treacherous nature had accumulated. Because despite his truly monstrous behavior, there was something, there was . . . I don't know. To some limited extent, I had always been drawn to him, too, just like the other boys, but wouldn't have admitted it or acted on it and had in fact gone out of my way to become his archenemy. Was it some crazy extension of *my* father's vendetta against *his* father? Something in the blood?

Watching him stagger across the dance floor, a thirty-nine-year-old man dodging the line dancers, I felt the sad, sad slipping away of time. Like when you suddenly notice that your dog has grown a gray muzzle. Or when you attend any kind of reunion, family, class, whatever.

I found Willie with Jerry and his entourage, the Panthrex boys, I figured. "Gentlemen," Jerry boomed by way of centering attention on himself and then, with broad, sideways glances, on me. He wrapped his single arm tightly about my shoulder and, with a wide grin, looked around at the others. "This is the one and only Toomey Spooner, my late cousin Virgil's boy and, let's keep our fingers crossed, the next mayor of Oceana. Also, he who will lead what I know will be our oh so *successful* hunt on Sunday." Now they all nodded and turned to one another, shifting and murmuring bored assent. Moo.

We shook hands while Jerry made the introductions. Thirty seconds afterward, I couldn't have told you a single one of their names. Then Jerry moved in a little closer to me, as if to speak privately.

"Listen, Toom," Jerry said. "We gotta be scootin'. Because, let's face it, this party is a pretty dismal affair and it's making me feel bad. You stickin' around or what?"

"We won't be long. Why?"

"Thought I might drop by. Have a drink. Couple of things I'd like to discuss."

"Sure. We ought to be back at my place by eleven or so."

"I'll see you right around eleven then, give or take." With that, Jerry and the Panthrex crew wound toward the exit.

After that, Willie and I took our turn on the dance floor. The band was on break and George Jones was coming at us over the p. a., "The Grand Tour," I believe, but in any case a slow one, and we held each other close, cheek to cheek, Willie's hand cradled in mine. The armory smelled of new leather and stiff, starchy denim, but Willie smelled like sun-warmed hair, musky, sexy.

"Talk to Dickie?"

"Mm-hm, I did, more or less. He wasn't really in the mood."

"Tell me more."

"He and Inky've split up and he's kind of taking it on the chin. All preoccupied. And his eyes were aflame."

"Can I take that to mean you weren't helpful."

"Afraid so."

Carry Me Home returned to the stage and Willie and I sought refreshments. Hot Dr Peppers with slices of lemon and baby smoked oysters on toast squares with a dab of bright French's mustard. I had seconds.

Then I made the strictly political rounds, the candidate's self-aggrandizing side trips that Willie had so counted on. I knew it was necessary but had thought I'd do it in my own way and in my own time, as it was natural and convenient: in other words, never. Willie, who never even knew my father—and who knew nothing of his detached, self-defeating approach to politics—understood that better than I did. Anyway, I smiled and nodded dumbly and shook hands and asked about decrepit family members I'd neither seen nor thought of in years. Some had even died, though nobody seemed to begrudge me not knowing. Small towns will infinitely indulge the social faux pas of their own reformed drunks—and somehow, everyone seemed to be aware of my recent flirtation with sobriety—because in the back of everybody's mind is the likelihood of the backslider's dramatic, career-ending bender. And if the proportions are biblical, as they often are, it is something the entire community can participate in. Like a 4-H dance or a county fair. Only better.

I took a perfunctory but necessary interest in long, pointless anecdotes, vague laments about local government and what all it didn't do for the speaker, and grim medical dispatches. Just doing my job. But I listened with real interest to an old woman as she recounted her year-long war with the state road commission. They had claimed eminent domain, paid her fair market value (which is to say nearly nothing, at least around here), and rolled down four lanes of asphalt over her ancestral home last spring.

"It's where I raised up two boys and countless hogs and buried my Charles when he give out after sixty-one years is all. Now I'm in a condo and his headstone decorates a doggie walk at the rest area. Looks across to a Rite Aid in town, my condo does."

"Where are your boys now?"

"Pff. They give me a computer last Christmas. Why, do you suppose?"

"They thought you'd like it, I'm sure. I've been thinking maybe—"

"Arizona. They're in Arizona." She paused, eyes fixed on my chest. "Both of 'em took to the desert. Doesn't that beat all? The *desert*, my eye."

Was she poor, living on Social Security and keeping herself

patched together with Medicare, here to collect her necessary share of the fund? Or did she have something squirreled away, some minor wealth she felt compelled to share? I couldn't tell. Either one or the other was no more than accident or luck.

I poured another steaming Dr Pepper, sized up the room, and wandered down into the slough of despond, the zone of want. Votes is votes, I thought. Then I felt like an asshole, an actual politician as opposed to the Jeffersonian ideal of the citizen-legislator. I knew I'd better watch myself, too, because a thing like that could get away from you before you knew it. The evidence is everywhere.

I sipped from my cup and milled around, trying to catch an eye, start a conversation, but there was an abiding sense of suspicion crowding those drawn faces, and I was roundly and thoroughly ignored for a time. Finally, I just sipped at the Doctor and watched the band and dancers like everybody else. Like watching *Hee Haw* with a crowd.

"You runnin' for mayor?" I turned to a slim, bedraggled man, long of face and limb, thirty-five, thirty-six. "I heard somebody say you was runnin' for mayor."

"I am. Toomey Spooner." I offered my hand but he ignored it.

"Things have happened to us that we didn't never ask for, mister." His delivery was rote and flat and full of defeat, downright Gregorian. And I knew him from somewhere.

"Well. Like what?"

"Like had to move to Davies' Bottom, for starters." He made a gesture to indicate the "we" around him. A woman, obviously his soul mate, a boy and a girl; and I remembered: the Ponderosa. Grannie was absent or dead, but probably at home in bed, watching TV in a hot, humid room with the sound turned high. "Lost my damn job and ended up down there with the coloreds. That would seem to be the long and the short of it. And, God, you oughtta see how they live down there!" I wasn't sure what he meant. I had seen how they lived down there. And I imagined that in truth it was probably a step up for the fellow before me.

"Your job doing what?"

"Well. Just between you and me"—he slit his eyes, rolled them left and right—"I was working a dope field for some boys over to, well, a *neighboring* county. Hoeing and watering and shit. Whatever. Come harvest, though, and I was just naturally thowed outta work."

"Any other experience?" I was thinking maybe I could put him to work digging postholes or something out at my place.

"Dug graves out to Serenity Gardens. Creeped me out, though. Got to where I couldn't sleep. Not to mention my wife didn't want me touching her." He gave me a doleful look. I took in his family gathered about him. The boy's eyes weren't exactly focused and floated a little, and I wondered if he needed glasses. None of them looked as if they'd been surprised by anything in a long time. "So, Toomey Spooner, let's pretend you're mayor. What're you gonna do for me?" The man poked his chin out at me, defiant, and, honestly, a little annoying.

I had no idea. Of course, hiring him myself, what with his past experience, was now out of the question. Last thing I needed was an ex-professional gravedigger hanging around the place like the Grim Reaper.

"Well, you understand, I'm naturally foursquare on the side of full employment, I mean, hell, I suppose that goes without saying, but there're other considerations, too, such as extending worker's comp benefits by thirteen weeks, though probably not to marijuana farmers, no offense, and convincing new industry to relocate in the area, except not by way of tax credits, which is always a losing proposition in the long run, plus—"

"That's horseshit, mister. We ain't on TV. C'mon." He swept his clan together with a motion of his arms. "Looks like it'll be nigger-town for a while, kids."

It *was* horseshit. Any fool would've thought the same thing. I had to get serious about this thing, I knew, reinvent myself on some grand yet folksy scale. Master a rhetoric of the people. Resonate. Did that necessarily mean that one had to become something of a fraud and an asshole? Or was there some other way? And would it oblige me to pander to some goddamn cracker who shot off at the mouth and quite casually slung around words like "niggertown"?

Willie. Where was she now? I hadn't seen her for a while and I was now anxious to head home. I had some big thinking to do. I had seen that simple desire falls short without a master plan. Execution, that's what it's all about, Buster. I saw that the old woman was now sharing her loss with Dickie Fitzgerald, who looked supremely, exquisitely bored—and yet as if his shoes were nailed to the spot—as she unscrolled her sad story. And it seemed to me then that so few things ever change. That Dickie Fitzgerald's son, even Dickie's great-grandson, would one day stand right over there, too, bored to tears by the pain of an old woman, keeping one eye out for *his* mother, who would be teetering, a little drunk, a little too loud. And that the boy who needed glasses would have a son, and his son's son would no doubt, at five or six, aspire to replicate *his* father's life, to one day be all that his own old man had become: an ignorant, unemployed, white-trash gravedigger stranded in Davies' Bottom for now, but with many rungs left to descend even yet.

My cousin Jerry's high beams slashed through the night and shot off at improbable angles as he approached my place, hitting deep potholes full tilt and crashing high out of them. Hick town rogue with a nose for ins and outs. He slid to a stop out front, gravel crunching under radials, and marched across my lawn through the shadows, ducking low apple- and peach-tree branches. Unlike so many overweight older men, Jerry didn't move as if underwater: he'd retained an eager young man's gait and surety of bearing which seemed to owe nothing to banal, prolonged defeat. I met him at the door. I didn't want him to ring unnecessarily, as Willie was already asleep upstairs. Politicking at the Stocking Stuffer had done her in.

"Toom." A friendly nod, a toothy salesman's smile, Jerry bounding up the steps and onto the porch, hand automatically extended, a reflex action, a hand ready to seal a deal. Any deal. Of course I shook it. We scuffled through the door together, past the empty coat rack, the dark foot of the stairs, and into the kitchen. Jerry seated himself at the table and I leaned against the sink, smoking, curious, tapping my ashes into the disposal. Almost of a motion, he withdrew a flask from an inside coat pocket, uncapped it, sipped, his Adam's apple bobbing against his collar, set the flask on the table, and spun its cap back into place. Looking from me to the flask, he said, "Help yourself." I thought I heard Willie moving around upstairs. Floorboards creaked overhead.

"Something passed across your face back there at the Stocking Stuffer," he said. "Something when I mentioned our hunt. Like maybe you were thinking about not coming." He leaned forward, resting his elbow and sleeve-enveloped stub on the table. "If you don't mind my asking, what the hell's going on? I was under the impression we were all set. You know, had, like, a *plan*."

"For starters, you know I don't hunt."

"Yeah, but you've gone with your father and me a lot."

"That's right. For the companionship. But there was that bit about me 'leading the hunt.'"

"Point taken."

"Actually, Jerry, as it turns out, I've also got some questions that I don't think have really been answered? Such as, who exactly are those gentlemen, and what precisely do they do?"

"Well, like I told—"

"I know. Waste management. That just seems a little vague. Anyway, I believe these are reasonable questions. So let's just say I'm on hold for now."

"Goddamn, Toom," Jerry said, calm and low and sleepy-eyed, "it's not like I'm asking you to submit your dick for scientific inquiry," but he flushed and swelled at the neck, straining for, or at, or against *something*. "Listen, not to get off the subject, but what'd you make of Dickie Fitzgerald's big news?"

"That it's long overdue, I'd say. Now Inky can pack Dickie Junior off to military school where he belongs and get on with the shambles that are her life."

"Mm . . . you're referring to what exactly, Toom?"

"Divorce. Looks to me like they're about to crash-land in district court. Although Dickie of course is in denial, which figures."

"Yeah, right. *That*." Jerry hit the flask again and lit another cigarette. A slow smile drew his face tight behind a curtain of blue smoke, a thought obviously dawning on him as he put two and two together. "Sumbitch didn't tell you, did he?"

"Tell me what, Jerry?"

"Well, one, since you brought it up, he's got the drop on Inky McCoo big time, and they *will* endure in holy matrimony. Guaranteed. Something to do with a quid pro quo in the prenuptial, I think is how I heard it. But anyway, that's really beside the point. Fact is, Toomey"—Jerry took a drag on his cig and started to laugh, but ended hacking and hawking smoke into his lap. He looked up, smiling and red-faced, thick carotid artery visibly pulsing. He shook his head and looked back at his lap, still grinning. "Goddamn, I can't believe he didn't tell you himself."

"C'mon, Jerry. The suspense is killing me."

"Well, Toom, here's the thing: your ol' buddy Dickie Fitzgerald is running for mayor, too."

"You jest."

"Ho no. Here. Just in case you didn't quite believe your own ears." Jerry extracted a long white pamphlet from a pocket inside his jacket and handed it to me. Sure enough, "Fitzgerald for Mayor" was emblazoned in red and blue letters across the front. Christ. What was Dickie thinking? "So you see, Toom, you and Dickie are now adversaries in a new and potentially meaningful way. No more kid stuff."

"I wouldn't expect his campaign to stay on a lofty, uh—"

"No, neither would I, Toom. Low road all the way." Jerry made a wavy, submarining motion with his hand. Then he lit two cigarettes at once and passed me one. "Prepare to tread shit, son." Jerry rose as if to go, patting his pockets, and spoke past the cigarette he clenched between his teeth. A long ash fell to the floor. "So what do you say, Toom? Sunday's the last day of deer season, and in all likelihood your last best chance to butter up those Panthrex boys. Who'd really welcome the opportunity to advance your campaign, don't forget. Now why don't you plan on spending Sunday morning in the woods, hm? And maybe slay a big old buck in the bargain."

"Jerry—"

"I know, I know. Just kidding."

I agreed, and we made plans for me to meet Jerry at his place just after first light Sunday, to meet Jerry and his business acquaintants from out of state, that is. Coffee at dawn—probably spiked with bluegrass whiskey—hot country ham and scrambled eggs, and a long, unhappy morning crouched low in a damp blind or high on a windy stand with more than likely unprincipled sportsmen and captains of ambiguous industry.

Right before my eyes, Sunday had shaped up onerously.

That night I again dreamt of General Truman Spooner his own gallant self, twisted into some painful configuration among his fallen boys on the banks of the Potomac, all of them yet warm in the sweet morning sun. Faint magneto hum of flies. A saddled, riderless horse, confounded, picking his way among the dead. And a bereted, downy-cheeked private huddled in an eruption of wild roses, shivering, gazing out over the fresh necropolis and, beyond that, the wide river, absentmindedly gathering the coils of his wet, dusty viscera and slipping them back through the long, jagged incision across his abdomen—he is gradually going into shock, retreating into his own memory, to the smells of his childhood, to the comfort of his mama's bosom *carry me home carry me home carry me home* and finally, before he drifts irretrievably away, there is the sound of his general's voice *we are good men, and we are brave men, and we have fought for what we believed, but never forget that a glorious failure is no failure at all.*

CHAPTER FOUR

The next morning, after breakfast, Willie and I went for a walk. The long Indian summer was finally over, and the bare trees stood spidery and crazed against the colorless hills. The sun was a dull white disk out ahead of us, obscure behind thin clouds bunched in the east. Willie crunched through the dry autumn leaves beside me, and Zero brought up the rear, zigzagging from tree to tree to tree, wagging his big head back and forth, nose close to the ground. A rifle exploded in the distance, its echo quickly damped by the gathering moisture. Hunt's place was just over the next rise, though still a ways off.

"You know, Toomey," Willie said hoarsely, a little winded from the hike, "working with those peckerwood desperadoes on a regular basis, not a lot surprises me anymore. But I swear, the goddamned *audacity* of Dickie Fitzgerald!" Referring, I understood, to Dickie's mayoral bid—which of course she'd first heard of this morning—and the pall his historical imprudence must surely cast over any aspiration of Dickie's to public office. Not to mention that there existed a vivid and very public (if not exactly conclusive) record of said turpitude. Willie had stopped and I turned to her.

"I know," I said, shrugging, "I don't get it either."

Beginning, I suppose, with the fact that Dickie had twice come under indictment, though actually in neither case was he finally convicted. Still. Everybody around here knew he was guilty. *He* knew he was guilty. He knew everybody knew he was guilty. Once for fraud resulting from a low-bid contractual obligation to the state for roadwork never completed. Never even broke ground, yet the money nevertheless disappeared. The other time for conspiring to ventilate his old buddy Doggie Phipps in what amounted to a botched midnight bushwhacking. *Somebody* ruined Doggie's empty cruiser, directing a shitstorm of .12 gauge slugs and buckshot against it. Doggie, who was then the sheriff of Mann County and probably well deserved what he almost got, was at the time investigating the locally murderous marijuana trade, working with, and at the behest of, federal agents. After that, Doggie lost his taste for law enforcement altogether and declined to seek a second term in office. (It was a bad period for marijuana farmers, a time when only the worst were in the business. Over time, though, most of the real bad guys ended up in jail and left the commerce to local boys who really didn't mean anybody any harm.)

Plus there were the dreary domestic misdemeanors, never fully adjudicated. Charges filed in the heat of the moment, dropped in the morning like nothing but a bad idea. But still the primary evidence of Dickie's liability skulked around Oceana. Inky Fitzgerald (nee McCoo) in big dark glasses, purplish skin edging from behind one wide lens as she sniffed a cantaloupe at the IGA Foodliner or sat at a red light on Main Street, gazing neither left nor right and grinding her teeth. And Dickie Junior had suffered an unlikely series of injuries requiring casts and braces and slings. Not to mention an affliction the family termed Tourette's syndrome that manifested itself as exhaustive banshee cursing, often in public. Social workers were known to have visited the Fitzgerald manse. Unannounced and frequently. Though no more than that was known. Nevertheless.

But the substantiations—or *trans*substantiations—of Dickie's real depravity, the now aged sons of Pearl the goat, presently gorged themselves on an ever diminishing hedgerow of wild roses at my place: Meshach, Shadrach, and Abednego.

The summer I turned fifteen, I spent fishing for carp, mainly. Just for sport, of course, because at that time, around here anyway, only Negroes actually ate carp. But I liked fishing for carp because they were far and away the biggest fish plying the North Fork (excluding the apocryphal catfish, "big as men," supposedly bottom-feeding down by the corps of engineers dam): I tossed them intact back into the slow, black water—their splashes sounding deep and bottomless tones rather than the glassy, glittering ones of lesser fish—and watched them vanish like ghosts into the deep, still pools. That fall Dickie and I entered Mann County Senior as sophomores, and the American Farmers of Tomorrow end-of-summer show fell halfway between the start of school and Halloween, on the last Saturday of September.

The show was sponsored by local businesses, mainly ag related, and everywhere there were bright banners stretched across corrugated metal barn walls—Ripsaw's Grain & Feed, Dewey Implement, John Petticrew DMV, et cetera—and long strings of triangular, red, white, and blue flags alternately snapping to and falling slack in the capricious breeze. Low white clouds edged with gray scudded west to east in an otherwise profound and blue sky, and a lot of pale brown dust hung in the cool autumn air in expanding, billowy columns above rowdy horses and temperamental bulls, who huffed and stamped and snorted and just generally showed off for onlookers. Mostly out of sight but on every side, chickens and goats and hogs and cows clucked and bleated and snorted and mooed. I hadn't entered any beasts in the show, but most of my friends had, and

I was just loitering and wandering the grounds, stopping to talk here and there and vaguely hoping to hook up with a girl. Killing time on a Saturday afternoon. I didn't much care for animal husbandry nor horticulture, though it pleased me when my friends took ribbons, and I was happy to be there among the exhibitors, the popcorn and soft drink and hot dog vendors, the clattering hooves and wind-blown feathers, and the myriad, evocative odors of salves, manure, hay, and sun-warmed fur.

I didn't then smoke among known adults—though if I were in an adjacent county or town, I smoked boldly and with what I took to be a certain amount of savoir faire—so I skulked off into the peripheral woods at the south edge of the show and walked along a ridge looking for a path just to the downside of the hill. Something a little out of the way. Soon I came to a path and slanted down it, tapped out a Camel and lit it, the wind gusting and rustling the dead and dying forest, when I heard, faintly and nearly whelmed in the wind, the mournful bleating of some creature, a goat. I tilted my head against the wind so it wouldn't whistle in my ears, closed my eyes, and listened intently. It seemed to come from below.

At the bottom of the shadowy gorge, the air was cool and humid and green and it chilled me, raising goosebumps along my forearms and thighs. I stood still for a moment and listened again; then I followed a muddy rill strewn with soft, rotted logs and limbs uphill, apparently toward its source, and climbed the flat, mossy stones along its bed like steps. Here and there I stopped to listen before I continued.

From a distance, and through a dense mesh of sumac and rhododendron, I spotted the goat, a black nanny with a big, snowy white spot on her side, and I remember thinking: Pearl—as if that were her name even then. She was sipping water from a small pool, in a grotto at the foot of a soaring limestone wall. A chain around her neck, glinting in a shifting beam of sunlight, looped away and was fastened to an anemic tree that had struggled from a crack in the vast rock face. She paused and looked up in my direction; either she'd smelled me or she'd heard a twig snap. Her ears flicked like switches, first one and then the other. After a moment I recognized her as Dickie Fitzgerald's goat; he'd shown her that very afternoon at the AFT show and drawn for himself a lot of adverse attention when she'd failed to earn him a ribbon: he'd sworn blasphemously and kicked savagely at a fence post before a small, silent, shifting knot of onlookers, cross-armed and askance and studying their boots and shoes, as country folk are wont to do (that is, as if they weren't really paying any attention whatsoever, when in fact no detail escapes their lapidarian scrutiny, saving for later their semi-private expressions of grim disapproval, for the days and months and years to come).

Then a figure whom I took to be Dickie appeared—despite that I could not make out his face—and I crouched there where I was, at considerable remove, and watched. He was at that time a full head taller than me, and maintaining my voyeur's attitude seemed like the prudent thing. But, squatting like that on my haunches, my view was even further obscured, though I could still make out bits and pieces of the panorama through narrow openings between the fleshy leaves of mountain laurel. My abdomen stirred as if my lower viscera were slowly revolving, and I harbored some dreadful suspicion I couldn't have named.

All I could see from my new vantage—or *dis*advantage—were blue jean-clad legs from the knee down (rolled up, faded jeans over old cowboy boots with curled tips), as well as the goat's, Pearl's, shifting there in the dry, superfine dust beneath the limestone overhang, where it had not rained for many, many years, perhaps ever; so little clouds rose now at the least disturbance. Boots scuffed through the dust and pulled up flush to Pearl's hindquarters, the curled, pointed toes nearly touching her fetlocks, knees almost resting upon her hocks. Then there was a rocking motion to the legs, as if Dickie (and I was *certain* it was him) were trying to dislodge the goat, but Pearl held her ground—though she rocked, her hooves had found firm purchase in the thin dust—even as she bawled in the echo chamber of the cavern. Unsuccessfully, I strained to get a better look without shifting in the brush. I needed to confirm my strong, sickening suspicion. But it was not to be. Nevertheless, I knew.

Dickie had been gone for hours by the time I crept from my blind. He'd left Pearl tethered to the scrawny tree, and I kept thinking he might return. The sun had disappeared over the ridge and it had gotten quite dark in the gorge, but the sky was still blue and streaked with diffusing trails of jet vapor. But at least there was a little light left.

I unfastened Pearl's chain and led her by it through the woods, around and over the limestone wall to the next ridge and then down to and across a long, flat valley—filled with wildflowers in the summer—I knew to be owned by Caesura Toller, Jerry's former sister-in-law and, as I vaguely understood it, at that time his girlfriend. Finally we reached a gravel backroad that intersected another backroad that eventually led out to our place. Pearl and I pulled in about midnight. Insects and amphibians buzzed in the ditches along the road, and a gaudy harvest moon, orange and abundant, sat fatly on the horizon out ahead of us, lighting our way.

Come spring, and I bought an old billy goat—he had a graying goatee and yellow eyes—from our forever neighbor Tirey Loy (a contemporary of my grandfather's), and he and Pearl took immediately to one another. They nuzzled and gently butted heads and slept curled together, and they rutted when Pearl came into heat. The first two times, the billy goat's seed failed in its calling, but the third time, as if to nullify the disappointment of their previous efforts, Pearl grew large with kids. Three of them. And the old billy goat stood proud guard over his wobbly-kneed brood, lowering his twisted horns at any provocateur, real or imagined. But just as his three sons—Meshach, Shadrach, and Abednego—were coming into their own and sprouting furry little knobs on top of their heads, the old billy goat, who I now regret to say I never named, succumbed to a large tumor that had blossomed between his ribs and his heart. In another year, less, actually, brucellosis claimed Pearl, and it was only luck that she didn't infect her now orphaned sons. With Deddy's permission, I buried her on the periphery of our family plot, up there on the mountain, and I marked her grave with a big, flat riverbed stone onto which I'd etched "Pearl" with a claw hammer and a rusty railroad spike I found in the toolshed.

My class graduated from high school that spring and Deddy suggested a celebration at our place, kegs on him. We drove to Lexington together and picked up the kegs at Big Daddy's liquor store (Mann County was still dry in those days). I put the kegs in an old claw-footed bathtub in our barn and stacked bags of ice around them. Mama in the meantime had strung multicolored Japanese lanterns through the rafters of the barn and thereby canceled out any ostensible hoe-down effect, pretty much inevitable there among the stacked bales of hay and overripe horse stalls. Almost as an afterthought, I herded the sons of Pearl into the paddock that led into the barn, where they'd be unavoidably visible through the wide, raised barn door. All three took pretty directly after their mother,

Shadrach and Abednego almost identically: only in Meshach had any of the old billy goat shown up.

By six o'clock my classmates had begun to arrive in twos and threes and fours, and by seven the barn was crowded with ebullient teenagers, supercharged and hopeful with respect to the night and the rest of their lives. Oblongs of beer foam flew end over end from jostled plastic cups, pocking the talc-fine dust in the barn, and big plans were laid out in rash, ill-considered particulars. I had watched Sewell's friends languish around here for years after similar declarations of verve and independence, following *their* graduation.

At last Dickie rumbled into the sideyard, pulling in between the chicken coop and the back porch in his huge new Ford pickup, a graduation gift from his mother. He climbed out, cradling a pewter stein, and said hi to my mother through the screen door—I'll say this for Dickie, he never passed up an opportunity to flatter and wheedle. Then he ambled over. Soon he was flocked around by pretty girls and square-headed jocks, all jabbering away and competing for his attention: Dickie was probably the most "popular" kid in our class. I was frankly near sick at the sight but closely attended to the scene nonetheless, hoping the initial hubbub would soon subside, and it did. I watched Dickie glide athletically across the paddock and into the barn—smiling, nodding howdy do—duck the low-slung Japanese lanterns and head for the kegs propped in the bathtub.

But he stopped dead just short of the kegs, and a curious, impenetrable look passed over his face. He'd seen the goats in the opposite paddock through the barn door, and he seemed to be studying them, and something in him knew something was fishy, something *he couldn't have named.* It was as if I could see the machinery at work in his head, making all the necessary, unhappy connections: the gears spinning, the magneto humming, the cylinder firing, and the hammer falling. Some other boys had by now caught up to him and were taking turns at the keg and telling lies that would pass forevermore as gospel. But Dickie was lost to them, assessing the moment, deaf to the commotion around him.

Being considerably taller than the other boys, when his head swiveled in my direction the effect was that of a water-borne crocodile locating its prey: only Dickie's eyes were visible above the heads of the others. It was the moment I'd been waiting for. I nodded at Dickie—yes, yes, it's just as you think, you fucking turd—but I surprised myself by taking no delight in the moment. I took no delight because in fact it made me feel sick and small to have orchestrated this awful thing and to realize that the world would have been a better place if I had simply saved the goat and kept it to myself. Regardless of how I felt about Dickie, and regardless of his own demonstrable depravity, it was the most devastating thing I'd ever done to another human being.

But Dickie glanced again at Pearl's orphans, who were so clearly her progeny, and back at me and took one stupid step in my direction. Stupid because—well, what was he going to do? Then, thinking a little more clearly, he stopped, reversed himself, and strode, with his empty pewter stein dangling at his side—his back as angular and obdurate as a piece of plywood beneath his silky western shirt—back to his new pickup. In a moment he was gone, and through the open barn door, beyond the goats, I watched a cloud of pale dust form over the road that followed the contours of the mountain.

Still advancing through the woods towards Hunt's place, I said, "Willie, are you aware that Dickie's Christian name is Richard Hedley Fitzgerald?"

"No." Willie's class was six years behind mine and Dickie's. If

Drema had graduated from Mann County High, she and Willie would have been in the same class.

"Yep. We—some of us, anyway—used to call him Dick Hed."

Willie said, "Well. What's he thinking right now is what I'd like to know."

"I wonder," I said. Not even Willie knew about Pearl the goat. I'd never told a soul. Not only because it was so awful, but because—in a critical sense—I hadn't actually witnessed anything. I'd had to make an imaginative leap, albeit a very small one, no more than a short hop really. Still. It had always been enough to keep me silent on the issue. Though maybe not for much longer. "But I guess it's honest. Dickie's of an audacious clan, honey."

"You could say that again."

Hunt's cabin was in sight now, just down a long, slow slope, among a thicket of ginkgo trees planted and nursed long ago by old Agee, Virgil's father and Hunt's stepfather. The ginkgoes' leaves were uniformly, brilliantly yellow and would fall en masse any day. A feathery plume of smoke curled from Hunt's chimney, and I thought I saw movement through one of the windows. Willie had never visited with Hunt at his place before.

We noisily surmounted Hunt's front porch in our heavy hiking boots, Willie wide-eyed and a little aghast at Hunt's exterior decor: here he exhibited to the world his extensive collection of animal skulls, each one carefully scrubbed of any remaining hide, bleached and exactingly placed into the context of some larger design known only to himself. But I'd watched him consider a new acquisition, turning it over in his rough hands at some distance from his cabin, glancing down at the skull, up at the cabin, squinting, tilting his head first left, then right, until its position in his menagerie was made manifest to him. At any rate, for Hunt it was not a random process. Most of the skulls swung heavily on lengths of fishing line, from the porch railing and along beneath the eaves of the cabin. They brushed one another in the breeze, and sounded the warm deathly notes of clay wind chimes. Others sat in windowsills and hung from nails against the side of his cabin in arranged clusters, in diamonds and circles and crosses. They represented the last earthly remains of many species: squirrels, possums, deer, skunks, cows, and I don't know what all. But Hunt did. He could estimate their ages at death by examining their teeth. Among other things, he was a sort of self-made naturalist. He idolized David Attenborough, the PBS guy, and in reference to him always punctiliously included the title "Sir."

"This far exceeds your rather underplayed description, Toomey." Willie stepped off the far side of the porch and disappeared around the corner of the house. I knocked and waited; then I lit a cigarette. Soon Willie appeared from around the opposite side of the house, having completed her preliminary tour of the grounds. "Hunt didn't, hm, you know," she said, admiring one of his configurations and raising a phantom rifle. She sighted down a phantom barrel, and pulled a phantom trigger.

"No, he didn't. He scavenges. In the woods, along the road. He just takes what's there." I knocked again and stood looking at the door. "Hunt! Hey, Hunt!" I tapped on the window. Still nothing, so I went on in and Willie followed me.

There was a big fire banked in the fireplace, recently stoked, the top logs not even yet scorched where the flames licked at their undersides; the wood was green and it hissed. An empty plate, a piece of Mama's china—the whole set had somehow passed directly to Hunt upon her death—sat on the table; next to it a steaming cup of black coffee and a fork on a folded paper towel. There was a thick buckwheat pancake in a cast-iron skillet on the stove, still warm to the touch, and a full pot of coffee. I poured two cups and handed one to Willie. And, as usual, the whole place smelled like wet dogs. Which would have been one thing had Hunt actually kept dogs.

"What's wrong?" Willie asked, reading my expression.

"Just . . . *Hunt*." He'd seen us coming and withdrawn, an old tiresome trick of his. When and why were unforeseeable. "Have a seat." I rolled up a butt out of Hunt's stash of Bugler. It was the least he could do.

Willie wandered around the one big room, sipping her coffee and examining the artifacts along the walls and shelves; the interior collection was primarily inorganic and altogether less macabre than the exterior one, though still suggesting misfortune and conjuring a dead, dead past—yet somehow reminiscent of a more innocent epoch, too: a yellowed baseball with rotten threads curling out along its seams; an old hobbyhorse in one corner that somebody had used for target practice, pocked and splintered by bullets, its lips drawn back and forever frozen over long teeth in defiant mid-whinny; Drema's baby shoes, not bronzed but dry and flaking away to dust on the mantel; an upturned hubcap full of gleaming arrowheads Hunt and Deddy had dug as boys from the fields and hills; a little glass globe, within which the Tin Man, the Scarecrow, and the Cowardly Lion trooped across a field of bright poppies, in a snowstorm if the thing were turned up, then righted; and, among numerous photographs elaborately framed but hung askew, a black-and-white eight-by-ten of Hunt and—I swear to God—a young Elvis Aron Presley, both boys smiling unaffectedly and leaning in close to the lens of the anonymous photographer. Hunt and Elvis appeared to be on the midway of some backwater fair. Next to where this photo hung was another, taken on the same spot, of Elvis and a young black guy, about the same age as Hunt and the King.

"Toomey?" Willie had removed the Elvis/Hunt photo from the wall and held it in both hands.

"You'll have to ask Hunt, honey. I *really* don't know." And I didn't. Getting a straight answer from Hunt was just about impossible. On all subjects equally, he tended to speak obliquely and elliptically, never quite addressing himself to the matter at hand, nor finishing whatever loopy discourse he *had* embarked upon.

Almost ever since I could remember he'd been on a trajectory increasingly eccentric and solitary. For a time, not long after he'd moved out here to be alone, he collected radiator hose. Miles of it. I remember it stacked and strewn among the ginkgoes and far into the cedar woods beyond. Hunt said it was all that stood between us and the collapse of civilization, and his aim was to horde enough of the stuff to ensure that very same collapse. Before long, though, Deddy'd had just about enough of it, and one Saturday afternoon he hired the Needham brothers to back their dump truck in here and haul it all away. I remember Hunt watching the Needhams from his front porch. All day they hauled armloads of black hose to their truck, and periodically they trundled a load off to the dump. Hunt didn't raise a finger to stop them; he just sat there on the top step with his chin in his hands, looking forlorn and like he might cry under Deddy's uncharacteristic scowl. It was one of the saddest things I had ever seen.

I told Willie all this and then poured us each another cup of coffee. I looked around for the sugar this time but couldn't find any.

We finished our coffee and, when it became apparent Hunt wasn't granting audiences, put on our coats to leave. On the way out, I stopped at Hunt's writing desk, where one volume of the old family journal was laid open. They were thick, dusty things bound in leather, and Hunt often pored over them at night. Impulsively, I closed it up and tucked it under my arm. I hadn't really looked at any of them since I was a kid. Virgil, my great-grandfather and my father's namesake, and then Agee had kept the journal and made detailed, daily entries. Through the years after Agee's death, other family members had scribbled periodic entries, but it suffered then for its lack of continuity, its loss of preoccupation with the *dailiness* of tribulation. I left Hunt a note telling him I'd taken it, as he tended to become unnecessarily alarmed.

Willie and I headed back through the woods toward my place, and Zero ran out ahead of us, smiling now and then back over his shoulder, his tongue lolling over his teeth and trailing spittle. We took the long way back and walked along a ridge over the North Fork. The iron-colored water was visible below, through bare trees.

It was nearing noon, and dark, empurpled clouds now ran across the sky in heavy folds, like a plush old theater curtain. A distant boom betrayed a jet pilot somewheres a-way up there, slipping into the heavy cover and then pushing out, above it and into the sunshine, wisps of cloud vapor trailing away from the tips of his wings, the polished nose of his jet reflecting spiked, dazzling rays of light. Some square-headed kid from Tuscaloosa or Boise or Akron, patriotic, well intentioned and crew cut, probably thinking of a girl or a game of pickup with the guys or an ice cold beer—or *whatever*— but at any rate certainly not *there* there, soaring at thirty, thirty-five, maybe forty thousand feet ("Who knows, Willie!") over Oceana, Kentucky, faster than the speed of sound and accomplishing like crazy.

CHAPTER FIVE

P-POW!

"Well, hoo fucking ray!"

"Nailed that cocksucker!"

Big men—dilettantes, as it would happen, despite that prevaricating asshole Jerry's assertion that they knew what they were doing—churned about seemingly at cross purposes on the rickety platform, desperate to alight and give chase. I kept a close eye on their long blue rifle barrels, recklessly waved in the morning sun. The buck, preternaturally cool and abstracted for a moment after he was hit, his shoulder already dark and slick with a bucket of his own blood, had suddenly vaulted into the nearby trees and brush. Poof: it was as if he'd leapt out of existence. But even these inflamed amateurs knew better than that, so I followed them at what I took to be a safe distance and reminded them to keep their rifles aimed at the ground. "Otherwise," I said, and then vaguely added "well," and left it at that. I hoped it conveyed an ambiguous but gloomy portent.

The morning had begun pretty much as I'd had it figured. I pulled into Jerry's yard just as the sky was paling and parked among the pickups already nuzzled up to his porch. His house was painted blue, and the trim and porch white, in honor of the University of Kentucky's colors. A patina of frosty barnacles had settled over everything during the night, and I came *that close* to busting my ass on the way up the porch steps. Inside it was warm near the wood stove and there was a superabundance of the weird camaraderie that wells up among men who are strangers to one another but who nevertheless bond as brothers in the hours and minutes preceding blood sport. All for one, et cetera. Hearty smiles flourished.

Vincent Bologna, with an oily grin playing over long, piano-key teeth—one of the Panthrex advance men from the Stocking Stuffers'—circled the room with sweet black coffee and a little cream pitcher of whiskey and kept every cup full to the brim. Mine included. It was necessary fortification for the work ahead and meant nothing in the long run. Jerry, meanwhile, proved anew his monodextrous proficiency: he broke the bright, creamy yolks of perfect over-easy eggs on biscuit halves and grilled thick slabs of country ham; he ran plump oranges through a manual juicer; he fried potatoes with celery and onions in sizzling drippings and kept Vincent Bologna supplied with fresh coffee and hundred-proof Turkey.

"Lawdy, Miss Clawdy," Jerry said, gesturing with a greasy spatula, "I declare I do believe in the superiority of country cookin', the beneficence of fellowship, and the . . . the irrefutably *salubrious* effects of expensive bourbon whiskey."

"Here, here."

"To Jerry." Coffee cups were tipped in Jerry's general direction, then drained. Vincent made another pass of the room with the coffee pot and cream pitcher. Before long, and as if on cue, we stood up and began to rummage the room for our discarded coats and down vests and hunting caps.

We drove over to Pearce County in four pickups, through the Stonecastle River Gorge and into an area known as Long Meadow, near the Sheilsburg Correctional Facility; there we parked along a service road and split into two groups to hunt from a pair of stands on either side of a wide valley. Me and three of the Panthrex guys—

Bob Gregorio, Anthony DeRossi, and Tommy Iarusso—on the north rim, and Jerry, Dolin Smits, Lester Coombs, and Vincent Bologna, the senior member of the Panthrex exploratory phalanx, on the south. Dolin was a humorless, bovine man who was nevertheless on the school board, a body wielding considerable influence where the allocation of public land was concerned. He was also a well-known associate of Dickie Fitzgerald's. He'd somehow been implicated in the state contract scheme but, like Dickie, had walked. Lester was a lifelong friend of Jerry and my father, and an old-time country doctor with stiff white hair jutting from his jug ears. He composed weird fiddle tunes he could no longer play because his big hands were gnarled with arthritis, but regardless of which he hunted deer each season, fished throughout the spring and summer, and climbed rocky slopes to birth unlucky infants in overheated, one-room trailers. He had, years earlier, been mayor of Oceana himself. In fact, he had whipped my father's ass but good in one election. Lester didn't take much shit nor happily endure wheedling flummery, and all morning I'd been wondering how he and Vincent Bologna were getting on. Or Lester and Dolin the Ponderless for that matter. Always the team player, Dolin—in his bland, chummy way—was clearly in the Panthrex camp. I couldn't help but wonder how come. Dolin, again like Dickie, was known to steer entirely clear of nonprofit alliances.

All of which brought us to this: a miserable cold morning with us hunched on a stand sipping Jim Beam, Bob Gregorio's preposterously lucky shot, and the depressing chase, which was characterized by an unattractive desperation, way beyond what would have been reasonable—the men wild-eyed and greedy, fearful of losing the animal to the forest, unnecessarily so not only because the buck didn't have long to live and wouldn't get far, but because he'd left a seriously consequential trail of blood that even a blind hog could've tracked from here to Lexington.

"Lower those goddamn barrels," I shouted up ahead for the third time. Mottled by sunlight streaking through the bare trees, they jogged on, glancing at me over their shoulders and sheepishly lowering their rifles.

Bob Gregorio called back over his shoulder, "Couldn't've got too far. Not the way he's leaking."

Indeed not. We very soon came upon the buck where he'd collapsed across a shallow rill, one glassy eye aimed skyward, the other, beneath, sunk in silt. The corpse acted as a dam, the water rising against his belly, flowing around either end, past nose and tail, tail fluttered in the rippling current. Blood still trickled from a perfectly round little hole in his neck and mixed with the water, in which the red fanned away and disappeared. From here, probably, to the Stonecastle River, which emptied into the Kentucky, then the Mississippi and finally into the Gulf of Mexico. His big ribs were so still. Eight points branched from the crown of the buck's head: four of those poked into the wet gray clay.

Bob Gregorio was hovering over his kill when he looked dead at me and said, "Now what?" He looked back down at the buck and nudged it with the toe of his boot. *Now* what? Well, *now* I could quit wondering whether or not Jerry had lied to me. *Now* I knew these guys came up at least somewhat short of being "real pros at this sort of thing," as Jerry had put it.

"Evisceration, Bob. And don't kick at your trophy like that."

"Wha'd'ya mean?" He had gone sort of blank and his face sagged a little, as if gravity had just been turned up a few notches.

"You know," I said, stepping in toward Bob and his buck and drawing a finger vertically across my own sloshables, "gut him."

"Hm." Bob adjusted his balls and looked past me, somewhere off into the middle distance. "Here's the thing, Toomey," he said, hitting an earnest, man-to-man note, "I've always hunted with a guide . . . or *some*body." He nodded as if a guide—or *some*body—were now present and being acknowledged. "You know? I mean, I shoot things. But the next time I see it, it's on a plate with a side of mashed potatoes and candied baby carrots."

Of course I saw where Bob was headed, but one of the reasons, *the* reason, I refused to hunt—and even on this day I carried no weapon—was sheer gut-churning revulsion at such an intimate transaction with a largish fellow mammal. It stirred things up in me. So my qualms weren't moral, at all, they were constitutional, and there was no room for flexibility on the issue. The upshot of which was that I'd be a son of a bitch if I was going to clean up Bob's mess.

"I can walk you through it, Bob, but that's about it."

"I guess that'll have to do."

"OK, let's see," I sighed. I looked the thing over just to sort of get my bearings. "All right. Slip your knife in right there at about his breastbone and draw an incision around to here," I said, tracing a line with my finger down from my sternum. "Not too deep, though, cause you'll want to avoid engaging the organs. That can get pretty awful. 'Bout like that." I raised my index finger and marked a knuckle with my thumb, indicating what I imagined was the proper depth. "Maybe less than that, even. Otherwise, it'll get messy. Then you've got to reach in there and sever the esophagus and trachea, which you'll recognize right off. Sort of like hoses. Grab ahold of them and pull. And scoop out everything that doesn't look like steak or ribs or something to eat. And there you are. You've field-gutted your trophy."

"So that's all there is to it, huh?"

"Pretty much, yeah. It's not rocket science. Except you'll probably want to stuff that cavity with leaves. The meat keeps better that way." Bob, Tommy, and Anthony were all hovering like high school wrestlers, bent a little at the waist and warily circling the carcass, Tommy and Anthony edging almost imperceptibly away, creating a little distance.

I withdrew Deddy's hunting knife from the army knapsack I carried. It was about a foot long and razor sharp and had a long, curved bone handle. And a pronounced blood gutter. Its wide blade flashed in the sun. Deddy had carved game with it and had once waved it in Hunt's face. I could remember that. But I didn't know why. I also remember Mama pleading with Deddy, but nothing specific. And then Hunt moved out of the old house, my house now, and into the cabin. To be alone? I must have been four or five, an age at which life is vast and vivid and wholly unpredictable. More than any full-grown person could stand.

"Here you go, Bob."

Bob slipped the knife in his belt, and he and the other two dragged the buck out of the water and tilted him back so as to rest him flat on his spine. Tommy straddled the buck's head and held its front legs aloft and apart. Anthony positioned himself identically, only aft, straddling the tail. Bob, knife in hand now, circled the buck, figuring where his advantage might lie. It was a unique approach, but I didn't really see anything wrong with it. Not that I'm an expert. I sat on a log at a little distance from this experiment, lit a cigarette and withdrew a plastic flask. The whiskey burned going down.

Bob at last settled into position on the buck's right side and bent to his task. He looked the gravity-flattened white belly up and down and, after some false starts, finally slid the knife into position in the buck's chest. I think he actually slipped it in and withdrew it before he stood and took a couple of heavy steps away, his face drained and grayish, the back of his hand raised to his lips. A couple of deep breaths, his bony back expanding somewhat radically beneath his checked pea coat, and he was back at it without hesitation this time. He carefully slid the knife in and drew it steadily toward the buck's nether region, down along its belly toward its sexual apparatus, just to where I'd shown him. From where I sat it looked like a clean, effective incision. But evidently it was not.

Anthony gagged first, but only by a millisecond. His whole body sagged dramatically and he released the two hooves he had held suspended and took two or three steps back, clapping his hands to his face just as his heel caught on a stone, and he sat down hard. Tommy, too, abandoned his position, violently flinging the fore legs away as he backpedaled. Only Bob held his ground, squatting there by the buck undeterred, though frowning; and, with the sudden retreat of his partners, the buck flopped over onto its side and Bob watched intestines released from the buck's gaping belly pile up in warm wet coils around and over his boots.

"Jesus Christ." Bob said this under his breath, and with no special emphasis, like a resigned, reluctant groom uttering "I do." And at that moment, I kind of liked him.

"'I'm afraid you got into the stomach there, Bob." I knew he had because now I could smell the bile, and I was beginning to taste hot juices creeping around on the back of my own tongue. "But don't stop now. Get the trachea and esophagus, quick. Otherwise you'll taint that meat and this is all for nothing."

Without hesitation, or even a glance in any direction, Bob got to it, vigorously and perhaps a little indiscriminately. I mean to say the blood and guts flew. Finally, bloody and winded, Bob stood amidst the steaming entrails and turned to me. "Now what?"

"Well. Prop that cavity up with a couple of sturdy sticks and stuff it full of leaves. Then you can use that tag you already paid for and we'll haul him back up to the truck."

After we'd taken care of Bob's trophy, which had dressed out at probably one forty, one forty-five, we had to abandon the stand and take to the fields in hopes of flushing prey. By then the sun was high enough that I doubted any deer were still at large, foraging in the wintry, wheat-colored hills and meadows for the odd new shoot or tender sprout. Spaced at perhaps thirty paces, the four of us advanced slowly over the wide valley toward its mouth, where we cut on through to an adjacent valley, which was longer but narrower, wedged as it was between steeper, less hospitable hills. Finally a small button buck sprang from cover out ahead of Anthony, who winged it, though not fatally. When we found the exhausted animal, panting and sprawled in a ditch, I stepped down to it, the gutting knife already withdrawn, and cut the frightened animal's throat, quickly and severely, and dark blood, thick with coagulants—thick with *fear*—oozed over and into the cracked, frozen earth. Bob helped Anthony gut it. I smoked a cigarette and sipped at the flask again, hoping to stanch a rising nausea.

Towering cottony clouds sailed through the otherwise bright sky over the valley, their vast shadows rippling over the dead grass and bare trees of the bottomland, and then up and away, climbing the slopes of the hills and disappearing at oblique angles over the rim of the encompassing ridge. The whiskey tasted good. As the hard-edged outline of the here and now fell boozily slack, I capped the flask and began to look around; and I felt strongly that I recognized this place. False memory? Maybe. I knew enough to suspect it. And so many places around here look so much alike. A cloud passed over the sun and I was suddenly chilled. Bob approached, his thin shoulders peaked and in sharp descent to where they met his long neck. Like an ambling M.

"Mind if I hit that, Toomey?"

I handed Bob the flask. Looking past Bob, I could see he'd left Anthony and Tommy the grunt work of scrounging for leaves. Which seemed fair. Anthony was hustling around while Tommy idly kicked at something in the tall grass. When three pistol shots echoed through the valley, Tommy quit kicking at whatever it was and started looking left and right, like a man trying to cross a busy street.

Bob said, "What's that, you s'pose?"

"Just Jerry. They're headed back to his place, calling it a day. Which strikes me as a pretty good idea." Bob handed the flask back and I hit it, too. When I tipped my head, I saw that a chicken hawk was riding the thermals above the northeastern end of the valley, circling down and away in a wide arc and disappearing into yet the next valley.

"It's beautiful here, Toomey." He took another big swig and said, "Not a lot like north Jersey." Some bird or the other piped a long, high note. A breeze kicked some leaves along the ground around our feet and rattled the dry undergrowth.

"You know, Bob, I didn't know where you guys were from. Actually, there's plenty I don't know."

"Well. Like what?"

"I don't know. It's just that Jerry's been kind of evasive. All I've gotten out of him is 'waste management.' But I don't know what that means. Nor have I arrived at any understanding of what exactly it is you all want with me. Provided I win this election, of course."

Bob laughed. "My guess is Jerry's stringing us both along just to see what all it adds up to for Jerry. He's been assuring us you understood our . . . *agenda.* And that you were definitely predisposed to be cooperative."

"Did he?" I lit a cigarette. I smoked for a minute in silence, kicking rhythmically at a big limestone rock embedded in the ground. "So, Bob: tell me what I need to know."

"What?"

"About Panthrex. Bring me up to speed here."

"Oh." We passed the flask again, draining it this time. "Well, what the hell. I'm certainly not married to the corporation, though I believe the others are. Real company men." He nodded to indicate Tommy and Anthony and I guess Vincent Bologna. "We incinerate medical waste, Toomey, which folks have an emotional reaction to. But you know, something's got to be done with all the unspeakable refuse our health care industries generate."

"Do you smoke dope, Bob?"

"I . . . *could.* I mean I haven't, but." Bob shrugged and smiled.

So we smoked a fat doob and blew big, swirling blue clouds into the wind. I borrowed Bob's thirty-ought-six and let go a deafening round at a B-52 flying over. The USAF made bombing runs out of western Arkansas to eastern Kentucky and back. It approximated the distance from a sprawling airbase in Stuttgart to the presently sundered Soviet Union's eastern frontier.

"They say the cold war's over, Bob." I sighted the sky again, as if tracking skeet across it. "But they might be lying. So. Panthrex."

"Right." Bob scanned the cold ground for a place to settle. With an air of resignation, he said, "No more whiskey." Then he bent down and stretched out among the weeds, propping his head on his palm, elbow to the dirt. He looked up at me.

"I guess you could say we've got a number of irons in the fire, Toomey. We're not just medical waste, although that's as far as my concerns go. We have a division that constructs bridges all over the world, for instance. That's all they do. We have a film production company, and we operate a chain of stores that sells nothing but discount designer eyewear. We have a huge chicken processing plant in Arkansas, a textile mill in North Carolina, and a urea plant in Louisiana. Just to give you some idea."

"Urea?"

"Yeah, synthetic piss, more or less. We use it in plastics. Lawn furniture, beach balls."

"What all's involved in medical waste? Specifically."

"Specifically? Well, let's say some guy—Joe, let's call him—Joe's got the chronic crick in his elbow, just won't let up, right? So finally he's had enough and he goes to see his GP, who, being broadly trained and something of a hack to begin with, refers Joe to an osteopath who suspects cancer, and who refers him to an oncologist, a golfing buddy of his. And the oncologist confirms the osteopath's grim suspicion: bone cancer. Surgery is scheduled chop chop, no pun intended, and poor Joe has his arm sawed off at the elbow—a life-saving operation. But now what?"

"God, Bob, I don't know. You didn't have to be *that* specific."

"The hospital can't just toss the arm in the dumpster, can they? You bet your ass not. And that's where we come in. Rather one of many places we come in. Of course not in every instance are amputated limbs delivered over to us. You'd be surprised how many people bury them. Why, I've even heard of memorial services for the doggone things."

Now I wondered what had become of Jerry's arm.

• • •

Bob and I rode back in my truck, following Anthony and Tommy. The deer were loaded into the bed of their truck. Bob had asked if he could drive and I let him. My guess was it had something to do with his maiden dope voyage. You know? Like wondering what it would be like to take a bath stoned. Or watch TV. Or sit over there in *that* chair.

The countryside scrolled by through the window. A red-and-white patchwork quilt, whose swirling diamond pattern seemed to tighten and knot at its center, was stretched in front of a tilting, ramshackle porch as a sort of privacy screen, it looked like; but privacy from what, up this twisting, desolate hollow, is what I wanted to know. At one point, as we crossed a broad meadow, an immense flock of migrating starlings lifted from the surrounding trees and faded west briefly, then cut south with clear intent. Nearing the paved road, we passed a school bus lodged in a tobacco bottom, a stovepipe soldered into place on top of it billowing smoke. Pink curtains with a scalloped lacy trim hung over every window. Someone inside lifted the corner of one, held it for a moment, and then let it down.

We bumped up onto the blacktop, turned left, and Bob accelerated. A coal truck roared past, its turbulence first pushing us toward the shoulder, then the vacuum in its wake sucking us back toward the center line. I looked at Bob.

"Would the medical waste originate locally?" It sort of made me feel ghoulish, just asking it.

"Some, naturally," Bob answered casually. "For instance, we'd certainly service the area encompassed by Lexington, Ashland, Hazard. But you know, Toomey, I don't think you really comprehend the scope of the thing. This is a big operation, I shit you not. You have another joint?"

"No."

"Hm. I think I like that stuff. How 'bout a cigarette?" I tapped out a ciggie. "See, Toomey, there's just not enough—*material* in the area right around here to fire a big Panthrex incinerator. Think of it as fuel. To be efficient, we need to run twenty-four hours a day, seven days a week. And that, basically, into infinity."

We were chugging up a steep grade in too low a gear, the Ram's transmission clanging like a loose chain lashing around under the hood, when another coal truck blasted past us on its way downhill, and—somewhat curiously, because it was such a common sight—I was awed by its nearly unfathomable kinetic energy, and the skin on the back of my neck prickled.

"How big an operation, Bob? Can you give me an idea?"

"Well, we expect to service the eastern third of the U.S., at least. Not exclusively, of course, but in competition with other waste man firms. WWM, GlobalCon, T-Net. It's really a matter of, uh—holy shit!"

I knew without looking that Bob was reacting to the spectacle that was Abel Goforth's place, set against the foot of a hill off to our right. Abel left Mann County in 1969, I think, right out of high school, tall and loose-limbed, wiry new whiskers gathering about his chin; he returned a couple of years later, thickened, brooding, and hairy, heavily tattooed and in the habit of affecting aviator glasses and raggedy, sun-bleached army fatigues. And he began to paint his pictures. Not like a hobby, but full-time, with an obsessive, single-minded intent that marked him as a lunatic of some sort and set him forever apart from his community. Hundreds if not thousands of sweet, sentimental scenes precisely rendered on junk body parts—hoods, roofs, fenders, and trunks mostly, but even windshields and bumpers for panoramas: scenes of almond-eyed fawns sniffing the cold air in a wintry wonderland; of rascally squirrels high on a limb bedeviling a frustrated bear cub; of baby geese trailing their mama single file, one smart-alecky gosling nipping at the tail feathers of his or her immediate predecessor. Humans were absent in Abel's work, all of which was on display, arranged over the neat yard and into the trees and up the hill such that passersby might shop in transit. Lately Abel had been discovered as a "primitive" savant and his prices had soared. Out-of-state cars now often crowded his gravel drive.

"How's Panthrex fixed as far as pollutants?"

"As far as—hm." Bob was still a little distracted. "Well, frankly, Toomey . . . you know, hell, let's be honest. What do you suppose we'd be doing kissing ass in Oceana, Kentucky, if our operation were *wholly* desirable? Right? I mean, well, otherwise it just stands to reason we'd set up shop on Main Street in Santa Barbara. There's got to be some downside to it. Let's say we operate at full capacity and ninety-nine point nine-nine percent efficiency, three hundred and sixty-five days a year. We'll still emit eighty-three thousand tons of *something*. I won't insult you by pretending to know what exactly. Smoke—I know there's a lot of smoke."

Anthony and Tommy and the two bucks, whose legs and antlers flared appallingly from the bed of the pickup, disappeared over the top of the hill, and as we climbed toward it, too, the clanging under my hood grew louder. Downshift, I was thinking but was reluctant to say because I hate to make a man I've nothing against feel smallish, like he didn't know any better.

After I'd dropped Bob and his buck off back at Jerry's, I called on Woodson Walker, a bootlegger operating out of a kudzu-covered double-wide on Swanky Creek. I drove along a narrow dirt track until I pulled alongside Woodson's trailer; time-lapse photography would have revealed its gradual implosion. The yard was filled with four-wheelers and ATVs and a big satellite dish. A small dish was fixed to the side of the trailer. Woodson met me at the door.

"Toomey Spooner. Well, fuck me." Leaning against the door jamb, Woodson alternately picked at something crusty-sounding behind his ear and checked the end of his finger, pulling the cuticle back with his thumb. Growing up, he'd been a bullet-headed boy with a brain like a No. 3 sieve through which numbers and letters and dates leaked pitiably; but somewhere along the way he'd picked up the habit of making money hand over fist. Or at least making money. Strictly on the nefarious side, of course, but still I had to admire him some, knowing what he'd started out with.

"What brings you all the way out here on this," Woodson said, glancing beyond and above me, past me and through me, presumably at all creation its own self, "this day of our Lord?"

"Four half-pints of Beam does."

"That'll wet a feller's whistle, sure." He shot looks left and right, up and down Swanky Creek trail. "Right back," he said, and ducked into the gloom, stirring up the deadened interior air. The odor of mildew wafted from the door.

A pistol shot exploded within. Then Woodson reappeared with four half-pints, evidently unaware of any domestic calamity. "Twenty bills, Toom. And I hope you know I 'preciate your patronage."

We transacted and I left, four bottles clinking together in my jacket pockets when I hit rough patches along the frequently washed-out Swanky Creek Road. A frosty crescent moon rose, splintered behind bare, arterial branches.

When I got home, I shook some kibbles into a bowl for Zero and poured myself a long, strong bourbon. I added a couple of ice cubes and a splash of tap water. It felt like I'd been gone for days. I touched the replay button on my answering machine and leaned against the counter, swirling two cubes in the bottom of my—already?—empty glass. That interim—the time between hitting the replay and the sound of a recorded human voice—was a curiously lonely moment. The tape whirred and the heating ducts ticked, expanding with warm air. I busied myself by freshening my drink. Idle hands and all that. Whirrrrrr . . . whirrrrrr . . . click.

"Shit. Hi, Toomey. I hate talking to this goddamn thing. You didn't make it up last week, and I was just wondering how you're doing, how Willie's doing. How your campaign's doing, because there hasn't been much about it in the *Herald*." Drema was silent for a moment, and I heard a TV in the background. "That's not true. Well, it is true, but it's not why I called. Toomey. *Shit*." Her voice was cracking, filling with tears. "Fucking Odel, Toomey. He barged into our apartment last night, all fucked up and bellowing about his hurt and his dick and what all he's going to do. I don't remember how it all happened, but it ended up with me shoving a pistol down his throat and lecturing him about what an awful end he'd met. And Toomey, he finally shit and pissed all over himself. Then I felt sorry for him and I let him go, which is looking right now like a pretty big mistake, because the fact is, he's not taking it lightly. I'll call you later or tomorrow. Lorraine and I are seeking safe haven."

Click.

That fucking idiot Odel, goddamn him. I wished Drema *would*'ve filled his throat with hot lead. Hell, she practically owed it to society!—well, no, I don't know, maybe not. Who's to say? What I could say beyond doubt was that after a day traipsing through the woods and detonating firearms with the express purpose of murdering herbivorous mammals, a little global calamity as it was reported by CNN and another big drink or six sounded pretty doggone good. Wasted days and wasted nights. I could get back on track in the morning. Become my helpful, reliable self again.

Hunt banged through the kitchen door without knocking. I was still leaning against the counter with a drink, and I said hi. But Hunt ignored me. Completely. He crossed the kitchen and went straight to my rolltop secretary in the corner, snatched the old journal I'd taken from his cabin the day before, and left just as he'd come, banging the door shut behind him. I couldn't help but envy Hunt's unaffected contempt for social conventions. Because to tell the truth, in a broadly democratic way, I was pretty sick of people, too.

I poured another big undiluted drink, took my place on the sofa, and turned on the TV. Then the numbing images unfurled over the screen, one after another: rioting Third World mobs stampeding into the camera, past it, just beyond the reach of whistling batons; enormous earth-moving equipment with shovels the size of tract homes rumbling over misty, stump-studded moonscapes; hollow-cheeked refugees with eyes like burnt fuses streaming pointlessly across sub-Saharan Africa, eastern Europe, southeast Asia. The world as we know it wrenched apart into all of its discrete components and reassembled in startling configurations.

Then the whiskey really kicked in, and I hovered between consciousness and coma, my head lolling over my chest. I drooled onto my shirt. And, as if on some special edition of CNN, there were Mama and Deddy and Willie and Drema, Dickie and his mother and Inky, Hunt, Jerry and Bob, even Doggie Phipps and Vincent Bologna, and I can't remember who all anymore, all silhouetted in high relief against a flickering orange video sky and cast vaguely as ... I don't know, survivors perhaps; survivors it seemed of some vast natural catastrophe from which no one escaped, toiling without discernible purpose in rags among the jagged ruins, silently, solemnly, stunned. There were myriad ambient creakings, low concussive booms. A steady whistling wind swirled debris around their raw, rag-wrapped feet.

I woke up lying crosswise on my bed—though I had no memory whatever of making it upstairs—face down, arms and legs sprawled uncomfortably over the edges. The sun was streaming through a crack in the drapes and warmed my back through a flannel shirt. I was a little relieved because I'd at least made it to bed. I smelled piss, though, and when I twisted my hips a little, I am so sorry to report, my jeans clung cold and damp to my skin, and I knew that the bedspread and the sheets below me were wet, too, and that later I would have to stand the mattress in the corner to dry. The scene as it played in my mind was suggestive of a sickness unto death, so I didn't move again for some minutes, concentrating for future reference on exactly how I felt: sick and tired and a little ashamed, my skull pounding behind eyelids closed to the sun, pounding out what ought to have been the natural and happy rhythm of systole and diastole, my heart.

A while back, that night at the Ponderosa, Willie asked a pertinent question that I either couldn't answer or just out and out evaded. Or perhaps it was a little of both. Anyway, her question—which concerned Drema—went something like this: How in the name of God does a girl wind up in Drema's predicament?

Well, let's see. I can't really provide an answer, but I can provide some historical perspective. So—

When Drema was nine, her big brother Sewell disappeared (which I'll come to shortly). When Drema was ten, a tiny capillary detonated with fatal results beneath her mother's skull (which I won't come to at all, I don't think, no). And when Drema was eleven, there was her father's entirely accidental—if highly predictable—suicide, which ended Virgil's long-term program of pain management even as it apparently triggered Drema's own.

A precise, disastrous progression, as well as a sort of object lesson; one by one by one, a confirmation of the gloomy universal syllogism (I remember this from school)—*All human beings are mortal; I am a human being; therefore, I am mortal.* Now you tell me: Who can remain indomitable in the face of that?

It was a tough four years for me, to be sure, but it was Drema whose course in life was most radically recast. And mostly for the worse.

In the days and weeks and months following Deddy's funeral, Drema and I embarked on Act II, settling into our new life as orphans, as well as trying out, testing and probing, our newly reconfigured affiliation—for I was now much more than Drema's brother, I was her legal guardian, her de facto daddy-o. Neither one of us was prepared for that, but we managed to cobble together a more or less plausible power relationship. Drema was twelve and I was nineteen. Plus, I was a whole lot bigger than she was; and although the effect was subtle and entirely psychological, it was an eminently practical one.

Then, the day before Drema was to start the seventh grade, a Mann County constable came by the house. A swarthy guy named Cantees with a hooked beak, whose scent was of garlic and lemons. Very matter-of-fact, very business-like, he delivered a summons into my hand. The following week there was to be a hearing in Lexington to determine whether or not I was fit to continue as Drema's legal guardian.

I called Jerry and he said he'd get back to me as soon as he knew something.

I explained it to Drema as best I could, but my own understanding of it was pretty limited. As the week rocked along, and for no good reason, I began to wonder if I *was* fit to continue as Drema's legal guardian. Yes, I knew her very well, but as a brother, not as a parent. What could I teach her about becoming a young woman? About young men (or women, as I was beginning to suspect) with only one thing on their minds? About anything?

On Tuesday of the following week, we dressed for court and left the house at seven. Drema obviously felt as though this were no more than some complicated rhetorical exercise, something adults felt like they had to put you through every now and then. I, however, was about to throw up. Jerry had informed me that the whole thing had been instigated by Aunt Lou, our mother's much-older sister.

Lou Weems and her husband, Eustace, were creepy old people who'd never had children of their own. All yellow fingernails, thin hair, and receding gums. They lived in Lexington, in a dark funny-smelling house in an old downtown suburb that was now mostly black—so they kept their curtains pulled, their doors locked, and their front gate fastened. There were plastic runners on the floor, pomade- and hairspray-darkened doilies on the furniture. Aunt Lou was an extroverted alcoholic, whose special talent was making my mother, her little sister, cry. In person, of course, at any family gathering, but more frequently over the phone. Eustace was, I now realize, an obsessed anti-Semite. He'd go on and on about the Rothschilds and the international Zionist conspiracy and Federal Reserve and the Bavarian Illuminati. And he was as fastidiously sober—in his own grimly funereal way—as Aunt Lou was unabashedly drunk. Mr. and Mrs. Hilarity.

For one who's been reared in the mountains, the drive to Lexington can prove more than a little unsettling. The mountaineer is not only used to strictly delimited direct sunlight and niggardly small patches of sky pinched between rough-hewn ridges, he takes comfort in it; there's a hidden quality to life in the mountains, an implicit guarantee of privacy and safety. It's *cozy* in there. But a traveler hurtling west-northwest over the highway toward Bluegrass country sees that somewhere about thirty miles outside Lexington the mountains abruptly give way to grassy rolling fields and a neat infinite grid of white plank fencing—but it's the *sky*, that's the thing. Suddenly opening up, it just goes on forever, like a pale inverted ocean, and you can't help but feel a creeping vulnerability. It's as if *anything* could happen.

And anything did.

Our counsel, a young fellow named Tubby Searight, was worse than useless—with a barely concealed nudge and wink, he seemed to side with my aunt and uncle. Searight fell all over himself fawning before the judge, who was clearly uncomfortable with the idea of Drema and me constituting a family. That's about all I can recall from the hearing, because I couldn't concentrate. Odd details are all that I now remember. Dust motes in a ray of sunshine. The sound of shoes scraping on hardwood. The faint odor of dust and flatulence.

And then it was over. Drema left the courthouse with Lou and Eustace.

I drove home to Oceana alone. I stopped by Jerry's place. He let me drink too much of his bourbon and sleep it off on his couch. He also said he'd "fix that Searight sonofabitch's goddamn wagon." But I never heard anything more about that.

And then I embarked on what I now recognize as my first bender—and which I also recognize as the first time I chose to get hammered as a direct substitution for actually doing something, the world premiere of what would turn out to be a lifelong inclination. At any rate, I stayed stoned for weeks—I still had a stash left over from a misadventure of Sewell's in the marijuana trade—and I drove all over three counties, visiting bootleggers (the sale of liquor was not yet legal in Mann County). It got to where nobody—including the *bootleggers*—was happy to see me coming. I was intentionally cruel, my mouth was poisonous, real potty. For instance, just before he whipped my ass but good, and in front of a crowd of men and boys drinking beer on Hansel Owen's front porch, I told Jimmy Giamatti that *my* father told *me* that *his* mother had been the undisputed hum-job queen back at old Mann High (and not a single word of it true: go figure). When I refused to take it back, Jimmy got very busy, and blood shot from my mouth and nose in squibs and squirts. *Well,* I quickly reasoned (if reason it was), *I expect I had that one coming!*

At the time, the Weemses' interest in Drema made no sense to me, but sooner or later it began to dawn on me what Aunt Lou and Uncle Eustace—that is to say, Aunt Lou—had been up to. They (she) had counted on controlling Drema's inheritance—it was as over a couple of jagged spots hidden beneath the snow, extending his arm for balance. "Toomey! Ha, ha. Take a goddamn look, son."

He held out the papers and I took them.

"God, Drema," Jerry said, between gulps of air, "it's really been too long, darling." Jerry put on his warmest, sincerest face, the weirdly broad one with a curling smile and twitchy brows. "How are you, hon?"

"Jerry," Drema said, "since you're family, I'll confide honestly: not all that good, really. Nope, not well at all."

"Aww. Sorry to hear that. Toomey—" Jerry clearly didn't want to hear the particulars.

"No, Jer, I've fled my happy home, for one, abandoning all my earthly possessions. I'm penniless, or very nearly so, and unemployed without prospects. My girlfriend—oops!—a friend of mine's on the verge of a nervous breakdown, or something. You know, it's been like that. Oh, and did I mention? I'm number one with a bullet on a certified psychopath's shitlist." Drema untied her motorcycle jacket from around her waist, put it on over her sweater, zipped it and snapped it up, up to her chin. "But never mind all that. How are you, goddamnit?"

"Hm. Well, pretty good, actually," he said, smiling weakly and trailing off at the end. He looked around. Down the hill, into the sky, finally at his shoes and back to me. "Well, Toom? What do you think?"

I handed the papers back to Jerry and started back up the trail. Drema fell into step beside me and Jerry trailed us, trying to catch his breath and slipping on rocks in his wingtips. "I don't get it," I said. "Could you spell it out for me?"

From where we were, I could see where the mountain plateaued, leveling off around the mine entrance.

"OK, here's the thing, Toomey." Jerry had stopped following us now. I turned around. Even from here I could see a thick blue vein throbbing on his neck. The top of his huge, bald head was bright beneath the sun. "This is what we've been waiting for, goddamnit. EPA approval and a fat tax break from the commonwealth. It's all right here, except for one thing."

"Which is?"

"Why, you, of course. Or somebody very much like you. Somebody who can talk sense to the dopers and basket weavers who'll want to pull the rug out from under our little project." Jerry turned and started back down the mountain. "Yessir. Ten thousand dollars directed to the campaign coffer of the candidate whose views they find friendliest," he called back over his shoulder. "Or least hostile. *Whatever.* Oh, and by the way, Toomey. Were you aware that in the state of Kentucky a candidate can pocket his unused war chest?"

"No."

"Not that this is meant to be a for-profit operation, *but.* Well, you think about that. Happy new year, kids." I watched Jerry as he slipped and slid back down the trail, grew smaller, and finally disappeared around the bend.

Drema said, "I take it that's your out-of-state businessmen."

"Mm hm," I said, "it is."

I wasn't anxious to discuss it with her. I felt like going back to the house, where presumably all that good holiday cheer still presided. But Drema didn't pursue it, and so we forged on, just as we had time and again. We continued up the hill, slipping now and then on flat, icy stones, just as Jerry had, though to less overall effect. We weren't, after all, wearing wingtips.

Without coming right out with it, Bob Gregorio had certainly been trying to steer me clear of Panthrex's ten grand, or whatever sum they'd eventually dangle. And he had to have had good reason,

I told myself. He was on the inside, after all, with a front row seat to Panthrex's misanthropy. But, on the other hand . . . well, I *could* use the money.

Soon Drema and I stood on the broad terrace carved into the mountain that wrapped around to the mine. Swift low clouds, isolated individually against the blue sky, had marched out of the west and now passed overhead, and everywhere the day glittered around us in the rapidly shifting shadow and light. It was too cold for the snow to melt, even too cold for it to snow anymore, and we hiked through it, around to the partially blocked-off shaft, blacker than ever against the otherwise unbroken plane of snow rising before us.

"Let's go inside, Toomey. Warm up, have a smoke." Drema took my hand to pull me along. We stepped through the rotten boards and into the dark. Just under the lip of the mine entrance, but still within the gloomy penumbra of daylight, I stopped and sniffed for gas—which is of course odorless, but nevertheless. And for the next few moments the day just ticked away, like nothing at all, the way days do when you're suspended between this and that, when there's no telling what comes next: a Christmas puppy yapped idiotically in the distance, a light wind rattled some dry leaves, the ice on the river groaned.

"C'mon. It's warm and still."

A match flared against the dark, lighting Drema's face Halloween-orange for a half-second. The diminished flame was drawn to a point and a right angle, sucked into the end of a cigarette, then flared anew as Drema took two or three puffs. I followed the beacon of Drema's waxing and waning coal, and soon enough I could make out her silhouette, squatting on her haunches, back pressed to the wall. I slid down next to her, identically positioned myself, and lit a cigarette, too.

We smoked for a minute in silence. "You know, Toomey," Drema finally said—sounding distant in the dark, reverberant, as if through a home emptied of furniture, drapes, carpet—"I just don't know what we're going to do. Any of us, really, but Lorraine and me in particular." Somewhere water dripped into pools, echoing in deeper recesses: *poip, poip, poip.*

"We can't go home. Not even back to Lexington, I don't imagine, not as long as Odel's lurking about."

"I guess you know you can stay here as long as you want."

"Yeah, of course I do." The coal on the tip of my cigarette flared. Then Drema's. "And I appreciate it. But . . . you know, the thing is, I don't really feel the pull of the place. Not like you do, anyway. Lorraine and I've talked about going to Louisiana, staying with her mother a while. In the same way you like being close to all this, a part of it, I prefer having a few miles between me and home. More like Sewell I guess."

Drema flicked her cigarette away. It arced across the shaft and exploded in a shower of sparks against the opposite wall.

More like Sewell. That got me thinking. For three or four days, anyway.

See, here's the thing about our eldest sibling (whom Drema had barely known, really): Once upon a time—and what a way long time ago it now seems—Sewell hid out in Louisiana, too. Hid out, flaked out, and—finally—checked out. Although there exists no empirical evidence for that final assertion (*ah, so it's only circumstantial, then* . . .), it is nevertheless as true as anything I know. I won't be denied *my* closure by a mere technicality: so what if Sewell's remains were never recovered?

Real quick, here's another succinct and gloomy truth: Sewell was a fuckup. Through and through.

Yes, it's true (and *verifiable*), my big bro Sewell "The Jewel" Spooner (after Earl "The Pearl" Monroe—we were big basketball fans, as are all Kentuckians) set himself on a trajectory that had to end just about exactly the way it did. He was a young man who seemed to deliberately stake out only the most difficult positions, to unerringly select only the roughest row of all to hoe—from his early teens on, but especially after he'd spent a year cruising up and down the Mekong River, during which he lost his taste for sitting idly on the sandy shores of the North Fork, just sipping a Stroh's, puffing a joint, and watching the dark water purl away, and during which he evidently lost his taste for things Oceanan altogether. But that's the least of it, really, except perhaps as a harbinger of what was to come. Because thereafter Sewell lurched and lunged headlong, living at every moment as if on three-day pass in some exotic dystopia: Bangkok, Mombasa, the Black Hole of Calcutta. The kind of steamy, miasmic port where it's always five minutes til midnight. Where it's always last call.

By the time Sewell turned sixteen he'd begun to rail against the Vietnam war, but I was a little confounded by what was evidently this highly provocative stance he had appropriated for himself. What I failed to understand was that Sewell, lying awake in his bed at night, had projected far enough into the future to imagine himself keelhauled in blood and guts at the exact tolling of midnight that would signal his eighteenth birthday. Which *was* in fact rapidly approaching.

Hoping to dodge the draft by way of an educational deferment, Sewell left home for Lexington in the fall of 1970 with his best friend, Truman Sturgill (who was a distant cousin and who was in fact named for General Truman Spooner) and enrolled as a freshman at the University of Kentucky. But that first year didn't go well, to say the least. He had to pay for an illegal abortion. He was twice arrested—and treated very badly in lockup—following antiwar demonstrations. And he finished out the year on academic probation.

Sewell returned to Oceana in late May, blithely planted a fallow river bottom with marijuana and, judging by appearances, settled in for good as Sewell Spooner, gentleman farmer. He enjoyed talking shop with the old boys down at Mike Jennings's Feed & Seed, who of course had no idea Sewell wasn't growing tobacco, corn, melons, pole beans, and 'maters. Although they *were* a little suspicious of him, because Sewell had by then affected an evolution of deportment and mien. Night and day, he sported tiny, wire-rim sunglasses, and he smoked long dark clove cigarettes. He had grown a wispy Fu Manchu and he pulled his hair into a short ponytail. He wore tie-dyed T-shirts, Levi's, and knee-high moccasins. In short, he was the aborigine returned to his tribe sporting top hat, jodhpurs, and tennis shoes.

And he did not return to Lexington in the fall. But he did harvest his dope. I sat on a stump one afternoon and watched him as he swung a sharp new machete in the bright sun and sang "Bringing in the Sheaves." Then, in late November he received his induction notice.

I don't really know very much about Sewell's tour of duty, except to say that it was in Vietnam where Sewell lost any interest at all in accomplishing anything. Following his discharge—and lacking anything that might reasonably be thought of as a long-term scheme for his life—Sewell slunk back home to Oceana. It was if he'd made a list and set out to alienate all his old friends, one at a time. The Jewell even got himself expelled from Truman Sturgill's for pissing on the True Man's guest bed. As far as his friendships were concerned, Sewell was evidently in a winnowing phase.

Then one spring afternoon, I looked down our gravel drive just in time to see a massive, gleaming chrome grill and bumper swing toward the house, followed by a 1955 turquoise-and-white Ford Crown Victoria. It rolled up and slowed to a stop, and Sewell got out grinning—though I could see that he was struggling to contain it—and he patted the hood as he walked around in front of it. He'd bought it that afternoon.

The next morning, following a breakfast of bacon and eggs, and with only the briefest, and most confusing, preamble, he left. Just like that. For about two months we received picture postcards and notes scribbled on bar napkins. Some of the postmarks? Belfast, Maine; Key West, Florida; San Ysidro, California; and Walla Walla, Washington. Sewell seemed to be circumnavigating the nation.

Finally he landed in New Orleans, with some notion of taking up residence, it seemed. He rented an apartment in the Quarter; and shortly thereafter I received a long letter from him, an invitation to please come and visit that summer. But shortly after he settled (if that was the word) in New Orleans, Sewell disappeared.

For good, too. There are no surprise reappearances. Not in this story.

Auf Wiedersehen, bro.

And as I now know—now that I can fit all the pieces snugly together, with benefit of hindsight and with actual history on my side for once—all that then remained for Deddy, his final moment of transcendence, would arrive in the form of his barnyard egress. But first, of course, Mama would have to suffer her sudden mortal stroke. She wouldn't even make it to the hospital. And now the causal chain is finally apparent, even to me: Sewell's disappearance led to Mama's death, which in turn led to Deddy's.

And although the whole cycle—from Sewell's disappearance to

Deddy's death—ran an exhausting nineteen months (or was it nineteen years?), it seemed to me then that I had been orphaned overnight.

Drema, of course, being the exception proving the rule.

So far.

CHAPTER SEVEN

"Louisiana, hm? Where exactly in Louisiana?" I asked and then shoveled in a big mouthful of scrambled eggs. Mm-mm-*mm*.

Drema, who clearly didn't know and hadn't really thought much about it, stopped buttering her toast and looked to Lorraine for an answer.

Lorraine wiped away a tomato juice mustache and said, "Lake Richard." This she pronounced in the French manner—ree-SHAR. "Over next to Texas and down by the Gulf of Mexico. The bottom, left-hand corner, mapwise."

"I don't know whether or not you remember, Drema, but Sewell lived in New Orleans for a while. Right before—"

"Oh, yeah." Drema was still half asleep. "That thing with Sewell. Right."

That *thing* with Sewell? I was about to push myself away from the breakfast table and begin to bluster, but I couldn't really blame Drema because nearly a dozen years separated her and Sewell, and he couldn't have seemed to her like much more than an acquaintance. An old family friend who might drop by for a plateful of food and a cup of cheer on holidays.

It was the very end of January, and for more than a month, ever since Drema had been back, I'd put my campaign—if you could even call it that anymore—on hold. But the election was to be held the first Tuesday in May (which seemed to me like sometime after the next appearance of Halley's comet), and Willie had been after me to get back on track. Not only that, but I was determined to avoid a slow Virgil Spooner fade. So I was going to haul my most ingratiating and aggrandizing self into Oceana this morning to, to—what? I didn't know, really. Talk about what all I was going to do for the community, I guess. Trouble was, I still hadn't bothered to cobble together a plausible platform. That was a little ways off. Willie's advice was to just be myself. Hm. I wasn't at all convinced that my unvarnished self was what right-thinking folks would finally vote for. And, predictably, I was beginning to regret getting involved in the thing. But on the other hand, and unlike my father, I *was* going to see it through.

And Drema had said earlier that she wanted to drive into town with me.

I shoved the last little wedge of toast into my mouth, poured a half-cup of coffee, and lit a ciggie. "Can you be ready around, oh," I looked at my watch, "how 'bout ten-thirty?"

"No problem."

Zero ambled over next to me, sat down, and gave me that pathetic doggie look. Anything good left on that plate? Hm? Something I might like? His tail thumped against the linoleum. I set a yolk-smeared plate on the floor. Zero pushed it around with his tongue.

"So." I exhaled a blue column of smoke that mushroomed against the ceiling. "Louisiana, huh?"

Ahhh. To be out of the house and humming along a well-maintained public highway at fifty-plus miles per hour, windows cracked and wind whistling through, snaking along at the foot of the hills, this valley leading to the next, snow visible at higher elevations, an improbably blue dome overhead! It's good to have the radio on, too.

It hardly even matters what station . . . *the cat's in the cradle with a silver spoon, hm-hm-hm and the man in the moon.* . . .

Drema was thirty-three years old, slim and boyish, and decidedly attractive, after a fashion: and that fashion included spiky white hair, probably four or five inches long, insouciantly belied by its very dark roots; a pair of wrap-around Ray-Bans, perched low on her nose; a flannel shirt with the sleeves torn off, worn over a thin, gray sweatshirt; a long cotton skirt, in a flower print; long johns; and a pair of heavy, shit-kicking Doc Martens, lowcuts, laced with rawhide. And she looked great, she really did, she was fully herself; but in the immediate environs of Oceana and Mann County, well, she might just as well have been Sewell trying to pass himself off for one of the gap-toothed plowboys over to Mike Jennings's Feed & Seed.

Since we'd made plans to have lunch with Willie, I parked just around the corner from the Stonecastle River Detention Center, a brooding, gothic edifice constructed of large, limestone blocks. Leering, splay-toed gargoyles—somehow suggestive of an aberrant and energetic sexuality—secured its low, dark entryways and had frightened me as a child. Actually, just thinking of them makes me uneasy, even now.

Drema and I stood on the sidewalk, looking up and down Kenton Avenue, trying to decide what to do next. Campaign, of course, was the easy answer. But where? And how, exactly? I was beginning to feel like an asshole. No, that's not quite right. I was beginning to feel like I was *going* to feel like an asshole, which was much worse. Because now there was an element of dread mixed into the psychic stew.

"I know," Drema said. "Let's head over to the courthouse. We'll renew your driver's license."

I was puzzled. "It hasn't expired."

"Then you *lost* it, Toomey." Her tone of voice insinuated that she was stating something just *too* obvious. She lit a cigarette. "Look, it'll give you an opportunity—a perfectly *natural* opportunity, I might add—to tour the seat of government, you know? Hang with the big dogs! Let them know you're around, Toomey Spooner, that you're a contender, too—a presence, a player, a fucking *inevitability*!"

Wow.

So, the courthouse it was. I wasn't at all convinced that this was a good idea, but at the time it seemed easier than arguing with Drema about it. So:

We mounted the expansive marble steps obliquely, passed boldly between titanic Doric columns, and pushed wide the ponderous oak doors. And then, after a thorough—and ultimately futile—examination of the building directory, I stopped a young man wearing the top from a pair of pale green surgical scrubs, a shower cap, and voluminous jeans hung very low on his ass, pants that looked as if they had been sewn from enough denim to erect a ship's sail. He had a single golden hoop through each pierced earlobe. He also wore a lot of heavy, cheap jewelry: a chunky metal watch on each wrist, several big rings, and a chain around his neck from which depended his name, I supposed, in crusty gold script—*Brian*. His hair was cut into a white boy's "fade." He sported a dirty blond, pubic-looking goatee and looked as if he hadn't seen the sun for months, years. His pasty white skin was pocked by purplish acne scars. I asked him where I could find the department of motor vehicles office.

"Fuck I look like, Jack? Mu'fuckin' imfo-*may*-shun kiosk?"

A what?

Drema took my elbow and we walked the length of the hall. At the opposite end, we climbed more wide stairs to the second floor. And at the other end of *that* hall, we discovered the DMV licensing office. It was a tiny room with a tall service desk and a photo rig—a stool set against a blue backdrop and facing a big, accordion-like camera. Behind the desk, a young woman I recognized but couldn't place—Lester Coombs's granddaughter?—was working the crossword puzzle in *TV Guide.* When she heard us walk in, she looked up and smiled. Plump, plum-colored lips circumscribed substantial, dazzlingly white choppers—like big pearls nesting on a tiny purple pillow. "Listen," she said, "four letters, second one's a T. Mayberry denizen."

In unison, Drema and I shouted, "Otis!"

I left the courthouse with two driver's licenses—my old one, of course, and another one that was still warm with fresh lamination—and eight fewer dollars in my wallet. That was the net effect of our visit there. There hadn't been even a single big dog about, and it had become apparent while wandering those cool, quiet halls that the real business of governing the commonwealth transpired elsewhere. But where? I wondered how I could not know that. Well, at least we still had our lunch with Willie to look forward to.

Walking in the sun toward the SRDC, and without looking at me, Drema said, "You've got to admit, Toomey, it sounded like a pretty good idea."

Yes, I did, I had to admit that. And once upon a time . . . well.

We passed the SRDC and then turned right, walking along its east face. Then we turned onto a walk that sloped down and ended at an SRDC basement door. To enter the building, we had to pass beneath and between a pair of the glowering gargoyles. A scrap of cloud blotted out the noon sun.

I realized I was a little edgy. But why? The gargoyles? The election? Something else? . . .*the cat's in the cradle with the silver spoon, hm-hm-hm-hm-hm the man in the moon.*

I tapped on Willie's office door, pushed it halfway open, and ushered Drema in ahead of me. Willie was facing us, seated behind her desk. Randall, wearing the orange jumpsuit with SRDC stitched across its chest, sat in a chair against the wall, facing Willie. Again? He stood up and extended his hand—both hands, really, seeing as how they were cuffed—to shake. This time he smiled broadly and genuinely. His protracted eyetooth poked into his lower lip. "Hey, Toomey. Good to see you again, man."

"Randall, do you pay rent here?" I took his right hand and his left flopped up and down like a vestigial appendage as we shook. "Randall, Drema." I nodded toward my sister.

"Howdy, Drema."

"Randall."

I said to Randall, "Sorry to see you're still stuck in here."

Randall shook his head, while refusing to let go of my hand. "Naw, man. I'm back." Then he laughed.

Willie said, "Randall, our session's over, so I'm going to call the guard now. See you tomorrow?"

"Aw, sure, Miss Rains." Then he turned to me. "Hey. I just wanted to say, good luck at the polls, Toomey. I heard about you runnin' for mayor and everything. That's great. And just to think, I might know the mayor more or less personal-like. Do you know what little things like that do for my self-esteem?"

After a squat, ill-tempered guard with a barely concealed contempt for the holy work Willie did—"I used to think I knew a thing or two about a thing or two," he said cryptically, shaking his head—retrieved Randall, Willie, Drema, and I decided we'd go to Grambos' for lunch. There really wasn't a lot of choice, not after we'd ruled out the Dairy Queens and Mickey Ds that had in recent years appeared along the highway. What it came down to was Grambos' and the Crossroads Truck Stop, which was fine if your tastes ran toward chicken-fried steak and milk gravy—which mine, often enough, did. But Grambos' served grilled lamb kabobs and warm, pleasantly sour dolmas and other Grecian delights. Nick Grambos had not forgot whence *he* came. But neither had I. Somewhere in the recesses of my imagination, the word "OUZO" materialized, glittered and shimmered there for a moment like Excalibur risen from that dark and haunted lake, then slowly sank away into the deep neurogloom once more.

It was nice enough out for an afternoon in late January, and so we decided to walk. Willie grabbed her coat off the back of her door, and I helped her into it. We all donned sunglasses and strode into the sunny day. Once more beneath the gauntlet of gargoyles. We walked three abreast, me in the middle. Past the Hi Hat Boot Shop, the Auto Zone, a row of old frame houses perched high on a hill overlooking the sidewalk and backlit by the sun. We had to make way for a little red-haired boy who roared past on a Big Wheel. Looking neither left nor right, his focus on some point straight ahead was unblinking and chillingly absolute.

"How do you deal with those losers all day long," Drema asked. "I mean, doesn't it get to you? Screw up your sense of what to expect from people?"

"Oh, I don't know," Willie said and shot me a quick smile— meaning ... *what?* "Most of them just got off on the wrong foot and didn't have the resources—intellectual, emotional, or otherwise— to figure out some other way of coming at life. Like Randall. Essentially a sweet man who nevertheless does some pretty awful things.

Which makes a kind of sense when you consider his childhood—all I can say about *that* is that Randall learned some terrible lessons real early, a fact which accounts for his father's continuing presence in the penitentiary at Eddyville. You can probably infer the rest. No, most of them are *still* children. And it's just heartbreaking, is what it really is."

I offered Drema my hankie.

Willie smiled sweetly. "Don't be an asshole, Toomey."

We were passing an old Ford pickup, fifties-ish, bulbous, some scoured anticolor. A meaty black elbow sprouted in its open window. Then, as we passed: "Hey, Toomer." Only one person in this world conflated my name thus: Isenhower, or Ike, Chandler. "Got a minute?"

I turned toward the truck, then back toward Drema and Willie to wave them on—we were only a few doors from Grambos'—and stepped over to Ike, who was sitting behind the wheel, smiling and puffing a cigarette. Ike was six-two or -three and probably weighed three hundred pounds, but he was not a soft man. Like me, he lived on his ancestral lands; but unlike me, he actually farmed his. Ike grew fabulous cantaloupes and honeydews, tended a pretty fair-sized tobacco base that meandered along a bottom by a creek, and raised some of the best dope for miles around, in discreet but myriad patches all over his property. Ike and I had attended school together from the first grade on—we started school together the year integration came to Mann County, me from one side of town, Ike from the other—and had always gotten along well.

"Yeah, of course I've got a minute, Ike. What's up?"

"Well, me and some brothers've been talking, you know, about our interests," he said. "It was out to the Swahili Elks the other night, and this mayor's thing came up, and we did a lot of talking about

table, silently negotiated among themselves by way of sharp glances and frozen smiles, and found seats. Folks returned to eating and drinking and talking among themselves, the commotion subsided. *Crack!*—an old boy with big veiny Popeye arms and tiny teeth about the color and size of curried rice broke a tight rack—nine in the corner. The jukebox whirred and groaned, pressed its worn-out needle into another scratchy 45. A-one, and a-two, and a—*An empty glass . . . a last cigarette . . . it's clo-sin' time . . . and I'm drunk again. . . .*

After we'd finished eating—gobbled the last of the falafels, mopped up the last of the gritty but sublime tahini sauce, scooped away the last sliver of expertly seasoned lamb—Willie had to hurry on back to the SRDC, where she said she had a *very* full afternoon ahead of her. The prisoners, she said, were more prone to debilitating depressions during the long gray middle months of winter than at any other time of the year. Just like the rest of us.

Grambos' had by this time emptied out by more than half. The regular Joes with one-hour lunch breaks written into their union contracts were long gone, while the suits remained, sipping coffee, nursing tall, weak, business-lunch bourbons. Dolin, Judge Thackerey, and the Fitzgeralds yet lingered over precariously stacked dirty dishes and sweaty glasses puddling water over the table. They were leaning in close and speaking in hushed voices. Clearly, some big-dog action.

I heard the bell over the door tinkle and, looking up, saw Antoine Crawford moving toward a stool at the counter, where he took a seat. He snatched a menu out of a little clip that held two. Like Drema, and like Sewell before either of them, Antoine himself was something of a rara avis in Mann County.

Antoine was one prickly brother—or Ethiopian, as he was wont to declaim, to the complete bafflement of many an Oceanan. But he and I seemed to get along well enough, even though our brief encounters always left me feeling a little tense. Antoine was extremely well read and well spoken—to an unnerving extent. Thirty years earlier, he had gone away to college—to Berkeley, on academic scholarship—and had only returned to Oceana in the last two or three years, after working for many years as some kind of counselor in a free clinic in Oakland. When he came home, he had a tumultuous Medusa's head of graying, waist-length dreadlocks, a wife and two teenage daughters, and a hair-trigger sense of injustice, along with a pretty much unchecked willingness to express his outrage in the vividest terms. And he scared the shit out of, well, probably every last ofay I knew. For this alone, I was personally of the opinion that Davies' Bottom—as well as the rest of Oceana and Mann County in general—could use a lot more cats like Antoine Crawford.

Drema decided she wanted to shoot a game of pool. Best two out of three, actually. We lit fresh cigarettes and climbed out of our booth. Sunshine poured through the front window and, like silvery fog at sunrise, illuminated the layers of tobacco smoke. I could hear the kitchen gearing down, pots and pans crashing on their way to the dishwasher. Behind the bar, Nick Grambos laughed at some story the salesman was sharing with him. A sample case sat on the floor next to the salesman's barstool.

Acting on some baleful impulse—and to demonstrate something, though I've no idea what: my stouthearted intrepidity, perhaps?—I called over to the Fitzgerald table. "Hey, Dickie." Dickie Junior looked straight at me, but his daddy looked left and right and then *finally* at me, as if I were the last person in the world he expected to call his name. Some bit of complicated and very prissy one-upsmanship. So: Dickie was demonstrating something, too. "How 'bout you and your boy Dickie Junior there versus Drema and me?"

Dickie spoke to his son across the table. The boy smiled and nodded.

Drema scowled and turned her back to me, chalked her cue furiously. I'd pissed her off.

"Sure, Spooner." The Dickies Senior and Junior pushed themselves away from the table, while the grimly matriarchal Alma Fitzgerald—that is to say, the *sober* Alma Fitzgerald—reached out and steadied a stack of teetering plates. Inky smiled . . . *bravely*, is the only word for it. Knowing as she did from long experience, I guess, how her husband's adventures frequently turned out. And worried, too, about her boy and his precarious confidence, his explosive bouts with Tourette's. Or *whatever*, as Jerry might have put it.

We flipped a quarter, and Dickie Junior broke. Six in the corner, cue glancing away and ending up in the opposite corner. Scratch. Drema's shot. Six in the corner again. Good. I liked being solids. Drema then banked in the two before she sank the three but scratched in the side. Oh, well—two, zip. A pretty good start.

Papa Dickie spotted the three, cued up. He chalked his stick and blew pale dust from the tip. Chalked, blew. Chalked, blew. Inky wandered over unobtrusively to watch her boys, leaned in a corner where the sun fell across her face. She squinted against the bright light but stayed put. Dickie, still chalking his cue and peering cross-eyed at the worked-over tip, said, "Spooner, my man, I hate to come right out and say it, but prepare yourself for a glimpse of the not-very-distant future. May second, to be exact." He motioned with his cue, somewhat vaguely, and it seemed to me he indicated the nine ball in the corner pocket. Both the nine and the eleven were snuggled up in the corner, wedged between the cushions. The cue ball kissed the eleven and it dropped with a satisfying smack into the empty leather pocket. Then he walked to the other end of the table and began to line up his next shot.

Drema stepped in close to Dickie, and I could see what was coming. I expected he could, too. Drema squared her shoulders, puffed herself up a little. "Uh, Dickie, just a sec there. It seemed to me that you called the nine in the corner on that last shot. I mean, that's what that nonverbal pointing stuff led me to believe, anyway. You wanna clear that up before we move on?"

Dickie looked up, smiling uncertainly. "Uh, sure. Eleven in the corner. How's that?" he said. "But you know, I thought this was a friendly game, hon. The honor system. You know, just us *guys.*" Drema didn't say a word, nor did she budge, but Dickie bent to line up his shot anyway. Dickie Junior had moved over next to his mother, and, detecting the nascent tension—which he was probably pretty good at by now—he was getting a little fidgety and beginning to punch at the air. Then, and although it was barely audible, he barked. Then twice more, sharply and a little louder. Yappy, like a small dog. We all pretended not to notice.

Still lining up his shot, but evidently ready to go, finally, Dickie Senior said, articulating very clearly now, "OK. This time, nine ball in the corner. *This* corner." He poked his stick into the pocket, lest there be any mistaking. But it was obvious and it was a gimme, and he sank it. Then he called the fourteen in the side and made it, before he missed the fifteen in the corner. It ricocheted between the cushions—too hard—and popped away, rolling to the other end of the table.

"Shit fire." Storm clouds scudded across Dickie's pinched brow.

Drema said, "Aw. Real tough luck, *Fitz.*" She smiled.

My turn. Dolin, Judge Thackerey, and Alma had drifted over one at a time to watch. Stalling for a moment, I chalked my cue. But perfunctorily. No Cincinnati Kid, I. Nevertheless, I sank the seven ball in the side, just as I'd called it. Maybe a *little* tricky, but. Then, returning to form, I blew an easy combination.

Back to Dickie Junior, on whom the pressure of competition appeared to be taking its toll. His right hand was punching furiously at the air as he approached the table, and he seemed to be emitting a low, but swelling, magneto-like white noise. Dickie Senior said, "Relax now, son. Easy. That ten's got your name on it. Right there in the corner."

Dickie Junior—thank God—relaxed enough to knock it down. Easily. And I think that helped everybody else relax a bit, too, because the little guy—and we along with him—had seemed to be escalating toward, well, something *big*. Dickie Junior circled the table, more confident now, markedly less spasmodic.

"Uh, twelve in the side," he said, looking to his father for affirmation—Dickie Senior said nothing—"I guess." He bent to his shot, drew his stick back slowly, across his bridged hand, slid it forward, drew it back, gently tapped the cue and sent it toward the twelve. Unlike his father's, his was a game of finesse. The balls kissed and the twelve dropped in the side. Then he put the fifteen in the opposite side, and left himself a real good look at the thirteen sitting along the rail. A straight shot to the corner. It was beginning to look like a bad day at Black Rock for the Spooner clan.

But as Dickie Junior's shot slid along the rail, it got too much of it and came off to tap the thirteen back against it. Angling off the rail, it rolled just right of the pocket. The boy walked around the table and handed his father the cue, as if the act marked his resignation from something. "Sorry, Dad, I, uh, uhm, mm, mmmmmm—

muh, muh—fuckfuckfuck, errrrrr—" He swallowed—I mean, actually visibly swallowed—whatever was coming next. His right hand began to punch at the air again. Then a big facial tic set in.

Drema went on a run. She nailed the three, four, and five balls in order, then banked the one into a side pocket. I couldn't help but wonder where she'd picked up these deadeye skills. Preece Thackerey and Mama Fitz were clearly fascinated, too. And because there *was* something sexy about it, I suspected Dolin of nursing a chubby. Drema walked around the table, studying the situation, figuring where her advantage might lie. But it was a tough shot. Eight against the rail, between a corner and a side pocket, cue right out in the middle of the table. She hadn't left herself with much.

"Eight ball in the corner," she finally said, pointing emphatically to the corner pocket on her side of the table. So it was going to be a bank shot. Probably the only way to go, really. That, or else force the eight to ride the length of the rail—no margin for error there. She put some bottom English on the cue, sent it toward the eight. The white ball tapped the black one, backed away as planned, and the eight rolled toward the corner, kissed the cushion, and came to rest right in front of the pocket.

"Shit. Shitshitshitshitshit." *Drema* said that. More or less under her breath, but still, I don't imagine anybody missed it. And I'm confident she was not mocking Dickie Junior.

Dickie Senior casually sank the thirteen, leaving only the eight, then turned to Dickie Junior, smiling. The boy, huddled in close to Inky, looked terrified. He knew what was coming.

"You do the honors, son." And while I have no doubt that Dickie was trying to do right by his boy—buttress his self-esteem, restore his wobbly confidence, etc., just pursuing his notion of fatherhood—this was so clearly the wrong move as to be stupefying. Or, as I've heard people around here say, stupid-fying. Partly because the shot was *so* easy that there would be no earthly way to justify missing it, no excuses. I watched this dawn on Dickie Junior. Nevertheless, he stepped toward his father and the proffered cue stick, egesting a strangled little yelp.

Inky, squinting into the sunbeam that fell across her face, spoke to her husband. "Dickie, you know, *maybe. . . ,*" she pursed her lips and tilted her head left and right, equivocating, ". . . *not.*"

Dickie the daddy either didn't hear her or pretended not to.

Dickie Junior's face contorted, screwed tight at the center, then relaxed. He took the cue from his father. Then, seemingly out of nowhere—and I think it caught him by surprise, too—he screeched, "NIGGERTOES!"

Antoine, who up until this point had remained disinterested, turned on his stool.

Christ. I was ready to forfeit.

Drema said, "Don't you fucking get it, Dickie?" She came up next to the table and leaned into it, establishing eye contact and speaking to—or spitting at—Dickie Senior across the expanse of green felt. "You bag of shit, shoot your own goddamn shot! Can't you see what you're doing?"

Now *that*, he clearly heard. He leaned over the table, too, pointing his finger at my sister, nearly, but not quite, stabbing her in the chest as he spoke. "Tell you fucking what, *Missy*—and I'd appreciate it if you tried real hard not to forget what it is I'm about to share with you." I could see that Dickie had entered that weird zone of lucid, superarticulate fury. Drema had gone too far. And I began to suspect that Dickie himself was about to go too far. "Whatever it is that comes to pass between me and my boy is pretty goddamn clearly none of your fucking beeswax. And furthermore, the next time you feel like maybe you gotta wild hair rooting around in your crack—"

Dickie Junior's simmering conniption finally erupted into a rolling boil. His lips formed a gaping O and his tongue appeared, rolled front to back, as if to stopper the opening. But it was no use. The facial tic reappeared, enhanced, redoubled.

"Uhnn—mmmmff . . . ffffff . . . FUCK-A-DUCK!"

Dickie Senior spun, shouting "Hey!," and slapped his son across the mouth. Hard. He bent to the boy, face to face, and pinched his son's mouth into a painful-looking 8. Dickie Junior was crying, and tears ran in glistening rivulets down his tiny, twisted face. "I've had about all of *that* shit I'm likely to swallow, mister! Do you hear me?" Dickie Junior was nodding against the arrestive force of his father's hand, and muttering something under his breath, straining to keep it in. "OK, goddamnit, from here on out—"

A pool cue, with Drema at the business end of it, whistled through the air and landed with a gut-tightening thwack against Dickie Senior's right ear. He shut up *right* then, for sure, but, other than that, for a moment he didn't seem to feel anything. Then his eyes went all googly, his jaw slack, and he slid into a puddle at his boy's feet. It was like a cartoon. A very slow feed to the brainpan.

And, as so often happens, it was left to family to defend the indefensible—namely, their miserable, awful own. Poor Inky, whose heart couldn't possibly have been in it, stepped in to take up the cudgels for the father of her only baby.

Tiny fists flew, and Drema pretty successfully blocked the inconsequential blows, backing away now, strictly on the defensive.

We left the eight ball sitting on the table.

Draw.

As Drema and I were hustling ourselves away—with a much-too-belated sense of stealth and circumspection—Antoine, thick dreadlocks sproinging every which way, turned on his stool and leaned toward me, as if he were about to share a secret. The slightest smile played across his lips. "Good game," he hissed.

"God, Toomey, how many ways can I say it? Shit! I'm *so* sorry!"

"I'm just tired of talking about it is all."

We were back on the road, headed home. The day had pretty much frittered away all the luster and clarity and promise it had so abundantly exhibited only this morning. Enfeebled blue-gray clouds had moved in, but threatened nothing, except, perhaps, a kind of meteorologically produced lethargy. A life-at-the-bottom-of-the-sea ennui. And about all I felt like was taking a long nap.

Call me when it's over.

I called Jerry at the dealership as soon as we got home.

"Well, if it isn't my favorite nephew—or, uh, cousin—*whatever.* How do, Toom?"

"Well—"

"Hey! Guess who's sitting here with me."

"Jerry, I—"

"Give up, do you? Abel Goforth. Har, ha! Finally sold enough of them glorified car parts to trade in that piece of shit he's been driving since I don't know when—no offense, Abel. Just a sec, Toom." There was a pause on the line. "Sent Abel out to the showroom for a cup of coffee and a cream horn. It's free and that'll please him no end. So."

"I may have a little problem, Jerry."

"No, you don't, Toomey. You don't have a problem."

"Well, I might. This afternoon, just a few minutes ago, actually—"

"Yeah yeah yeah. Forget about it."

"You know?"

"Of course I do. My agents are legion."

"It's just that—"

"Look, what's ol' shit-for-brains gonna do? Press charges? You've gotta be kidding me. Do you know what kind of goddamn panty-waist he'd look like? Can't you just see it in Wednesday's paper? 'Candidate Fitzgerald's Clock Cleaned by Spooner's Baby Sister.' Never happen, my friend, and *he'll* see to that. Far as you're concerned, just go on about your business, pretend it never happened. Hell, for that matter, you could maybe even take advantage of the situation Dickie now finds himself in—get Drema to whip his ass on a daily basis, for instance, every day between now and May second. And he would have absolutely no recourse."

There was a long pause while I tried to decide whether or not Jerry was kidding.

Then he said, "Oh, my God, Toomey! I've got a fucking brilliant idea—I almost missed the forest for the trees!"

Geez, Louise. What now?

CHAPTER EIGHT

Well, I'll say this for Jerry Toller: I'll be a son of a bitch if he wasn't dead on right about how the whole thing finally shook out. No sheriff, no state trooper, no inflamed deputy dog of any breed whatsoever came fishtailing up my gravel drive, clambered in shiny leather shoes onto the front porch, rapped on the door with big raw cop knuckles, wearily demanded to speak with the littlest Spooner. None of that, and nothing in the paper. Not a whiff of the incident elsewhere, either, not as far as I could tell—no rumormongering, that is. It was something not unlike a miracle. For all the world, it was as if Drema's assault on Dickie had never occurred at all. But it had, hadn't it? It seems to me a fledgling malaperp could be forgiven if he (or *she*, though I don't think Drema marveled over it as I did) began to wonder.

Oh, yeah, and Jerry's "brilliant idea"? That we ought to initiate a whispering campaign, get the word out that Drema had indeed whipped Dickie's ass—which wouldn't have been fair, not even on the face of it, because Dickie had been bushwhacked—and make Dickie either admit it or deny it in some public forum. If he admitted it, well, the implications for his manhood were obvious (homo); and if he denied it, twist that into an admission that he wasn't above roughing up the little ladies of Oceana (homo again, because he had no history whatsoever of similarly engaging men). Force the bastard into a lose/lose situation, as Jerry put it.

"Is that the same as a no-win?"

"You bet your ass it is. And I don't see any reason at all to get smart with me, goddamnit. Listen: this is what *you* wanted."

"Weeelllll. . . ."

"You know, I distinctly remember saying you couldn't tread shit without taking in an occasional mouthful. Did you think I was kidding?"

Then, visibly softening, and with his chin cocked toward his chest and peering at me as if over bifocals, the suddenly patrician Jerry said it was "politically speaking, son, the right thing to do." I told Jerry to forget about it, adding that as far as I knew I still had veto power over this or any other bad idea of his. But I could tell by his tone of voice—preemptive now, *yeah yeah yeah we'll get back to this later* is what I was reading between the lines—that I'd not heard the last of this line of thinking.

I discovered shortly thereafter, and through Jerry, of course (which was getting more than a little tiresome), that Dickie had seen a doctor and been diagnosed with nothing more than "a very mild concussion and a egg-sized knot on his damn thick skull. Which nevertheless ought to render his a more cautious candidacy. I don't believe he understood til now that *anything* can happen."

I passed this information along to Drema, who pretty much literally shrugged it off.

"Yeah, well, that confirms it for me then. I *didn't* catch him quite right."

A few days after that, Ike Chandler of the Mann County marijuana cooperative called. It was early, the light slanting in low through the windows, and though I was working on my second cup of coffee, I was still a little fogbound. I hadn't been out of bed long, and in any event had hardly slept at all: that nettlesome trinity—

abandonment, impotence, extinction—had borne down on me throughout the long night. All alone on a broad dark river, rudderless, sailing swiftly toward the falls beneath a close—and *closing*—night sky, when. . . .

Oh, never mind. I'm sick of hearing about it, too. From here on out, it's strictly the verifiably concrete world.

I answered the telephone. "Hello."

"Toomer?"

"Speaking, Ike." The wind-tunnel respirations of a very large man whistled through the connection. "How're you this morning?"

"Well, not bad, actually." He said this as if he thought I'd be surprised to hear it. "Not bad at all. My ex called this morning to say she's marrying some badass nigger over to Morehead, a Lee's Famous Fried Chicken franchisee I think she said. Which means the burden of alimony will soon be lifted, and for that I'm a grateful man. I'm fucking humbled, actually. Course none of that's got anything at all to do with why I called, but since you asked."

"Well, congratulations!"

Why Ike *had* called was because he and his colleagues hoped to set up a meeting for that evening, provided I was available, of course. I assured Ike I was, and that I was just as eager to meet with them. Then we agreed on the Swahili Elks Lodge, not much more than a roadhouse with a meeting room, really, not far from Ike's place just outside town. I had some reservations—which I kept to myself—about the introduction of spirits into what ought to've been an otherwise sober political confab, but what the hell? Maybe it would be just exactly what the proceedings called for: something to soften the sharp edges, dull the mulish will of those suspicious, isolated, up-from-slavery bottom-farmers. But maybe not, too—we'd just have to see about that.

(Not to suggest that there had ever been any slavery around here. Pretty much everybody has been more or less equally poor ever since the first white folks hiked into this area through the Cumberland Gap.)

Drema wandered bleary-eyed into the kitchen just as I was hanging up. She cinched her bathrobe together and swirled cream into a cup of coffee. "Who's that?" Sleepy indifference. Just asking.

"Ike Chandler. I'm going to meet with him and some of his buddies tonight out at the Swahili Elks Lodge. Discuss what it'll take to earn their support, which will amount to I don't know what all. In fact, I can hardly imagine."

Drema gulped, watched me sleepily over the rim of her cup, then set it on the counter. "Huh." She withdrew a pack of smokes from her bathrobe pocket, tapped one out, and lit it. She coughed. Smoke swirled around her head. "You know, Toomey, I haven't been out to Swahili Elks Lodge since—"

I had to cut her off right there, just had to, because I could see where she was headed.

"Huh uh, Drema, I'm sorry, but not tonight. I hope you'll understand, darling, but I really can't afford another wacky adventure like our last one. All things considered, it just seems like the way to go on this thing." She didn't understand. Without saying a word, she turned and left the room, trailing blue smoke, disappeared around the corner. I immediately wished I hadn't sounded so snarky. But hell's bells—what did she expect?

I lit a cigarette, too, and sat down at the table. Zero wandered into the kitchen and plopped onto the floor at my feet. I stubbed out my smoke and called Willie, because I'd hoped she'd come along.

She was having dinner with her mother, though. I knew that, I'd just forgotten. Juanita was preparing a meal out of *Gourmet* magazine. Roast chicken with potato, apple, and prune stuffing; cranberry-quince chutney; balsamic-glazed pearl onions; pear and pumpkin pie with ginger crème anglaise. Or something about like that. They did this on a regular, rotating basis, a mother-daughter thing. The next month Willie would host her mom. Maybe something out of *Bon Appétit.*

Then the telephone rang again. I knew it was something I didn't want to hear, whatever it was. I absolutely fucking *knew* it.

Regardless: "Hello."

"Have you seen this morning's *Herald*?" It was Jerry. Again, damnit. He was referring to the Lexington paper.

"No. . . ." I could hear that it was not good news. Just as I'd suspected.

"Well, Toomey, although *I* don't personally take it as bad news"—aha!—"I believe *you* will." Long, portentous pause. Jerry's style. "Sumbitches got ahold of that Drema-Dickie story," he said in a sort of solemn, hoarse whisper. "Page B-1 this morning." I heard the newspaper rattle as Jerry located the piece. It took a long moment—the one-arm lag. "It's headlined, 'Mountain politics: In Oceana it's business as usual.'"

"Well, damn it all to hell, Jerry, goddamn it, how do you suppose this happened?" I had a strong suspicion I knew exactly how it had come to pass, but I wanted to hear it from the horse's own double-dealing puss.

"Toomey, now I can hear what you're thinking, but with God as my sonofabitching witness, I do not know. You'll just have to take my word for that. But if I find out. . . ." Another long pause, this time meant as a solemn threat against whoever had done this loathsome thing. Not very convincing.

"If you find out, what?"

"Well, uh, you know, I'll let you know, of course. Then, I don't know, I guess we'll take it from there. Cross that bridge when we come to it. You know. Et cetera."

Just what in the hell's that supposed to mean, I wondered, walking down to the mailbox to retrieve my own *Herald.* It was a mess outside, muddy *and* frozen. Overcast, beginning to snow. I sneezed when the air froze in my nostrils, blew a big sticky oyster into my cupped hands. Trying to negotiate the snot-storm, I slipped and fell in the cold mud. Shit.

. . . Huh, Jer?

It was February 2. I know, because Drema and Lorraine were watching CNN as I was getting ready to leave the house that evening, and there—as a light moment spliced in between the national news (bad) and international news (worse)—was poor, stunned Punxsutawney Phil, batting his milky old groundhog eyes against a brilliant sun. So. Six more weeks of snow and sleet and ice and wind. But after that the sun must shine. That's the deal, damnit.

Sewell, by the way, was born on Groundhog Day. But it never occurred to me on that particular day—as it has likewise failed to occur to me on many other Groundhog Days—that it was Sewell's birthday. And Deddy—this seems somehow related and worth mentioning now that I'm into it—was born on the Fourth of July. Until I was nine or ten years old, it seemed perfectly natural that the world should celebrate my father's birthday with fried chicken picnics, parades down Main Street at noon, and fireworks at night over the football field.

Ka-boom.

Not to mention that the Fourth of July is now a seminal date in my own ongoing drama. But I'm getting way ahead of myself, so first—

The Swahili Elks Lodge was, as its name suggests, a fraternal organization first and foremost, which, nevertheless, could get pretty rambunctious, and maintained, year in and year out, an extravagant casualty rate. Not infrequently, men exited on stretchers, escorted away by incredulous, head-wagging EMTs. Which does not make the place as dangerous as you might imagine, because here's the key to the mountaineers of the Bluegrass state, black or white: we only murder—or even seriously wound—family and really close friends. Around here, consequential violence is in no way random or diffuse—it is an act born of intimacy, and it is terribly focused. Which is a comfort in a way. Anywhere you feel like a stranger, or at least as if you have no close attachments, you're relatively safe. But woe unto the son of a bitch who chooses to resume some ancient quarrel at a family reunion, a wedding, or a funeral, where he's surrounded by loved ones. Because chances are good that he's a goner. And chances are almost as good that it's his brother or father who will serve time in Eddyville or LaGrange for dispatching the imprudent provocateur. Of course, within this system it's the mothers and wives who do the real suffering. Otherwise, it's really more of a spectator sport, like horse racing or basketball. Or politics. For all of which we harbor an immoderate (and some would think quaint) fondness.

At any rate, as probably the only white man in the Swahili Elks Lodge that evening, I'd be remarkably safe—which cuts against urban-style street smarts and all that and, in fact, sounds fantastically counterintuitive. But it was true then and remains true today, although, given the homogenization of our culture by television, how much longer it will obtain is impossible to say.

I pulled in right at eight, skidding across the gravel lot surrounding the lodge. I'd been listening to the radio—a locally produced show featuring twangy fascist windbags railing against the "media elite"—and had nearly shot right past the place. But I managed an emergency landing and slid in, narrowly missing several busted-up pickups and a mud-splattered backhoe, whose operator, I had no doubt, was inside fortifying himself with strong drink for the cold and wind-blasted ride home in an open cab.

I climbed down out of my truck. It was cold, but it felt as if it were getting warmer. Just slightly, though, because it was still well below freezing. The wind was picking up, too—some sort of front moving through. A few snowflakes blew down out of the starless, moonless sky. And, for someone walking across the parking lot on a night like that, the Swahili Elks Lodge generated an inviting ambiance: its gauzy, softly lit windows aglow, the southern-fried *odeur* of a busy kitchen, the muted, multiple bass rumblings of male voices.

But alas . . . well, what can I say? This *was* the Swahili Elks Lodge, and it *had* rather successfully targeted a narrowly defined, if somewhat frightening, demographic. Drunks. Roadhouse sluggers. Men who either did not want to go home or who, for one reason or another, were not welcome there. Not the broader (and kinder and gentler) constituency I was going to need. I was thinking big tent, just like you know who. With the really significant difference that I meant it.

Inside, big workingmen's broad shoulders and fantastically distended beer bellies swung and rolled and tilted this way and that, vying for space. Some men boomed or brayed, bared their teeth, slapped at one another, sloshed beer out of their mugs and over the floor. Others sulked or nursed some tragic personal failure or otherwise kept to themselves, hunched morosely over sweaty bottles of beer. There were perhaps two or three women about. Most everybody smoked, exhaled roiling blue blossoms against the low ceiling. Visibility was severely limited.

When I entered, the noise level dropped for a beat—a quick registering of my presence, it seemed—and then resumed. In self-defense against the dense smoke, I lit a ciggie, too, and slunk toward the bar, with this thought: it would only be politic to have a beer. Or two. I'd been thinking about it all day. It struck me as an issue of trust, of camaraderie. Or at least it could be construed as such, somewhere off down the road. And I was heading that possibility off at the pass, because if there was one thing I'd learned following my recent forays, it was that the last thing I needed was anything that smacked of, oh, loftiness. Airs.

"Shot of your house bourbon and a cold draft," I said, leaning in at the bartender and speaking up. And I swear to God I hadn't planned on that whiskey until I opened my mouth. It just leapt out. The cooperative gentleman set me up, though, chop chop, exactly as if I knew what I were doing. And before I had time to recant.

Twisting on my stool and looking around the place, I didn't see Ike. An old guy next to me nodded when I turned in his direction. I nodded back. He had a fuzzy halo of hair—like an old monk's wispy tonsure—full, cracked lips, and big swollen beak, pockmarked with ancient acne scars. Faintly through the din, I thought I heard him humming "The Girl from Ipanema," even as he took numerous delicate sips from a longneck he tilted to his lips. His Adam's apple ticked up and down. He looked familiar, but that was all. The waitress was a squat, powerful-looking woman with a wildly out-of-control Afro, who looked as if she could take it or dish it out, your pick, and whose profile was as cruel and indifferent as a hatchet. I wondered how she did in tips. I could imagine that working out either way.

Smacking my lips, I ordered another shot of bourbon. And another draft. And a pickled egg. I took most of the pickled egg in one bite and then popped in what was left. *Mmmm. . . .*

There was a slight tug at my elbow. It was the old guy seated next to me. I raised an index finger—just a sec—and washed down the last of the pickled egg with a swig of beer. "Yessir?"

He said, "Toomey Spooner?" I nodded, and he smiled, revealing two rows of crooked, tobacco-stained teeth. "Freddie Peeples." Still smiling, he extended a slightly palsied hand. We shook. "You don't remember me, do you?"

"Well, yes and no." Which was the truth. "I thought you looked familiar, but I was having trouble placing you."

"I suppose I'd've been surprised if you could. It's probably been thirty years. You've grown up, I've gotten old." Mr. Peeples paused, raised a dry, flaky knuckle to his right eye and squished around a bit, until it welled up with water. Then he dabbed at the tears on his cheek with a wadded-up gray hankie. "I used to run with Hunt mostly, but sometimes with your old man and Jerry Toller, too. We'd go fishing, mostly. Oh, and you know what? One time me and Hunt met Elvis Presley, down at the Shelby County fair, near Memphis. And I snapped a pitcher of them two, together on the midway."

"I know that snapshot, Mr. Peeples. There's also one of you and Elvis."

"There is? Why, I guess I've forgotten about that. Course we were young then, brimming over with piss and pickle juice," he said, smiling and lifting his beer to his lips, his demeanor vaguely implying a toast. He lowered the beer. "Now I'm happy just to *get* pickled." We both laughed.

"Toomer!" Ike Chandler was now steaming across the room, a big rubbery smile on his face. "Right on time, too." Ike loomed up before me, his expansive beer keg chest eclipsing the rest of the room. "Looks like you just beat the snow." I looked out the window and indeed it was coming down fast now. Big wet flakes, gusting silvery through a cone of light in the parking lot.

"I hate like crazy to cut it short, Mr. Peeples," I said, shaking his hand. I felt its tremors through my own. "But I'm supposed to meet with these gentlemen."

"'At's OK, Toomey. It was good to see you." He started to turn toward the bar, but turned back. "Hey. Good luck with that Fitzgerald boy, too. A chip off the ol' shit-eating block, that one is. Don't forget, I knew *his* daddy, too. Did day labor for that cocksucker more days than I care to recall." Mr. Peeples smiled.

I turned to Ike. "So. What's the plan?"

"We're in the back here, in the meeting room. There's eight or nine of us, and we're just happy to see you. With the weather and all, we weren't sure if you'd make it all the way out here or not." Ike was smiling, cutting his eyes toward the table where his comrades huddled, all of them watching Ike and me. I raised a shot of bourbon and tossed 'er back. When I looked back at them—through hot, whiskey-teared eyes—they were all smiling and waving Ike and me over. And now I realized I recognized most of them. The twins Roy and Ray Benson, who graduated with Ike and me. Johnny Omohundro, who was reputed to be half Cherokee and who was some kind of a self-styled preacher in something called the Institute for Divine Metaphysical Research. Butter Smith, who had gone to the University of Kentucky on a football scholarship but had returned to Oceana after only two years and pursued a series of odd jobs. And a real pain in the ass known as Tommy Cobb.

"You ever hear of Panthrex?"

Ike had all of the sudden assumed an earnest face and leaned across the table on his elbows to put this one to me. Unless I had missed something, it came out of nowhere and caught me up short, although I had nothing to hide. I shouldn't have been surprised—I mean, it would've been unlikely that I would be the only one who'd heard of Panthrex. Word like that gets around. It was just that up until then our powwow had been nothing but bullshitting and monkey business, flipping coins and drawing straws to determine who had to trundle his big ass back up to the bar for drinks (because if we'd had to rely on that grim and shiftless waitress, we certainly would've sobered up between drinks, and I don't think anybody would've stood for that). And I was beginning to wonder if there was actually anything substantive we needed to discuss, or if I was here on a simple get-to-know-ya mission. But now Ike—whose bearing suggested he was at least a little on the hammered side—had posed a serious question.

"Panthrex? I have, Ike. Why?"

At this point, and evidently taking his cue from Ike, Tommy Cobb—and everybody called him that, too: Tommy Cobb, first name *and* last—leaned across the table on *his* elbows. "Cause we thought that just maybe you might *of.*" That said, he leaned back, a smug little smile playing across his lips, apparently satisfied that he'd made some devastating point. I had no idea what dim bulb flickered within his skull. Nevertheless, Tommy Cobb—who was Ike's size, but altogether less cuddly—was a man whose murky but intensely felt passions only a reckless thrill seeker would disregard. "Too white for words," he snarled.

"You know, Tommy Cobb, I'm sorry. But I have no idea what

you're getting at." I leaned forward then, to demonstrate that I was serious, too. Twisting away from me in his seat, Tommy Cobb made some low, bearish noise. Butter Smith shot Tommy Cobb a look— *shut the fuck up, man.*

Ike jumped in. "Toomer, here's the thing. I suspect you know Panthrex is hoping to build a medical waste incinerator, right?"

I said I did.

"Well, then here's something you might not know. That facility is going to require a large and steady supply of water. A lake of it, literally. And to get that lake—and all this is in the official proposal over to the courthouse, Toomer—to get that lake, they want to dam Little Swanky and New Bethel creeks, create a reservoir. And that's problem one."

"'At's right," Tommy Cobb said. "Because there goes our fucking shit right down the goddamn drain, man. No pun intended, either, *bro*." Then Tommy Cobb rocked back in his seat, crossed his arms over his chest, and emitted an ugly sucking sound. Again, the effect was one of conclusiveness, as if we'd just reached the self-evident end of something—'nough said, Jack.

But not enough said to suit me. And I said so. I wanted to add that I'd not yet learned to interpret whistles and grunts. But I didn't. At this point, it was likely to have been construed by Mr. Cobb as an at least somewhat racist remark.

Tommy Cobb rolled his eyes extravagantly and exhaled loudly, completely exasperated with me, and I was beginning to think: Fuck you, Tommy Cobb, you ignorant and contrary sonofabitch you. But just then Ike leaned across the table again, his big black face the very picture of patience. His fingers were knit together before him: a church and a steeple. There was something a little sad in his eyes. He looked as if he were explaining something to a child. I looked around the table at the other half-dozen or so faces. Excluding Tommy Cobb, they all had that look. Tired but patient. And as if they all understood that I was a little simple.

"OK, Toomer. Little Swanky and New Bethel's our bread and our butter. I don't know any other way to put it. We all siphon off water out of those two creeks. But if Panthrex fills that reservoir, they're going to construct a culvert that'll divert those creeks away from our properties. You can see how that'd leave us high and dry. The next thing you know, not a pot to piss in nor a window to toss 'er out of. And we're back to living just the way we grew up. Good-bye satellite dish, hello soup beans, wild onions, and cornbread."

Everybody laughed, including Tommy Cobb.

Even though I finally understood—once it was all laid out for me with painstaking explicitness: they were irrigating their dope patches with creek water—I had some further questions which they gladly answered. I say gladly, but of course Tommy Cobb didn't look too happy about the pop quiz. Anyway, the upshot of our Q. and A. session was this: well water was impractical, because wells are dug close to houses—convenience, of course, being in the very nature of wells—and far from remote stands of marijuana; and they couldn't dig new wells because of the attention that would draw, especially from the National Guard helicopters—the dope patrol—that endlessly prowled the sky; city water was out of the question, too, not least because only one or two of those guys even had it, but even if they had, the use of city water, in the volumes required, would've been like waving a big red flag in the face of law enforcement officials; and *rain*, they insisted, well, rain (wagging their heads sadly now) was too capricious to count on, year in and year out. So it was creek water or nothing.

Johnny Omohundro said, "That's how it is, Toomey."

"But there's more to it than that," Ike said, looking graver than ever. His forehead was furrowed, his jaw set, his countenance utterly baleful.

"Lots more," added Tommy Cobb.

Ike nodded, his lips pressed into a hard thin line. "Tommy Cobb's right, Toomer. *Lots.* How much do you know about what all Panthrex'll burn, and what all will end up in the air and the water?"

The air and the water?—where on earth was Ike going with this? I was a little taken aback. These guys were *not* environmentalists. On the contrary. They worshipped at the altar of the logging and mining industries, voted for politicians who favored complete and total deregulation of our natural resources. Their toilets flushed into otherwise pristine mountain streams, made romantic day campers from Ohio deathly ill. They didn't recycle. They dumped worn-out appliances in gullies along remote roadways. They poured motor oil down the sink. Weekends, they drank beer, tore up the hills on their ATVs, and spotlighted deer—in season or out. Just like the white people hereabouts, they were fucking *traditionalists.*

"Not that much," I said, regaining my balance, "not that much at all. The guy I spoke with is supposed to get back with me on that." I was thinking of Bob Gregorio. I'd put off for too long getting back in touch with him. Which I obviously needed to do. Like yesterday. "But he did suggest that their operation wasn't altogether clean."

"Yeah, well, to say the least," Ike said, his eyes crossing as he lit a huge hand-rolled cigarette. It crackled and threw off sparks. "There's rumors going around, Toomey. You know anything about them?"

I told him I didn't. Now what?

"Well, mainly that Panthrex is a lot more dangerous than they're letting on. And it's not like coal, where maybe a couple of guys get crushed in a roof fall or blow up in a methane explosion. No, a Panthrex in the neighborhood could affect everybody. Look at this." Ike pulled a piece of paper out of his shirt pocket and—with one eye screwed shut against the cigarette smoke—unfolded it and smoothed it on the table. Then he slid it over to me.

* * * C O P S * * *

Citizens Opposing Panthrex
If we don't police our own environment, who will?

A Medical Waste Incinerator in Mann County?
For Your Information . . .

—**Panthrex** is a Canadian-based, multinational corporation. Its reach is global.

—**Panthrex** has had no previous interests in or ties to Kentucky. In other words:

—**Panthrex** has nothing to lose here, no stake in **OUR FUTURE!**

—**Panthrex's** proposed medical waste incinerator has been rejected by seven other communities in the southeastern U.S.—**WHY??**

Because a medical waste incinerator
emits **TOXIC** wastes!!

—DIOXIN. Ever heard of Times Beach, Missouri? Love Canal? Ghost towns.
Unlike CYANIDE, for instance, DIOXIN is "not known to be safe in **any** concentration." Exposure produces miscarriages and birth defects, not to mention behavioral and neurological problems—brain damage!—and **death**.

—<u>LEAD</u>. LEAD poisoning produces convulsions, brain damage, **death**.

—<u>CADMIUM</u>. Prolonged exposure to airborne CADMIUM results in kidney disease, bone marrow disease, emphysema, and **death**.

—<u>MERCURY</u>. Contact with MERCURY violently corrodes skin and mucous membranes and can result in **death**.

—<u>ARSENIC</u>. A well-known poison. ARSENIC produces diarrhea, cramps, anemia, paralysis, skin tumors, and **death**.

—<u>CHROMIUM</u>. Vapors from burning CHROMIUM cause lung cancer. Makes cigarette smoking look like a program of preventive medicine.

Is this what we want in the air and the water of Mann County? Well, it's what we'll get if we let Panthrex build and operate their proposed medical waste incinerator. For more information, call COPS at:

(606) 877-1558   ikec01@pogo.net

I was amazed. By a number of things. "Where did this come from, Ike?"

"Me," he said, obviously a little pleased with his effort, "by way of the Internet. That's my number there at the bottom. And my e-mail address." I hadn't noticed, but indeed it was. It had been sitting beside my phone for a week, scribbled on a yellow Post-it.

Isenhower Chandler—aka ikec01@pogo.net—had developed a well-known, if somewhat unlikely, interest in the so-called information superhighway, but it had never occurred to me he was doing anything more than downloading games and dirty pictures. But his interest was well known because he talked about it all the time, evidently spent a lot of time hunkered before his computer—and I had underestimated him. Christ, would I never learn?

His interest in computers was one of many unexpected side effects that the commerce in dope had had on folks around here. The dope trade afforded the growers—and, by osmosis, their acquaintances—contact with a more diverse group than this little patch of land had historically provided. Almost all the marijuana grown hereabouts finds its way to far-flung destinations—the invisible hand of the market at work—and that leads to associations that otherwise never would have been made. And thanks to those connections, Ike—and other men like him—had diversified his interests, broadened his horizons.

"And if this incinerator is anything at all like the others," he was saying, "and it's just about got to be, really, then we're in trouble is what it looks like. More trouble than just us losing our water, that is. I mean, look at that list. Now there's some shit I'll bet Panthrex isn't telling *anybody,* probably not even themselves."

That struck me as probably accurate. Of course, I'd met the Panthrex guys. They weren't evil. It's just absolutely ridiculous how easy it is to get in up to your ass in—oh! so, it was exactly as Jerry had warned me, after all—*shit.*

More or less completely humbled by now—my ignorance exposed, my embarrassing lack of understanding of others made plain—I walked out of the Swahili Elks Lodge and into an eerily lit night. There was a luminous, inch-thick frosting of snow over everything—the cars and the trucks and the looming, Jurassic backhoe; the state road curving away in either direction; the hills enclosing the valley, throughout which there was scattered irrefutable evidence that this entire area had once been an ocean floor. Glub.

But it had stopped snowing. Now there was the delicate ticking sound of ice raining over the landscape, a sizzling sound, like someone frying a skilletful of bacon in the next room. If the roads weren't yet treacherous, they soon would be. And then, if it kept up, impassable.

I had reached what turned out to be an easy and obvious decision: I would not, under any circumstances, oblige myself to Panthrex. I could hear Jerry already, sputtering some twisted-up Tollerism. *Well, you can chop off my legs and call me Shorty, but I think you're being just a little goddamn hasty, son.* What I *would* do is stick with my clan, my fellow Oceanans, Davies' Bottomers, Mann Countians. Which on this night meant Ike Chandler, his buddies, and yes, even that irritating prick Tommy Cobb.

Sure, they trafficked in contraband, grew powerful dope in the hollows settled and cleared by their grandfathers and great-grandfathers (sometimes for other people's grandfathers and great-grandfathers), but I enjoyed their product—when I could get it—and was trying above all else to avoid the taint of hypocrisy. But beyond that, we shared a history and a future, were inextricably bound together. I had known them in grade school, seen them weep with frustration over their multiplication tables. I remembered the baby 'fros and the sparse pubic mustaches they grew in high school. I knew most of their wives and kids. Their aunts and uncles and cousins. Even some of their horses and dogs and goats. In short, the shape of their very lives. I remembered whence they'd come, and had more than a fair idea of where they were headed. That's *my* community.

But where did Panthrex fit in? I couldn't answer that, but it seemed best to err on the side of caution. And despite the fact that he eventually got rich off the deal—unlike just about anybody else around here—all I could picture was old Agee scratching his name onto a piece of paper, signing away all rights to the land his own father had settled. Doing what he felt like he had to do, for his boys, Virgil and Hunt, and eventually for Drema and me. But that was another time and another place. Another *world*. And for reasons that made sense then, Agee wasn't looking too far down the line.

I was. Or at least I was trying to.

The roads were indeed treacherous, and getting worse, but I made it home. On the way, though, I passed three other vehicles that had slid gently off the road and become mired in half-frozen mud. Nobody hurt, not even the two cars and the pickup, it didn't look like. It was just embarrassing. Shielding their eyes from the glare of my headlights, the vehicles' passengers milled about resignedly and waved me away when I offered assistance, as if they had simply fucked up and just didn't deserve anybody's help.

My house was dark when I pulled in. This was a surprise, because Drema and Lorraine had been staying up until four and five in the morning, drinking beer and wine and watching old movies. I just assumed that for once they'd gone to bed early. Got their hands on some Percodan, maybe, or been overcome with passion.

But that didn't explain the dilapidated, seedy-looking Nova pulled around back and parked in my usual spot. I pulled in beside it, cut my engine, and climbed out. I slipped on the ice and almost fell before recovering, flailing at and finally clutching the door handle. I stood there for a moment, feeling more or less well-oiled and warm, more or less drunk, more or less pretty damn swell. The rain was still falling and turning to ice, still accumulating, and the trees, the bigger trees off at a distance, anyway, were beginning to sway and groan like fellow juiceheads with the weight of it.

I stumbled up the back steps and into the dark house, feeling my way from the mudroom into the kitchen, one hand sliding along the wall. I kicked something that went rattling lightly across the kitchen floor. A soupbone, I guessed. Zero's—speaking of whom. . . ? No doggie nails clicked over the linoleum. I found the light switch, and fluorescent tubes over the sink sputtered and flickered to life. I removed a tumbler and a bottle of Beam from the cabinet and poured a couple of fingers. Then a voice—high-pitched, but clearly a man's—addressed me from across the kitchen.

"Could you pour me one of them, too? I'm dry's a damn bone, man."

A small, wiry man sat at my kitchen table, looking all settled in, real comfy and at his ease. Probably in his late thirties, a slight, friendly smile. Some uncertainty in it, but not that much. He had a long, stalk-like neck, and a big shock of red hair erupted out of his scalp like plumage. He was enveloped in a big Arctic parka with a fur-trimmed hood and bright orange lining. A nickel-plated pistol rested on his lap. But it was his *size*—he was so small, I wondered if he hadn't been a jockey before . . . well, *this*. And with a few drinks under my belt, I was more curious than frightened. Panthrex? No. Too soon for that. Least you'd think.

"My pleasure." I pulled out another tumbler, poured a couple of fingers of whiskey into it. "Neat, or over rocks?"

"That'll do 'er just fine, thanks, just like that."

I stepped over and served my guest, slid into a chair at the table, and set the bottle of bourbon between us. "There. It'll be self-serve from here on out, stranger."

"Suits me," he said. Then we just sat there like that for a while, not saying anything, swirling our drinks, sipping, pouring a little more. The wind gusted outside, and frozen rain sizzled on the porch's tin roof. The big office clock over the sink ticked. Finally he said, "I guess you know who I am. I mean, you don't seem particularly surprised."

"Well, as a matter of fact, no, I don't. But I guess I just assumed,"

I said, nodding at the pistol on his lap, "that you'd bring it up when you were good and ready." I smiled. A shiteater, but it seemed warranted.

"Odel Dent." He reached across the table and shook my hand. "Happy to make your acquaintance, Toomey, and I mean that. Despite these circumstances." He glanced around the room as if surveying the aforementioned circumstances. "But I've got to caution you, I've still got this here pistol, and I aim to find out a thing or two before I go. Like where in hell a couple of double-crossing pussy bumpers might've got theirselves off to."

Odel Dent—I could hardly believe it. I had imagined any number of Odels, of many shapes and sizes, but the man presently seated across from me was not among them. He was hardly bigger than a schoolboy, which meant I had to assume he was lunatic, without concern for his personal safety. Because that *does* give a man an edge, and would account for his reputation with acquaintances and law enforcement officials.

Before I answered him, though, I splashed a little more bourbon into my tumbler, regarded the pheasant stamped onto its side. I thought, pleasant. A pleasant pheasant. "Odel, tell you what. I'm as surprised as you are. More. I thought they'd be here when I got home. Which is not to say I'd tell you anything even if I knew—"

"'Preciate your candor."

"—but I don't." Then it hit me. I really hadn't thought of it before. "I suppose you read about Drema in the *Herald* this morning."

"I did." Odel looked a little pleased with himself. "You could say that current events is like a hobby of mine. Read the paper every morning, front to back. And the Drema I read about this morning was a person I recognized right off."

"I expect so." The image floated up unbidden: Drema shoving a pistol down Odel's throat, and Odel . . . well, I couldn't afford to think about *that*. Not right now. "Odel, all I can tell you is that I thought I'd find Drema and Lorraine here when I got home. But instead I found you. So, what now?"

"I'm not sure. I've got to think about it."

"Are you going to shoot me with that thing if I get up to take a leak?"

"Of course not," he said mildly. "Why would I do a thing like that?"

I guess I could've been going for a pistol of my own, but I wasn't looking for trouble. Not *that* much trouble, at any rate. Besides, I didn't feel any real threat from Odel. Nor he, evidently, from me. I stepped into the bathroom and closed the door, set my whiskey glass on the sink. Drema's favorite sweater was draped over the shower curtain rod, dried stiff and rough. Lorraine's blow dryer was plugged in, propped onto the towel rack. So, theirs had been a hasty retreat. Well, that's *something*, I thought.

I opened the medicine chest, and there was the bottle of Antabuse Lester Coombs had given me. Unopened. He said it had helped him over a rough patch years before, but, since I clearly didn't have any real interest in total abstinence, I had no intention whatsoever of taking the drug myself. I drained the last drops from my tumbler and dropped one of the pills in. Then I ground it up with the end of my toothbrush. I peed, flushed the toilet, and returned to the kitchen. The scene was just as I'd left it.

"Well?"

Odel said, "I'm still not sure, Toomey."

"In the meantime," I said, snatching Odel's tumbler off the table. "The good stuff." I walked back over to the cabinet—where I'd set my tumbler—and pulled out a bottle of Baker's. Aged eight years, 107 proof, silky and lethal as a pit viper. I poured two drinks, returned to the table, and set what had been my glass before Odel. "Cheers."

And we drank. Then we reloaded and did it again. Once more for luck. I wondered how long it would take the medicine to kick in, but I also tried not to study Odel for symptoms, tip my hand. But I didn't have to. It was not a subtle thing.

Moments after that third shot, a pensive expression crossed Odel's face—his eyes a little crossed and cast down, as if he were trying to look inward, as if he were being made aware, for the very first time, of his own highly complicated and delicate machinery. But it only lasted a moment, a mere flicker. The first time. Then, hardly skipping a beat, the same expression gripped him again, held, matured into something else altogether, the death mask of a passenger on a plane nosediving toward an Iowa cornfield. Odel looked up. "The fuck?" Then his stomach gurgled, loud, like an institutional toilet slurping away the last of a turd-filled bowl.

"Man alive," I said, "*I* heard that. You OK?"

"Don't know . . . I . . . shit, mm . . . nngggg."

Now he was brightly flushed and bent at the waist. Big bullets of sweat had burst out over his forehead, and soon ran in rivulets down his face. He gasped and panted, then began to gulp as if trying to swallow air. Odel reached out for the table and tried to stand up, but his knees wobbled and gave out and he collapsed on all fours, gagging and trembling. Like a squirrel passing a jagged bit of walnut shell. Remarkably, though, the sonofabitch still gripped that damned pistol.

Then the torrents of hot, bilious vomit began splashing over the floor. After the first surprising jet, Odel collapsed completely, still dreadfully conscious, his cheek to the floor. Then it came in spurts. He just lay there, miserable, groaning, watching it shoot over the floor, his eyes lolling up to me, back to the mess he was making. I felt awful. It was like watching a poisoned dog die. I stood up and walked out the back door.

I was surprised Odel hadn't thought of it, or maybe he had: Drema and Lorraine were just about certainly Louisiana-bound. I assumed—correctly, as it would turn out—that they'd somehow been tipped off about Odel's impending visit. And for reasons I have since forgotten and would probably have to get very drunk again to recall—reasons whose logic, though, must have seemed compelling to me at the time—I decided I'd try to head them off at the pass.

It had stopped drizzling now, but the ice storm was complete for the time being, a finished work. The sky was beginning to clear. But there was a quarter inch of ice over everything, a crystalline glaze sparkling in the mist-diffused moonlight.

I stood on the back porch for a long moment, listening and thinking. Within: the muted sounds of Odel's miserable writhing, elbows and knees faintly thudding against the floor. Without: every half-minute a big limb snapping, falling through brittle frozen branches and crashing to the forest floor. Slipping and sliding, arms awhirl, trying to achieve equilibrium, I made my way over to my truck, scraped clear a little patch on my windshield, and climbed in.

The gravel road that led from my place down to the paved highway was strewn with limbs, which I was able either to miss or to crash through. I slid this way and that, but avoided the ditches. My headlights swept across the trees lining the road, spotlighted fresh wounds where limbs had snapped and peeled away, stripped away bark and even portions of trunk. A big crab apple tree lay in sad halves in a hay field, split right down its center, the weight of the ice too much.

I was suddenly thirsty again, and wondered why I hadn't brought the bourbon along.

As I drove through Oceana, it was then the heart of the night, the dead quiet time, eerie in the grip of ice. Fizzy streetlamps pooled yellowish light over the frozen ground. The only sign of life was a garbage truck, trolling up an alley behind the courthouse. On top of it, a yellow warning light slowly revolved. Two workmen in bulky orange coveralls and big rubber boots clung to its back, smoking or exhaling steam, I couldn't tell which.

I negotiated the on-ramp and entered the Foothills Parkway, heading west. Slowly, deliberately. The portal I'd scraped in the windshield had begun to expand, but I was still leaning in close over the steering wheel. Soon I passed through the Slashes tunnel. Out the other side, I slowed down, pulled to the left shoulder, bumped and slid across the median. Then I headed east, through the tunnel again, and once out the other side, I slowed down and checked my rearview for oncoming traffic. Nothing, of course. No other fools out on a night like this. When I came to the spot I thought I was looking for, I eased off onto the right shoulder, eased off and just kept easing, fully under the thrall of ice and gravity now. Eased all the way off into the drainage ditch, eased further, into the rock face just beyond. It was all painfully slow, and the truck ground against the limestone, and ground, and ground. A boulder loomed into view and the truck lurched to a sudden, if not particularly damaging, stop against it.

I got out and, with difficulty, climbed up to the shoulder of the parkway, and made my way back up the road. Then slid back into the ditch. Beyond the scree, I dove into the icy underbrush, combed the weeds and bushes. Frozen branches snapped. Finally I found Sewell's flask. I took a long drink, draining what was left. Then I walked back to the truck and tossed the empty flask onto the seat.

I wouldn't have admitted it then, but I was glad I'd wrecked. It had been a long night.

More than an hour and a half later, after a very difficult trip on foot, slipping and sliding and busting my ass more than a couple of times, I was staggering up Willie's walk. She opened her door to me, still half-asleep, blinking and tilting her head away from the bright porch light. Saying very little, she got me undressed and into bed.

As I've said before: God bless Willie Rains.

CHAPTER NINE

Willie didn't have to be at the SRDC until after lunch, so she let me sleep late. When I finally awoke, I hied myself to the bathroom, threw up—it was nothing really, despite a lot of gagging and kacking: just an infant's teaspoon of foamy sputum—and, with a headful of tightly packed cotton and slowly grinding gears, slouched into the brightly lit kitchen. There Willie made a fresh pot of coffee, fried a slab of country ham in a cast-iron skillet, dipped some apple butter into a saucer, and popped two biscuits into the microwave. Between lip-smacking mouthfuls, I told her about Ike, Panthrex, COPS, Odel, and my suspicions regarding Drema and Lorraine's southern itinerary.

"You probably don't remember, *but*," she said, with exactly that emphasis, "last night you went *on* and *on* about 'the implacability of evil.' Care to comment in the light of day?"

"No."

"Why had you been drinking last night?"

"Politics."

"Well," Willie said, surprisingly unperturbed, standing and moving toward the window, "I hope those girls didn't get caught in this." Through the window, the ice-covered world glittered beneath an absurdly blue sky. I stood up so I could get a better look—the devastation the ice had wrought was breathtaking. I'd never seen anything like it. From what I could remember, it had grown much worse while I slept.

Telephone and electrical lines sagged with the weight of limbs, and some lines were actually down, looped like a child's handwriting across the ground. Trees were bowed beneath the ice. Rain gutters had pulled away from houses, some had given way completely. Next door, a TV antenna was staked to the ground, trailing wires out of what was now its top, where it had once tied into the roof. And it wasn't over—the sound of splintering limbs and sundering trees continued, though the pace had slowed. Suddenly, something crashed heavily nearby.

And then the refrigerator chugged, the house seemed to sigh—as if to say, Oh, what's the use?—and everything went silent. The power had gone out. Willie and I just looked at each other. After a moment, I asked her if she could give me a ride home. If, I added, the roads weren't impassable.

Willie was running late for work—there were still detainees to minister to, even during a once-in-a-generation ice storm—and so she just dropped me off. Zero galloped up to meet us, smiling, saliva flying as his tongue jounced from side to side. Odel had evidently recovered sufficiently to make a getaway, because his Nova was gone. I was glad. Glad he'd recovered, *and* glad he was gone. But I wondered how he'd fared on the icy roads. It had been tricky enough in Willie's Blazer.

I jumped out, nearly fell yet again, and heard Willie grind the gears, searching for reverse. Blinking into the bright world, nearly snow-blind, I watched her back up my drive. Then she stopped, cranked her window down, and leaned out behind very dark sunglasses. "I'll drive back out here after work," she said, "and we'll fix some dinner. Huddle up next to the fire. Give me a call if there's anything I can pick up." She waved and I gave a feeble wave, too, smiled weakly. I was still feeling more than a little wobbly from the night before. Although Willie's delicious breakfast had gone a long way toward rehabilitating me.

I looked at Zero. "And where were you in my moment of need?"

I paused for a moment outside my door, dreaded going inside, dreaded what I'd find. But stepping into the mudroom, I discovered that I had electricity—I immediately detected the ambient drone of a house humming along. I wouldn't have taken any odds at all on that. I crept into the kitchen. And there I discovered, even more remarkably, that Odel Dent had cleaned up after himself! There was no evidence whatsoever of his volcanic evacuations. Bright white winter sun poured through the east windows, and the kitchen smelled clean, like lemony chemical cleansers.

Odel, Odel, Odel. And after the way I treated you. . . .

I needed to check on Meshach, Shadrach, Abednego, and Uncle Hunt—even though I was sure they were all fine.

And they were. The old goats I found huddled together in the barn, all sleepy eyes and bulging bellies, swollen and tight as basketballs. Ears switched—once, twice—and heavy lids tried to flutter awake, but it was no use. I wondered what they'd found to gorge themselves on.

I wasn't left to wonder for long, though. There was a pump room built in as part of the barn, and in the pump room were the washer and dryer. Reconstructing the scene of the crime, I figured that Drema and Lorraine had deposited a pile of dirty clothes outside the pump room—just prior to their sudden departure—and that they hadn't bothered to open the door and dump their dirty laundry inside. And now, what had been the better part of two wardrobes was being processed through the four-chambered stomachs of three aged, malodorous ruminants. I discovered zippers and buttons and bits of vinyl scattered about, still attached to ragged swatches of cloth.

Hunt had seen me coming—o'er the final hill, down through the bare, frozen ginkgoes, picking my way along through the sheared limbs that covered the ground—and stepped out onto his porch to greet me. Smoke billowed from his chimney. Ice covered the skulls adorning his cabin, and little stalactites of ice hung from snouts and eye sockets. Even creepier than usual—somehow just that much more suggestive of the Big Sleep itself. But Hunt was smiling, evidently happy to see me. This time. His eyes were slit against the bright morning, and he was puffing on a fat, hand-rolled cigarette.

"We may slumber 'neath the shadow of Damocles' sword, yet daily we wake to fine, forgiving light!" Hunt was drunk. I stepped up onto the porch. "I just made that up, Toomey. But come on in." Hunt put his hand on my shoulder, followed me inside, and closed the door behind us. A whiskey bottle—either half-empty or half-full, depending on one's turn of mind, I suppose—sat on the table.

"So, what brings you out on a day like this?"

"Just wanted to check on you, Hunt, make sure you're OK."

"Oh, yeah, we're *fiiiine*. Just *bitch*in'." We? Bitchin'? Hunt winked, shot me a thumbs up, and staggered over to the stove. Wielding a pair of tongs, Hunt lifted from a skillet something small, skinned, and seared. "Squirrel? I believe there's enough here for two, nephew."

I stepped back outside. And this time there was good deal more than a teaspoon available for disgorgement.

When I got back to the house, I called Merle Cooke at Oceana Body Shop, reported the location and condition of my Ram, and asked Merle—Cookie, to his pals—if he would take care of it. Course he would. But, he warned me, not right away. Evidently, I was about his fiftieth caller this morning—everybody who'd been foolish enough to take to the road last night had slid right back off it, generally with consequences. I told Cookie just to get to it when he could. And Cookie was awful slow—but good—even when he wasn't backed up. Hm. Then—necessity indeed being the momma of invention—I had an idea. I put on my coat and walked outside to the toolshed.

The toolshed's a long, low building, half-enclosed and half-open, with a corrugated tin roof slanting down toward the back. It sits just above the pond. The enclosed area is the actual tool portion of the building, a shop really, unused since I'd come into possession of it. Cobwebs had grown over lathes, saws, shelves. The open end of the shed was for storage. We used to stack hay there, back when Deddy kept a few cows, and we parked our tractor, truck, and car beneath it, out of the weather. By now, though, I seldom used it, and never parked my truck there. But the toolshed was where Sewell's Crown Victoria had been moldering all these long years. It had simply never occurred to me to get rid of my brother's trophy car.

I threw back the dusty canvas tarp, and went over the car, making a list. Tires. Of course they were flat, but I'd also heard they'd go out of round if left to sit for too long. I figured it had to have been "too long," *however* long that was. Then rusty joints shrieked when I prized the hood open. I leaned in, observed, extended my list. Tires . . . belts . . . fluids . . . oil . . . battery . . . I leaned in and out, in and out, scribbling away.

Finally I closed the hood and walked around the car once more before heading back up to the house. Inside, I called the Western Auto, dictated my wish list into the phone. The kid I spoke with assured me they had everything I needed, but said they couldn't deliver my order until late in the afternoon or possibly the next morning, at the latest. I told him either would be fine. He thanked me for my patience. And I thanked him right back.

I spent all that afternoon refurbishing the Crown Vic, hoping to return it to its former sharky glory. It hadn't rusted out at all, although its paint had dulled badly—it had developed broad flat splotches—putting it beyond my restorative skills. Nevertheless, by the time I was finished, the old car didn't look too much worse for the wear. Not at all.

That evening, just as Willie and I were sitting down to dinner, there came several long, insistent blasts of a car's horn. Out front, Zero circled a compact Western Auto pickup, barking ferociously. When I came close enough, I saw that the distressed driver was none other than Tommy Cobb, the surly prick at the meeting with Ike out at the Swahili Elks Lodge. He was cramped in the tiny cab—and embarrassed—his huge forearms crossed over the top of the steering wheel and filling half the front window. His Western Auto baseball cap looked like a comic prop, like Bluto's miniature bowler. *Toot, toooot.* I smiled at him through his rolled-up window, then herded away Zero—whose record, by the way, in the area of physical assaults, was spotless. Once extricated, Tommy Cobb muttered darkly about goddamn white people's dogs, fucking Christmas bills, and shitty temp work. He fumbled about, hitching his pants over his ass-crack every time he bent and straightened up, unloaded his delivery onto my front porch, and drove away with hardly another word. Zero chased his truck back out to the gravel road. Taillights flickered through trees, disappeared around the mountain.

Zero came trotting back up the drive, smiling, his head held high. He was proud of chasing the bad man away.

That night Willie fell asleep reading, her hand splayed across the pages of her book as if she were being sworn in to some office. I marked her place and turned out the light, curled up next to her and lay there for a long time, thinking and listening. Every now and then a limb groaned, splintered with a loud crack, crashed through all the lower limbs, and thudded to the frozen ground. The ice was still at work, finalizing its claim on earth.

After what seemed like a long time, I slipped out of bed and went downstairs to watch TV. Specifically, CNN. Our ice storm had made the national news—mainly because it wasn't exactly *our* ice storm. Much of the eastern U.S. was cooling off beneath a mantle of ice, from northern Louisiana and the panhandle of Florida to Virginia, southern Ohio, and southeast Missouri. And everywhere, the results were much the same as here.

I thought: There's only so much abuse that Mother Nature will gladly suffer, and we have evidently pushed the old gal too hard. Sooner or later, she's duty-bound to push back.

At six I turned to a local channel, just in time for sign-on. "The Star-Spangled Banner" was playing and air force jets screamed through the boundless blue sky in formation, cruising above silver-lined clouds and somehow mocking all of us gravity-bound bogtrotters down here.

Mercifully, it all began to thaw that morning. Outside it was a little warmer, warm enough anyway, and the sun was blazing away once again, angrily glinting and glaring from every surface.

Sitting in the kitchen and having a cup of coffee after Willie had gone, I heard water dripping through drainpipes and over the tin roof at the back—*patpatpatpatpatpatpat.* Oddly cheery. Then I climbed into some old brown coveralls that had been hanging in the mudroom for years—I had no idea to whom they had originally belonged—and walked out back to the toolshed, where I got to work.

I'm no mechanic, but for a few hours that morning I labored heroically under the fantastic misimpression that common sense and grit would see me through. I couldn't have been more mistaken. But I was thinking—as I seem to do about once every five years— you know, look at the legion of half-wits who daily disassemble and reconfigure automobile engines, both hobbyists and professionals. *I* ought to be able to do that.

But by noon I had put in an SOS call to Billy Estes, who was chronically unemployed and liked it like that. He lived just up the road with his wizened granny, an amazingly energetic bag of sticks who still donned a huge calico bonnet to work a big patch of pole beans every summer. She was a charismatic and attended a little frame church where they were known to take up serpents. But Billy drank beer, studied the TV, and stole dope from those who'd had enough gumption to grow it. He was consequently quite prominent on any number of shitlists. But he was *handy*, and I occasionally called him for help, usually when there was some task I loathed or was otherwise unable to accomplish.

Billy said he'd be right up. An hour and a half later he found his way up to the shed. He drained a can of beer he was carrying. As always, his paws were grimy and his fingernails sported thick black crescents. His longish red hair had been slicked back with water, but was beginning to sproing loose.

"How do, Billy?" He didn't say anything. I'd used the intervening ninety minutes to further complicate the mess I'd made. We stood there together for a moment, admiring my handiwork. Or at least the energy I'd expended. Greasy parts—no longer identifiable to me—were spread out on newspapers that skirted the car. Finally Billy spoke up. He was smiling.

"You know, Toomey, I wished you'd of called me," he said and belched, "before it got to *this*. Yessir. Just once I wished you would've."

Then, and without any further self-congratulatory asides, Billy got to work. I walked back up to the house and cleaned up. I found a beer in the refrigerator and carried it out to Billy. He was on his back under the car, but at the *psshht* of the pop-top a grasping hand appeared from below. I placed the beer in it, and it withdrew. I found an old, dry-rotted lawn chair and set it up, smoked a cigarette and otherwise pretended to oversee the operation. Soon an empty beer can sailed from beneath the Crown Vic, clanged end over end across the hard ground, and came to rest at my feet. I interpreted this as a request.

I marched across the spongy lawn to the house for another beer.

Outside the toolshed, out of the damp shade, it was warm— warm*ish*, anyway. No breeze at all. Sunshine zooming around, shamelessly celebrating itself. Ice still melting. Everything bright and wet.

I returned with Billy's beer, resituated myself in the lawn chair, and resumed smoking cigarettes. Billy worked in near-silence, only occasionally speaking harsh words to himself, and then only under his breath. His workboots scraped on the dirt and he grunted a little as he repeatedly repositioned himself under the car.

I turned when I heard tires biting gravel. A black Range Rover with blacked-out windows was turning into my place. Its inscrutability was irritating—a Trojan horse? Slowly, it rolled right up to the shed and stopped. Then Vincent Bologna emerged from the driver's side, Bob Gregorio from the passenger's. A back window slid down smoothly, mechanically, revealing Tommy Iarusso a little at a time—eyes, nose, mouth, and nearly nonexistent chin. Behind Tommy on the back seat sat Anthony DeRossi, looking grim. Team Panthrex. Attired today in crisp, new outdoorwear, Eddie Bauer-ish—but, like a GI Joe's uniform, weirdly bulky and not quite right, either.

"Howdy, Toomey." Vincent Bologna smiled, tapped the ash off a cigar. Long, gleaming teeth, too narrow but nonetheless overlapping, as if they'd all been crowded in. He squinted into the bright middle distance, toward the Crown Vic, back at me. "That's a helluva nice car there. I used to drive one just about like it. Course that was"—he rolled his eyes up, thinking for a moment—"goddamn, thirty-five years ago."

We all laughed. Billy Estes peeked out from beneath the car to see what all the commotion was about. Then, obviously disappointed, he disappeared again.

Bob Gregorio walked around the Range Rover, brushing the tips of his fingers over the hood, looking a little shy. He kept glancing at his feet. "How you doing, Toomey?" He smiled and leaned forward, past Bologna, and extended his hand. We shook, and Bob whistled through his teeth. "Some storm, huh?" He looked around, further surveying the damage. Then he said, "Man," without emphasis.

"So," I said, putting off the moment of truth, "what can I do for you fellows?"

"Hey, Toomey!" It was Billy, bellowing at me from beneath the car. We all turned. "This here radiator's rusted out from here to Pikeville, man. She's tits up."

"OK, Billy. I'll take care of it after while."

Still smiling, but somehow looking sad, too, or perhaps just weary, Vincent Bologna moved a little closer. Bob looked off into the woods. Bologna said, "Toomey, let me see if I've got this thing straight. We've been led to believe that you've—that your position regarding Panthrex has, mm, *evolved*. Anything to that, son?"

Anything to that, *son*? I could hardly take that "son" shit from Jerry. And where did Bologna happen to hear such a thing? Not that I minded him knowing before I told him, so much as that it just seemed to indicate some undercover work on somebody's part. Which was not only unnecessary, but insulting. As if I'd been found out.

"Well, yessir. E-*volved*. But I'm a universe. I contain fucking multitudes. Or whatever it was Whitman said."

"Whatever—*what*?"

"You heard me. Now get off my property."

That afternoon I received in the mail a check drawn on Ike Chandler's personal account, made out in the amount of twenty-five hundred dollars. It was a campaign contribution, the largest I would receive, by far. Tucked into the envelope with the check was a note: "We think you'll be a friend once you're elected, Toomer. And we'll do what little we can to help. But you know we can't promise many votes—that's just how it is. Davies' Bottomers aren't big on voting. Just wanted to be up front. Ike."

"Hello." I had been expecting this call and had already decided on a strategy—the old rope-a-dope.

Go ahead, hit me with all you've got, Jer.

"Toomey—what in *hell* are you up to, son? You're making this thing so much goddamn *harder* than it has to be." Well, evidently Jerry had decided on a strategy, too, because he didn't sound angry—and that's what I had expected—but rather dispirited,

"Finally, and just for the record, yes—if, that is, you come to your senses—I will *probably* agree to marry you. But I'm telling you right now, I can't have a husband who's no more than a bundle of irresistible impulses, whose idea of fun is sprinting purposelessly hither and yon, like a chicken with his head cut off, who—"

"I hear you, sweetheart, I really do, and if there's one thing—"

"Toomey!"

"Yes?"

"Relax." Willie tilted the rearview mirror her way, pulled a comb from her purse and ran it through her hair. Then, with both hands, she carefully squared her sunglasses on the bridge of her nose. "Now, let's get this show on the road. I've got work to—OH!"

A robin redbreast (the first of the year!) barreled smack into the windshield—whump!—startling us both. Or, not to be anthropocentric about it, make that all three of us. The poor bird lay stunned on the warm hood of the car for a moment, flat on its back, hyperventilating. But in the next moment, it was back up on its feet, staggering, circumscribing a small, wobbly circle. Then it was off, though on a flight trajectory less than plumb, but soaring nevertheless, looping crazily through the trees until it disappeared, prevailing, after a fashion, after all.

Then, somehow—was it an act of grace?—we tacked one-eighty and made love right there on the front seat of SEWELL-2.

And the day was good.

CHAPTER TEN

Early that spring—or, put another way, very late into the season of my stealth campaign for mayor—the University of Kentucky Wildcat basketball team met its annual Waterloo. This time it was in Elvis's adopted hometown, in Memphis's preposterous Pyramid (and just what is it, by the way, with Tennessee and its citizens' curious fetish for the classical architecture of antiquity? Nashville has its replica of the Parthenon, and now Memphis has its Pyramid. What's next? Chattanooga reconstructs the Hanging Gardens of Babylon?). It was late March, a cold, blustery, damp week that just reeked of perdition and ruin, and, sure enough, we lost in the regional finals of the NCAA tournament, 84–71, to one of the typically bland and characterless (but oh so fundamentally precise) Research Triangle teams—it doesn't make any difference which one . . . well, OK, it *wasn't* State.

I said *annual* waterloo. All that means, in practical terms, is that the Cats fell short of an NCAA championship—again. I wish I were big enough to shrug, say, So what? and get on with matters of some consequence. Like wrapping up a damned mayoral campaign, for starters. And whipping Dickie Fitzgerald's goddamned ass for him and the commonweal.

The thing is—with the exception of a few wicked perverts who actually cheer for the University of Louisville, and a smattering of sorehead Negroes who continue to hold UK accountable for Adolph

Rupp's antediluvian racism—the citizens of Kentucky live and die according to the vicissitudes of their University of Kentucky basketball team. Sure, we might be known 'round the world for our sleek and sinewy thoroughbreds, our silky bourbon whiskeys, and our smooth rich burley (not to mention our now-ubiquitous fried chicken outlets—for which I hereby apologize). But here in the trenches—down here at the bottom, that is, with Mississippi and Arkansas, of every quality-of-life ranking ever devised by a *Money* magazine editor or government bureaucrat: education, housing, employment, income, infant mortality, etc.—while we might take a vague and mostly abstract pride in ponies and corn liquor and 'bakker, we *need* the basketball. Exactly the way a junkie needs his dope. That is, so we can just sort of fog out on all the rest of it.

So every year that the Wildcat basketball team fails to bring home an NCAA championship trophy—which is to say, almost *every* year—the commonwealth, from the shores of the Mississippi in the west to the banks of the Big Sandy in the east, heaves a collective melancholic sigh and sinks into a deep blue funk, and the whole state just slows . . . way . . . down. Fast food lines creep along, the crime rate drops. And I am no better than the rest. I wish I were. But alas. I'm not.

I think it would be fair to say that for about twenty-four hours, I was soul-sick. Desolate, inconsolable, and woebegone I was, just utterly bowed down with grief. I did not, however, resort to spirits, the vanquished sportsman's traditional recompense.

Drema finally called—that very afternoon, of course, in the dark aftermath of the Kentucky defeat, hoping to ameliorate the pain through sharing. We commiserated all right. That is to say we ululated, we keened, we gnashed our teeth. Like those hysterical, skirt-flapping Palestinian mothers who lose their beautiful dark-eyed boys to the *intifada.*

But we wore that out soon enough and moved on to other things.

And just as I had suspected, Drema and Lorraine were hiding out at Lorraine's mom's house in Lake Richard, Louisiana—way down south in the land of cotton. It's right on the lake, Drema said, obviously pleased, but the particulars of her new home and life she left to my imagination. And all on my own like that, I quickly conjured the easiest image, something I already knew, something I had seen in photos and movies, a gray and weather-beaten cottage, raised on two-foot piers and towered over by sweet-smelling cypress trees and nearly enshrouded in Spanish moss. Further, in my mind's eye, the red sun was setting over the bayou, and Drema and Lorraine and her mother capered on a crumbling wharf within a stone's throw of *la maison Acadian,* pulling crab pots and casting seines and running trotlines. All in the service of a simmering kettle of gumbo. And somewheres a-way off through the darkening swamp . . . a fiddle sawed, an accordion wheezed, and the mournful dulcet music of some Cajun clan carried in over the water. . . .

On another subject, Drema was more explicit. On the night of the ice storm, when she and Lorraine abandoned the premises and hightailed it out of Mann County, it turned out that Odel's *other* ex-wife had called to warn them that "the crazy fucker" was on his way to Oceana even as they spoke (this, by the way, was the first I'd heard of an aboriginal Mrs. Dent). The first ex-Mrs. told Drema she'd tried everything to dissuade or distract her sometime man—and yes, she admitted to Drema, Odel had been her off-and-on luv thang even during his tempestuous marriage to Lorraine—but, in

ized by high anxiety, cold sweats, claustrophobia, vertigo, and dread.

Having a baby—man oh man: long fuse, big bang. Who could possibly know what the consequences might be, twenty or thirty or even forty years down the line? And once the whole thing's been set in motion—well, who would want to?

CHAPTER TWELVE

In my next life, I will not own a telephone. Write it down. Ideally, I suppose, I'd come back as a Bedouin driving camel trains across the blanched, sand-blasted Sahara, or a swampy coon-ass Cajun who lives in his pirogue. Whatever. Maybe a bum scraping cigarette butts out of a gutter in Louisville, or Memphis. But I can tell you this: I will not own a telephone.

When the dang thing rang, I wasn't exactly in the mood. I'd driven to a big electronics discount warehouse in Lexington and purchased a computer—3.2 gig hard drive, 32 meg of RAM, K56Ffex modem, etc., etc., or so the salesman said. Something like that. I hadn't been home long, and I was trying to figure the thing out. Not trying to figure out how to use it, but trying to figure out how to configure the thing so it *was* usable. Comm ports and IRQ conflicts, *shit!*—the modem, the thing I was really interested in, was just about exactly enough to make me want to burn down the fucking house in exasperation. And right then, as I was saying, the phone rang.

"What!"

"May I *please* speak with *Mister* Toomey Spooner."

"Speaking."

"I *do* hope I'm not calling at a bad time, *but*—"

"Excuse me. I don't mean to be rude, but is this a so-called courtesy call?'"

"In a manner of speaking, yes, it is. Mr. Spooner, you don't know me, but I'm Lorraine Basile's—Lorraine Dent's mother? Eugenia Basile. And I'm calling from Lake Richard, Louisiana."

OK, Ms. Basile had my undivided attention, and I had to assume it was bad news. But how bad could it be? An accident—that seemed likely. Drema and Lorraine had been drinking and been involved in a car wreck. Or maybe they'd driven to New Orleans or Houston—both about equidistant from Lake Richard—for the weekend and been mugged, perhaps even wounded. Mrs. Basile's tone of voice suggested they were both still alive, at least. It was absent the direst tones—those soft, comforting ones, or the studied flatness of an official call reluctantly placed to next of kin.

"Yes, ma'am. I'm sorry. What is it?"

"Well, Mr. Spooner—"

"Toomey, please."

"Toomey." Eugenia Basile took a deep breath, exhaled into the receiver. "Now I'm not about to suggest he didn't deserve just about exactly what he got, but—well, Toomey, it seems your sister, Drema, has pistol-shot Lorraine's ex-husband."

Drema was shooting to kill, there didn't seem to be much question at all about that. As one extraordinarily helpful physician—a resident at the charity hospital who had labored to save Odel's life, sort of—explained it to me over the phone, and in lay terms, the bullet had entered Odel's chest at exactly the point where it might ordinarily be expected to do the most damage. I.e., rip into his tiny black heart. But because of the unusual trajectory—Drema had evidently been perched high on a live oak bough shooting almost straight down—and the puniness of her weapon (a two-shot derringer, easily concealed, of course, but not much of a man-stopper), the bullet pierced Odel's breastplate—miraculously, as the doctor put it—but passed more or less harmlessly into his chest cavity. Actually Drema shot him twice, but the other bullet, her second shot, merely ricocheted off his forehead, and as far as the young doctor was concerned didn't even count. Not so, the Lake Richard police and district attorney, who seemed to evince almost as keen an interest in Drema's intent as in what she actually managed to accomplish. So add failed head shots to the short list that customarily includes only horseshoes and hand grenades, because the D.A.'s office was contemplating an attempted murder charge, in addition to the assault complaint already lodged against my little sister.

I asked Willie if she'd like to drive down to Lake Richard with me—if, that is, her condition did not preclude it—and she said, of course, you dope, and we left the next morning. And despite the unhappy occasion for our journey, when we pulled out of Oceana in the old Crown Victoria I was full of that sweet sense of possibility—OK, the sheer *joy*—of heading out. I love to see the highway unfurled before me over the earth, the thin ribbon vanishing in the rearview. Even an overnight trip feels like the start of something completely new, as if a new and better me may yet emerge, once I'm out *there*. It didn't hurt that curled there on the seat beside me, Willie looked like . . . well, like a morning glory at *dawn*, her face tilted to the soft morning sun.

And she was carrying our child. I just couldn't get over that.

It also didn't hurt at all that I was leaving behind Mann County electoral business.

We drove north and west out of the mountains, through Lexington and down the Bluegrass Parkway into western Kentucky, past Hillbilly Heaven, Wigwam Village, and the ersatz-modernist Corvette Museum that juts, ironically, like a glittery golden tailfin out of what is later in the season a lush stand of soybeans near Bowling Green. The sky was overcast, but pale and uniform and didn't threaten rain. Somewhere between Gold City, Kentucky, and the Tennessee state line, and while Willie snoozed, I watched a biplane do barrel rolls over a freshly plowed field in the distance.

Then we were in the mountains again, only this time it was the mountains of north-central Tennessee. A little after one, we stopped for Frito chili pie in Nashville, at a cinder-block diner not far from the interstate. An old neon sign sizzled and snapped over the entrance: Lorries Means Good Food. I took the road atlas in with us, to decide on a route while we ate. Birmingham, Hattiesburg, Slidell; or Memphis, Jackson, Hammond. I slid the map across to Willie and asked her what she thought. It looked like six of one and a half dozen of another to me.

Almost instantly she said, "40 to 55," hardly glancing at the map (that was Memphis, Jackson, Hammond). I asked her why. She let her sunglasses slip to the end of her nose and looked at me over them, amused. "Elvis. Eudora. Hel-*lo*?"

In Memphis, I got off the interstate and asked directions in a convenience store. The pimply, punky kids who seemed to be running the place were practically preverbal—*uh, you know, like, sort of, uh*—so I finally just bought a map. Then Willie and I drove around until we found the Pyramid—I just had to see it. After that, we cruised slowly by Graceland, which Willie wanted to see, though she didn't particularly care about stopping. And the whole excursion didn't set us back an hour.

We spent the night in Jackson.

And that night, trying to go to sleep in a Best Western next to the interstate, with Willie beside me and cool, slick, synthetic sheets pulled up to my chin, I couldn't help but feel bad about what all us

Spooners had put Odel through. I had to remind myself that he had, after all, brought it all on himself.

The next morning we drove to McDonald's and bought Egg McMuffins and cups of McCoffee. We parked in front of Eudora Welty's house and ate.

There's something about Louisiana. I mean, there's just no mistaking it—you can't help but know you're *there.*

A little before noon, we passed exits for Bear Town, Magnolia, and Chatawa—Mississippi's final southern outposts. Then we passed into the preternatural and fathomlessly deep Deep South of Gulf Coast Louisiana.

Just across the Mississippi-Louisiana border, I pulled off I-55 for fuel. For too long, the needle on my gas gauge had lain heavily against the red E. The off-ramp wound round, taking us full circle, through tall densely growing pine trees and brush. And it was as if the interstate above had never existed—out of sight, out of earshot. At the foot of the ramp, abandoned earth-moving equipment— rusting and dust covered—sat on hard yellow clay, where it seemed to have scooped away whatever green things had once grown there. We sat at the stop sign for a moment with the windows down. The vast southern engine of insect biomass buzzed all around us. It's almost impossible to explain satisfactorily—because it's more than just the raw data, the look of the place and its feel on your skin—but I had the distinct feeling of being in another country.

Down the road, through the dense green growth, I thought I spotted a gas station. I turned my wheel to the left and bumped up onto the narrow macadam state highway.

It was not the kind of place you see much anymore, and certainly not along the interstate. It was a big clapboard building, gray with weather, and its tin roof had rusted orange. A pair of cane-bottom chairs—one with its seat blown out—sat on the front porch. A flaking Evangeline Maid Bread push-plate barred the screen door. Most of the old metal signs attached to the place were thirty years old or better. Some—like the one that read "I'd Rather Fight Than Switch"—advertised products that didn't even exist anymore. Two mottled mongrels with prominent ribs and big hound-dog ears wandered by. One stopped, raised his muzzle, sniffed at the air, looked left and right, continued on his way, and disappeared around the side of the building. With a final glance back over his shoulder, the other slipped into the tall weeds.

I filled the tank of the Crown Vic and walked across the dusty lot. I climbed onto the porch, pushed through the screen door, and let it slap shut behind me. It was very dark and ripe-smelling inside. I felt the air from a fan blowing in my face, but it had been so bright outside I was now snow-blind in the gloom of the store. I stood just inside the door for a moment, waiting to get my eyes back. The rasp of a large, slow dog's paws scraped across the floor in front of me. I waited a moment for my eyes to return.

Willie had asked me to get some snacks, something we couldn't get at home, and I returned to the car with a small jar of pickled quails' eggs, tasso wrapped in butcher's paper, hot lengths of boudin and andouille I'd fetched with tongs from a steam bucket, a bag of Zapp's "Crawtator" potato chips, and two Cokes. Aside from the Cokes, we couldn't have got any of that at home. Mission accomplished.

By midafternoon, though, Willie was hungry again, this despite the predominant note of decomposition in the air. We'd driven more than halfway across the flat, wet, fecund southern tier of Louisiana, from Hammond to Baton Rouge, where we crossed from

East to West over the wide and muddy Mississippi on the Huey P. Long Memorial Bridge, which arced breathtakingly high above the water, the barges, the factories and mills and petroleum-processing plants that line the shore on either side. It was obviously an old bridge, looking as if it could stand some work, and hinted at least mildly at some element of chance in its crossing.

Then from Baton Rouge we traversed the spooky, stump-studded Atchafalaya Basin, and along the way either went through or passed exits for Whiskey Bay, Ramah, Breaux Bridge, and Grand Cocteau, and I couldn't shake that sense of having crossed a border into some foreign republic.

But by the time Willie was ready to eat again, we were passing close to a town with the unlikely and Capra-esque name of Iota, where a seafood restaurant that had advertised for miles along the interstate was situated. Boiled crawfish was their signature dish, evidently—so, we really had no choice. Not to mention Willie's stated desire for fresh culinary experiences. And as far as I knew, nobody back home in Kentucky had ever boiled, fried, stewed, roasted, fricasseed, or otherwise prepared a crawdad for human consumption.

We found the restaurant and ordered two big platters of steaming crawfish. A red-headed waitress with veiny workingman's hands and a huge rock-hard ass instructed us in the art and science of sucking the heads.

We pulled into Lake Richard around dusk. An orange sunset was spreading over the lake, which was adjacent to I-10. We exited onto a road that hugged the north shore and took us past riverboat casinos and the hotels and restaurants that serviced them. Neon piping winked luridly in the gathering night, inviting weary Texans to stop and wager a few dollars, spend the night, leave some of their hard-earned money right here in Louisiana. On the west shore of the lake, petrochemical plants sat next to the water, their bleeder valve flames licking at the pale night. Lorraine's mom had very graciously invited us to stay with her and had given me what appeared to be precise instructions to her house. I thought I'd drop Willie off there, and then visit Drema in the parish jail.

3222 Lakeshore Drive. That was the address Eugenia had given me. And as one might reasonably expect, Lakeshore Drive circumscribed the lake. But I could see across the lake, I could make out every shore, and all I saw, in addition to the casinos and the plants, were other commercial properties—and a row of waterfront mansions. Perhaps there around the bend, I thought, where I couldn't see, there'd be an outpost of more modestly proportioned homes, of the sort of Cajun cottages I'd seen squatting along the shorelines of other bodies of water and had imagined for Lake Richard from the movies.

By now, we were rounding that bend on Lakeshore Drive that I'd been waiting for. 3216, 3218, 3220, and . . . *3222?* I could hardly believe it, but there it was. A twenty-, maybe thirty-room Greek Revival mansion. Or I should say that it was after the style of Greek Revival out front, where the circle drive would naturally lead one to disembark, but it seemed to give way to, or otherwise accommodate, a number of other styles as it spread back and out over the grounds—Italianate, Romanesque, Gothic, and I don't know what all. Across the road, built over the lake, was what obviously had to be 3222's private wharf, upon which there was a boathouse that was considerably bigger than my regular house back home in Oceana. Surrounding the main house were fantastic live oaks, elaborately bearded in Spanish moss. There was a walled-off rose garden beyond the—let's see—*west* wing, and what seemed to be a fully and meticulously restored row of slave quarters beyond the east, half-hidden in the shadow cast by the mansion. What lay to the rear, well, I could hardly imagine. A private menagerie à la *Citizen Kane*?

Willie turned to me. "Were you aware of—well, Toomey, *this*?" she said, spreading her arms before the windshield and holding them there, spread before Xanadu, as if she were—like poor Susan Alexander—hitting the sustained final note of her aria.

Spaced artfully throughout the perennial garden, tasteful little brass oil lamps burned softly and cast the perfect golden glow. Cocktails in the arboretum. A warm gulf breeze induced the mildest flutter in the broader-leafed tropical flora. Dry palms rustled. Perched on the rim of a brick wall, a tiny lizard with a red throat performed rapid push-ups. Meanwhile, Mrs. Basile, Eugenia, who had extended to us the warmest welcome I could imagine, was expressing her amazement.

"Toomey, you mean to tell me you've never before sipped a mint julep?"

"I do propose to tell you that, Eugenia."

"Well, that's just criminal. I'd say the state of Kentucky's got some explaining to do." In utter agreement, Eugenia and I smiled at each other in the soft light and clinked frosty silver julep cups. I had taken to bourbon and mint and sugar water like—well, like I *would*. Meanwhile, Willie sipped a big slushy virgin something-or-the-other, something fruity with an umbrella in it, something that respected her condition, and didn't seem to mind the absence of alcohol. Lorraine was pouring shots from a bottle of Southern Comfort. And didn't seem to mind anything at all. She was, in fact, quite drunk.

As it turned out, by the time Willie and I arrived in Lake Richard it was already too late to visit the detention center. And the only phone calls allowed at the jail were outgoing. So Drema might call and she might not. At least according to Lorraine. She had already called three times that day. And it was now near nine, when all calls stopped.

"So," I asked, "where's Odel right now."

"Mr. Dent is presently lodged in the Lake Richard Charity Hospital, recovering more from quote unquote life-saving surgery than from any ridiculous gunshot wound," Eugenia said. "The hospital's not a half-mile from where we sit. But upon his release, which ought to be tomorrow or the next day, judging from the niggardly little bit of information they'll parcel out over the phone—honestly, you'd think it's a matter of national security—he will be charged with stalking the girls. Police are stationed in the hallway, just outside his room, awaiting his release." Eugenia sipped at her julep and dabbed at the corner of her mouth with a cocktail napkin. "So, the situation is not *altogether* devoid of justice. Nearly, perhaps, but not altogether."

Willie said, "It's hard to believe a jury wouldn't call it self-defense."

"Hard to say," Lorraine said. She was freshening our drinks from a portable bar, a stainless steel cart on wheels. "I can imagine a Lake Richard jury thinking the prick was well within his rights. Don't forget, his wife had run off with another *woman*. And don't underestimate the potency of that. The prosecution won't."

"Lorraine's right, Wilhelmina." Eugenia set her drink aside and turned to me. "But on another subject altogether, and if you don't mind my asking, what is this 'Vote the Goat' business all about?"

I explained that the goat is a stubborn and willful creature, et cetera.

The Charlemagne Parish Women's Vocational Facility was out in the hot flat clammy blues-harp country, fifteen or twenty miles south of town, out in the wetlands that ran to the Gulf of Mexico, yet another seven or eight miles away. The land was densely cross-hatched by canals, and nowhere was it altogether dry. Heat waves rippled in the middle distance and beyond. Like supplicants to Allah, oil pumps bowed rhythmically and drew fuel out of the earth. Eugenia had told me that the people there lived much as they had a hundred years before, hunting, fishing, trapping. They shrimped and ran alligator farms. Most of the intraparish commerce seemed to involve beer and bait, and there also seemed to be a not-insignificant demand for hand-painted signs, whitewashed on weathered boards: Rabbits 4 Sale, etc. In many respects, it was like a flat wet Appalachia, a teeming land of poverty funneling the wealth out, all of it set in motion a hundred years before by unscrupulous and lavishly financed mineral minions.

The sky was clear but hazy and merely hinted at blue, like skimmed milk. But over the flat treeless earth, it was vast. Which worked to diminish the scale of things on the ground, including the women's parish jail, reducing its significance in the panorama. Somewhere on its grounds, smoke billowed into the sky, as if from a brushfire. Sunlight winked on razor-wire. I pulled onto the grounds. Without asking me any questions, but nevertheless eyeing me suspiciously, a squat male guard—whose thick black belt emphasized his heavy gut—raised the gate and let me proceed up the long dusty drive.

Once inside, another guard—a matron this time—led me through a hall of glazed brick and fluorescent light, then outside into a dusty little yard, empty except for a picnic table. She left me there. Fat, surreal insects whirred past. I lit a cigarette, finished it, lit another. I began to wonder what exactly was going on. I sat down on the picnic table bench, leaned my back into the table, and lit yet another ciggie. But I turned when I heard the heavy tumblers of a very secure lock fall—*ka-chunka-chunk*—and I saw Drema emerge into the yard, squinting against the sun, followed by the glum-looking matron.

"Toomey!" We fell into each other's arms. The matron kept several respectful paces back, but watched us closely. She raised her fist to her mouth and yawned, without blinking, but without taking her eyes off us, either. "Toomey, Toomey, *Toomey!*"

"Hey, little sister." We slipped apart but held hands.

Because my visit wasn't scheduled—and this came as a big surprise—we were only allowed five minutes together and didn't really get much past inane but necessary greetings. Toomey! Drema! *Toomey! Drema!* But as I was leaving, I scheduled a visit for the following morning, for which we would be allotted thirty minutes.

On the way out, I stopped at the front desk and filled out a formal complaint. Five minutes? I'd driven all the way down from Oceana, Kentucky, et cetera. It was futile, of course, but something I had to do.

Back at Eugenia's, I called Jerry. Without being very specific, yet hinting that there *was* something exceedingly specific he just wasn't saying, he suggested that my time just might be better spent back home in Oceana. But I just didn't have the energy to pursue it, to drag it out of him. I didn't even bother telling him that I intended to leave Lake Richard two mornings hence. In fact, I consciously mimicked his studied vagueness. Then I called my house to see if Hunt might be hanging around, and if he was, if he might pick up. He wasn't and he didn't. Or he just plain didn't. And of course he didn't have a phone of his own, not down there in that goddamn cabin of his. But it wasn't as if I really needed to speak with him, either.

Then, suffering a fit of something not unlike contrition, I dialed Jerry's number again. He picked up on the first ring. "Do I really need to get back?"

"Well, Toomey, here's how I see it. There's not much time left and you're a thousand miles from home and a couple of percentage points behind your opponent. Dickie's right here, campaigning hard, near as I can tell. But I'll leave it up to you."

"So as far as you're concerned, this is just generally a matter of principle."

"Well, there's that, yes—not to mention some simple arithmetic." Jerry paused to chew on something and swallow. "Oh, and did I mention that Panthrex has evidently bought the Simpson place and is scraping away a site? Two bulldozers got busy this morning."

"What?"

"That's right. Either they know something we don't—which I doubt—or else they're toting up their chickadees before they've hatched. All I know is that it's something Dolin Smits is in on, and, as I understand it, that it was facilitated by some fancy footwork by Preece Thackerey." *Judge* Preece Thackerey.

"We're leaving day after tomorrow, Jerry. And we'll drive straight through." Shit. Fifteen hours behind the wheel.

"Thank God for itty bitty favors, son. And needless to say, I believe you've made a, let's say, *mature* choice."

It was the same procedure the next morning. I waited in the yard alone, smoked two cigarettes and lit a third before Drema appeared. I brought a carton of smokes for Drema, too, but had been asked to leave them at the desk where I checked in. Upon polite inquiry, I'd been assured she'd get them. That mistakes were neither made nor tolerated.

After an embrace in the hot sun, I led Drema over to sit next to me on the picnic bench. I said, "I've hired a real lawyer. When I called your public defender, he sounded more relieved than anything. I guess that's OK with you?"

"Oh, yeah. He made it pretty goddamn clear he wasn't real enthused about handling my case. The unusual particulars of it. That's a quote—'the unusual particulars.'" Drema looked away for a moment. "What I want to know is what we did, what I did, that anybody wouldn't have done? I honestly can't understand why I'm even here. *He* came after *us*. And I shot him. That seems reasonable. And fair as can be." Out there in the brush around us, there was a low sizzle and hum.

"I've got more news," I said, "some good, some not so good. Odel was released from Lake Richard Charity, so he's evidently out of danger. If he was ever in any, which seems to be a point of contention between his doctors and the police. Anyway, he was promptly arrested. Which is the good news. On the not-so-good side, miraculously, he made his bail. So he's at large as we speak. But at least he's wanted. I don't have any idea where he is or what he's up to. Ideally, I guess, he'll screw up. Which doesn't seem unlikely, either."

"No, it doesn't, but shit-fucking-fire anyway." Drema kicked at the dirt with her orange regulation-issue flip-flops. "Goddamnit to hell." She said this with deep resignation, which I took to be a good sign. For now, at least. I didn't think it was a bad thing at all for Drema to feel a little defeated.

I looked back at the matron. "Can we walk on down here a

ways?" She nodded. Her expression was friendly this morning. And I took that to be a good sign, too. "C'mon, Drema. Let's take advantage of the day."

The high concertina-topped cyclone fence actually took in a fair amount of real estate, I suppose because land there on the broad marshy plain is nothing if not cheap. Providing it doesn't straddle a substratum of oil or gas, that is. At any rate, the fence circumscribed what I guessed to be a hundred and fifty or two hundred acres, and included within its perimeter was a couple-of-hundred-yards stretch of some still, black, anonymous bayou, in the vicinity of which stood the only trees I saw on the prison grounds—elaborately bearded cypress trees, trailing moss almost to the ground, their knees protruding from the water and earth like battlements, and a lone, but magnificent, live oak. That was the direction in which Drema and I walked, the matron a little ways back, and, judging by the mildly beatific expression on her face, she seemed to be enjoying the day, too; I was guessing that she might be prepared to cut us a little slack, if it came to that.

Drema and I sat down on the bank of the bayou. "OK," I said, "tell me what happened. I can't get a straight story out of Lorraine. Not that I think she's covering anything up, I just think she got a little too excited to recall the event with enough specificity to satisfy me."

"Excited?" Drema laughed. "Hysterical's more like it."

"So. Tell me what happened."

"You know, Toomey, it's really just the same old story. Except this time we had the drop on *Odel*—see, he's always been the one that had the element of surprise working for him. I guess the other big difference is that we were armed."

"I know he favors surprise entrances."

collar and tie, and he presented a temporary restraining order to the two bulldozer operators. He explained it to them at length, and driving back into town I flagged the two bulldozer operators into the Stop-N-Go and bought them each a twelve-pack of beer. Then we all went home. And I think it's safe to say there were no hard feelings.

CHAPTER THIRTEEN

The highest-stakes political event of the campaign season—the Fogg Farm Family Bar*B*Q—was coming up in the middle of April. It was neither fair nor rational, nor was it intended to be. As a matter of fact, the thing was *so* irrational it actually worked against the interests of the electorate, what with so little emphasis being placed on an airing of the issues and so much placed on vicious rhetoric and withering lampoons. In many ways, the Fogg farm event was way out ahead of the times.

But the Fogg farm event was where candidates were more often than not made or broken. It was a public pecking party, a cock fight, a bombastic battle royal—to the death. But you could bet everything you owned that all the candidates would be there, too, all the men and women running for seats on the school board, for the county's minor elective offices, for judge-executive and sheriff and so on. And taking no prisoners, they'd all come prepared to inflict the goriest mortal wounds on their opponents. Folks they'd mostly known all their lives. But the most remarkable aspect of the event was that come the day after, they'd all act as if nothing at all had passed between them. Publicly, at least. Now, what murderous pent-up rage roiled just beneath the surface and could never be let go of—that was another matter altogether. And something I could only guess at.

The Fogg Farm Family Bar*B*Q really was a barbecue, too, and there'd be sweet roasted chickens, big smoky spareribs, and pit-barbecued pork—some nontraditionalist, an immigrant from western Kentucky, might even introduce mutton into the smorgasbord. Plus there was sure to be potato salad, corn muffins, macaroni and cheese, green bean casserole, cole (or cold) slaw, baked beans, and, lately at least—confirming that a little knowledge is indeed a dangerous thing—seven-layer pea salad. So, like I said, it really was a barbecue and family-style picnic, but the actual Fogg family had passed out of existence or simply moved on too long ago for anybody to know the story or why or care about it anymore. At least I never heard anything about it. But the name itself had stuck, and had of course taken on an unflattering and unintended meaning over time, given the nature of the event.

So I was gearing up. I knew I had some Real Bad News that would utterly poleax my opponent, some information that could catapult me into the big leagues and fully and forever eliminate Dickie from public life. But the question was whether I could use it. That would require not only a pile of guts, but a reckless, even awesome, disregard for one's fellow man.

Because what if I was wrong? I had not, after all, actually witnessed the absolutely crucial aspect of the thing I knew had happened. But it had, hadn't it? Yes! But twenty years . . . well, that's a long time. Youth, and the taste for blood that comes with it, was no longer mine. I could feel—literally, in my body—all my righteous certainty leaking away.

Just as Junie Sepulvada had predicted, the Charlemagne Parish D.A.'s office had refused to prosecute Drema and she was released the second morning after Willie and I left. But there was a condition: she had to agree to leave Lake Richard and the state of Louisiana. And Odel, of course, was conspicuously AWOL for a hearing to determine his status as a persistent felon. But it was conducted in absentia, and the news for Mr. Dent was not good. At that point, I was certain he would not be returning to the area.

So the irony now was that not only was Lake Richard the safest place on the earth for Lorraine and Drema to pursue their vision of life, liberty, and connubial tranquillity, it was also the only locale on the planet from which they were legally prohibited to reside as taxpayers and peaceable citizens. To no effect, but to her everlasting credit, Eugenia tried throwing around some of her not-inconsiderable weight, and I was grateful. But it was no dice. The girls were going to have to leave. The ban was informal but powerful, and there was no appeals process—from the authorities' point of view, the very beauty of the arrangement lay in its informality. Or so Junie Sepulvada explained it to me when I called to thank her for services rendered. I scratched my head for a moment after that one. But I forwarded her a check that very afternoon.

Late one night after Willie had gone to bed, several days after Drema's release from the Charlemagne Parish Women's Vocational Facility and her subsequent banishment from Lake Richard, Drema called from Houston to ask if she and Lorraine could come back to Oceana and stay with me a while. They didn't know for how long and they sure didn't want to put me and Willie out, but they didn't know where else to go, either. I told her of course they could, that they were more than welcome, and that I'd pick them up at the Lexington airport the next afternoon.

After I hung up the phone I poured a drink—OJ and Vichy water—and walked outside with Zero and we wandered on down to the pond together. I felt as if I were about to have a family for the first time in a long time. Willie and I had vague plans to be married before autumn. Now Drema and Lorraine were coming to live with us, and by Christmastime Willie and I would be parents of a child.

Holy smoke.

I lit a cigarette and blew a ghostly plume toward the stars. A pearly moon was rising through branches heavy with swollen spring buds. Zero stirred when some medium-sized mammal crashed through the brush, but then he circled for a moment, rearranged himself and settled back down around my feet. And I thought: Hizzoner Toomey Spooner. And I wished my father could be around to see it.

Whichever way the thing went, he'd have been proud enough.

I'm pretty sure.

CHAPTER FOURTEEN

Spring had arrived, the wildflowers were in bloom, I was drunk on nothing more than the clear warm days and the life taking ever-more-coherent shape in Willie's belly, and Drema—Drema!—for once seemed quite happy to be at home in Oceana. But at that exact moment, at that very time of year, well, who wouldn't have been? In the week or so since she and Lorraine had flown in from Houston, they had been canoeing on the North Fork several times, they had tilled and worked the garden and prepared it for seed, and they had packed lunches and taken more than a few very long walks lasting half a day or more. Drema had even asked me if she could put in a small marijuana patch down in the muddy bottom where Deddy used to keep cows (although perhaps "keep" is not exactly the right word, since as often as not the cows were escaped and on the loose, renegades roaming the countryside), and I said that would be fine with me. In fact, it was more than fine, it thrilled me—I took it as pretty convincing evidence that she intended to stick around, at least for a while. Longer than she had at any time since the day she was forced to go live with Aunt Lou and Uncle Eustace in Lexington.

Not only that, but I'd become very fond of Lorraine. She was shy, as it turned out, and had begun to open up. More and more, she smiled easily and engaged in mild banter with Drema and Willie and even me. I guess I was finally beginning to see what Drema saw in her. It also seemed as if Odel were no longer a shadow hanging over every moment. Shooting Dent had evidently been cathartic, just exactly what the doctor himself might have ordered.

One afternoon I found Drema out in the barn, wandering around the pump room, looking into and around dark corners. I asked her what she was looking for. She said she knew that she and Lorraine had left a big pile of clothes out here the night they left for Lake Richard, and it was almost everything they owned. I had to tell her that Messieurs Shadrach, Meshach, and Abednego had dined on their jeans and shirts and sweaters.

So, the next day, Drema, Lorraine, and I drove into Lexington and shopped for the better part of the afternoon at Fayette Mall. We dined in the food court, and then we shopped some more and didn't get home until nearly midnight.

Speaking of the goats. One afternoon I was leafing through the *Oceana Shopper & Gazetteer*—which was, for the most part and through no fault of its own (and not counting the front-page spread they'd done on my protest out at the Simpson place, which was really first-rate), no more than a small, gossipy weekly ("On Saturday the 19th, Mrs. Joyce Sommerville's sister, Peg Drumjelskii, and her husband, Larry, stopped by for a visit. Joyce served the Michigan couple country ham and potato salad and prepared one of her famous butterscotch cream pies. The Drumjelskiis were on their way from Travers City to Daytona Beach for their annual spring fling . . ."). I was reading the classifieds when I ran across an ad placed by someone who was desperate to give away several adolescent goats. Including three females. It was one of those right time, right place things, and, scratching my chin, I thought, *hm*. By noon I was standing in the showroom of Jerry's dealership, asking him if I could borrow a truck—mine was *still* in the shop.

"Hey, man," Jerry was saying, "what the hell is it with you and those goddamn goats?"

"*Jerry* . . . do you have a truck I can borrow or don't you?"

"Yeah, I guess." Jerry was put out by my request. He didn't say so, but I could see that he thought it was an odd distraction, at the very time I ought to have been "focusing," as he put it. But, somewhat reluctantly, he gave in. "Go around back and ask for that knuckle-head Pee Dee. Tell him I said to give you the blue truck. But you ask me, you need more goats about like you need a goddamn hole in the head."

The goats, it turned out, were the innocent victims in a bad divorce. A ghost of a woman—approximately my age but much, much older, too—floated out to the truck, led me around back to the goats and told me to take my damn pick. I loaded two frisky young nannies into the truck, and I thanked the woman. I assured her that I'd make a good home for them, and she said, yeah, sure, but it just seemed like more than she could think about right then. With that unsatisfying conclusion, I climbed back in the truck and drove away.

Usually I had to keep the goats tethered. Penned goats will quickly defoliate the area circumscribed by the pen, and every bit as thoroughly as a dousing with Agent Orange. Tethering allows a measure of control—a kind of selective scorched earth policy. So the trick is (1) to move them frequently enough that they don't completely devastate one area, and (2) to stagger the areas that will be negatively affected by their presence.

But on this occasion I chose to pen them. First I led Meshach, Shadrach, and Abednego by their chains into the pen. Then I backed up the truck, and shooed the girls in. For a few minutes, all five goats appeared to be perplexed by the presence of the others. But that didn't last long. Soon nature took its course, and they all realized that their lives had been immeasurably enriched. Everybody got frisky. I wondered what would happen when one or the other of the nannies came into estrus. The brothers were by now senior citizens, retirees in the life cycle of goats. And what I wondered is whether they'd respond to the heady whiff of estrogen like wizened castrati or like, well, old goats. I realized I might have been unleashing forces over which I'd have no control. No—over which I was absolutely *certain* I'd have no control.

Speaking of old goats, Hunt wandered up. He was exceedingly proprietary—*maddeningly* proprietary, seeing as how he didn't actually *do* anything—about any changes around the place, and this constituted a very large change indeed. We'd had three goats (not counting their mother, Pearl, who had now been dead for a long, long time), all billies, for nearly twenty years. Hunt walked up and stood next to me—chest out, stomach sucked in, exuding the sort of holy, masculine gravity in which Charlton Heston once specialized—and, without saying a word, raised his open hand to his brow as a visor against the sun and studied the goats for a few long moments. Then, without looking at me, he said, "Toomey, all I can say is I hope you know what you're doing, son. Yessir, I sure do. Because what you've done here is introduce an element that may or may not touch off chaos. Females. Absolute random chaos. This was a closed system. Which means we *had* control." I didn't answer him, didn't even look his way.

Then he left my side, marched with studied old-soldier dignity around the pen and disappeared—knees, waist, shoulders, head— down the hill, in the direction of his cabin.

CHAPTER FIFTEEN

It was a lovely Saturday morning in April. Blue dome overhead, the barest breeze, sixty-eight degrees. Hunt, Drema, Lorraine, Willie, and I gathered 'round the breakfast table and ate flapjacks and sausages (homemade by the usually worthless Billy Estes, of all people, who had evidently gathered the starch to slaughter a hog himself), wandered one by one out onto the lawn where we snapped a few Polaroids for posterity beneath the blooming crab apple trees—Hunt and me, Willie and Hunt and me, Willie and Drema and me, Drema and Willie and Lorraine, etc., groupings that would ideally account for every possible logical association—and gathered ourselves together and piled into SEWELL-2. Lorraine and Willie balanced covered dishes on their laps. Spinach madeleine and vinegar pie, respectively. I drove. And in my shirt pocket, I carried a stack of notecards. My speech. The really hot stuff, I carried in my head. And it wasn't going anywhere.

And I felt good, even fit and rested, despite that I'd been restless all night, tossing and turning, winding myself up in the sheets and then tearing at them to get out and cool off a little. Then winding myself up again. Willie responded to my thrashings by repositioning herself, over and over, facing me, then turning away from me, but I don't think she ever really woke up—not enough that she'd remember, anyway.

So we had all climbed into SEWELL-2, but we weren't quite ready to leave. I backed the car into the toolshed and hitched the trailer to it, packed up the temporary fencing and the stakes and banner; then I pulled around to the pen where I was keeping the goats (and, as promised, where they were well on their way to effecting desertification of the area). Hunt helped me load them in. Meshach, Shadrach, and Abednego, Barbarella and Mini-Pearl (who was an almost dead ringer for the mother of the boys). As they climbed the ramp, Shadrach sniffed at Barbarella's sex, which was something new. Sniffed *and* flared his nostrils. Hm. Anyway, I had decided on the goats as a visual aide for the picnic and barbecue. And as was the case with the evil-looking billies Abel had tattooed onto the Crown Vic, it was not only for the voters' edification, but for Dickie's mortification as well.

The Fogg farm was closer to town than we were, but on the other side of Oceana. So I drove through town, taking a roundabout circuit, down Main Street and back up Boone Avenue, honking and waving at those I knew, which meant just about everybody on the street. Sympathizers(?)—more than half—smiled and raised a sort of longhorn salute, clenched fist with raised first finger and pinkie, which in this instance stood for a goat rather than a Texas steer, as I understood it; or, more completely, as shorthand for my slogan, Vote the Goat (and never mind Hunt's muttered objection that there was something vaguely fascist in the salute). It seemed to me a heartening sign—that something like that had taken shape spontaneously, a popular expression from the enthusiastic electorate, something in which I had had no hand, so to speak.

Big tent, baby!

I made one more pass down Main Street and then kept going, following it on out of town this time, until it became state road 90, toward the erstwhile Fogg farm. We passed a Fitzgerald float, a jerry-rigged pickup with a sign and lots of tissue paper and chicken wire. It was pulled over onto the shoulder, into a ditch actually, with a flat tire. Scraps of tissue paper littered the grass and highway. I honked and shot my hand out the window, and gave the two ol' boys who'd been hired to drive the thing—it was the Needhams, the brothers Deddy had hired to haul off Hunt's collection of radiator hose—a goat salute. When I slowed down, the goats in the back began to bleat. Soon Drema and Lorraine were bleating at the Needhams, too. Getting into the spirit of the campaign now, Hunt saluted them, too, and shouted "Vote the goat!" through his open window. Philpot Needham laughed, but his brother, Sunny, whose disposition was notoriously baleful and altogether lacking in anything like levity (hence, Sunny), flipped us the bird.

We sailed down the highway, beneath a budding green canopy, and finally turned off the state road and onto the Fogg property. We followed the hand-lettered signs and bumped over a grassy field, where a tall gawky kid in a windbreaker directed us into a parking space. Before we'd even climbed out of the car, I smelled hickory smoke, still-tacky paint, and freshly sawn plywood. On a knoll in the direction of the rostrum were the food tables and barbecue pits, and men and women in novelty aprons—some had candidates' names stitched over the pockets, some simply said something like "Kiss the Cook"—hurried this way and that, waving spatulas and tongs, directing someone to the Port-o-Potties with a turning fork, bragging, trading recipes, or refusing to give out secret ingredients. Red, white, and blue bunting staple-gunned to the serving tables flapped all around them.

Getting out of the car, Willie looked at me across the hood. "Do you have the camera?"

"Back here," Drema said from the back seat. This brief exchange prompted me to wonder if I really wanted any of this captured on Kodak film for posterity, for the babe Willie carried, for the babe's babes and the babe's babes' babes and so on. Thinking about it like that was unbearable, I soon found. I had to focus on the moment—sky, grass, mountain, bird soaring overhead—to clear my mind of all the generations to come. I fingered the notecards in my pocket, just to make sure they were still there. Check. *There* there. Yes. Check.

"Hey, Toomey." Willie's vinegar pie had somehow been passed to Hunt in the transition. "What should I do with this?" I pointed out the serving tables to him. He gathered Lorraine's spinach madeleine from her, she thanked him, and he wandered off in the direction of the tables. When he returned, we scouted out a good spot for the goats. Then we unloaded the materials for the pen—plastic netting and metal stakes—and began to set up. It didn't take long, and then we loaded the goats into it. They loved people, and sensed something exciting. They quickly grew frisky, and shook their heads at passersby and bleated great bleats of joy. We erected my banner over the pen. "Spooner for Mayor—Vote the Goat." And I set up a stand with a stack of my manifestos on it, and placed a flat river rock on top of them.

"Toomey." Jerry strode across the crowd-flattened grass, a half-eaten hot dog in his hand and a dab of mustard on his chin. "Howdy, ladies. Fine day for a picnic, wouldn't you say? 'Bout all I still require is a fine bourbon to go with it. Which I am sure will not be a problem. Toomey," he said, a smile spreading across his mug, "before the day's over, we will be known far and wide, son, as the finest goddamn political team in rural America. If we can pull this thing off—and with your buddies here," he said, nodding at the goats, "heh-heh, we're certain to get plenty of air time. C-SPAN's setting up right over there." Jerry pointed with his one arm, still clutching the hot dog.

"What?!" That is to say, *what?* I was feeling a little edgy to begin with, but C-SPAN? As it happened, I watched a lot of C-SPAN, but mostly for all the wrong reasons. I was amused by the braying jackasses, the sound of wet gray laundry flapping on the line—as Mencken had once more or less put it. In short, because I enjoyed the humiliation C-SPAN's unblinking cameras heaped upon self-important politicians—for which I was now beginning to suffer some contrition—inadvertently it seemed, or at least as an unintended by-product of C-SPAN's style. Letting a guy hang himself, without interruption.

Looking at Jerry—well, speaking of Mencken, what else did he say? That every normal man must be tempted at times to spit on his hands, hoist the black flag, and begin slitting throats? I judged myself normal.

"C-SPAN," Jerry said. "They're a cable network that—"

"Yeah, Jerry. I know C-SPAN. Did this come out of the blue?"

"Completely." Jerry smiled more broadly now. I could have counted his teeth. Or extracted them without benefit of anesthetic. I had to remind myself that, for once, it seemed, Jerry had had no hand in this onerous thing. Or that he probably hadn't. Almost certainly hadn't.

Willie knew I was getting a little edgy. "Forget about it, Toomey. You've got your speech." She patted my pocket. "Now may the best man win and all that. No matter what happens, Citizens for Spooner will still be here." Willie ran an open hand over her belly and smiled.

Jerry said, "By the way, Willie, I understand congratulations are in order. But may I make a suggestion?"

"What is it, Jerry?"

"Well, since the two of you are now involved in politics and all, it might be nice if y'all tied the knot before you started to show. Not that I personally care one iota. Just thinking ahead, is all."

"Actually, Jerry," she said, "we're perfectly content living in sin."

"Yeah. Well." Jerry harumphed off, his empty sleeve flapping, the sun reflecting off the top of his hairless dome.

I periodically noted the progress of the C-SPAN crew. They were erecting a small scaffold to mount a camera on, directly away from the rostrum, maybe a hundred feet back. A couple of cameramen mixed in the gathering crowd, asking simple C-SPAN questions, creepily neutral, neither leading nor loaded. Do you come to Fogg farm every year? Who are you backing? Do you intend to vote on election day?

Around noon I saw the Fitzgerald for Mayor truck commandeered by the Needham brothers pulling in, and then, not far behind, Dickie in his gold-flake Lincoln. Dickie and the whole crew. His mother, Inky, Dickie Junior, Dolin. And behind them in a Range Rover, Vincent Bologna and Anthony DeRossi. No Bob Gregorio. No Tommy Iarusso. I was curious about Bob—though not, evidently, curious enough to ask.

Then Ike Chandler and several of his colleagues rolled in. Ike drove and his pickup was full, inside and out—several guys were bumping along in the back. One of them was Tommy Cobb. They were all drinking beer, and spilling it down their chins every time Ike hit a bump. They wore the official marijuana cultivators' uniform—work boots, worn-out jeans, T-shirts, jean jackets or flannel shirts. And straw boaters with SPOONER bands wrapped around them! I was genuinely moved. I gave them the goat sign, and they gave it back—that ol' Tommy Cobb with real brio. Then they hefted themselves down out of the truck and wandered off in the direction of food, the only black faces for several miles around. But Ike hung back. He walked over to where I was standing with Drema and Lorraine.

"So what do you think?" He removed his straw hat and held it between us, turning it round and round. "I had them made up. There's a hundred more in the truck. Thought I'd pass them out." He was looking out over the crowd when his eyes lit up. "Hey, I bet they'll look great on TV." He'd spotted the C-SPAN truck.

Drema said, "You mind if I go on over and get one?" Ike told her to help herself, and Drema and Lorraine moved off in the direction of his truck. Ike watched them for a moment before turning back to me, allowing himself for the first time to smile. "Well?"

I said, "Isenhower Chandler, goddamn, you've gone well above and beyond the call of duty. I feel like I'm about to cry."

I wasn't hungry but I had a rib with my beer. Just a single rib. And a half ear of corn. Eating something seemed like the reasonable thing to do. Then I had another beer. It was getting warm out, and I was getting thirsty. And the beers were about as cold and delicious as they could get, buried in a mountain of crushed ice. Jerry offered me a shot of bourbon, but I declined. The second time he offered, I accepted. Then I wandered away in search of a beer chaser.

Willie had gone off with her mom, who had come separately, later, to take in a quilting demonstration. Drema and Lorraine were watching Greasy Creek, a bluegrass band, and wearing their SPOONER boaters. Hunt—I didn't have a clue. Hunt had just gone off. Soon Ike came looking for me again and took me back over to his truck. We sat on the tailgate and sipped together from a Mason jar. The locally concocted potation scalded my gizzard on the way down, and then sat like a smoldering chunk of charcoal on my stomach.

"Pretty raw," I wheezed, "isn't it, Ike?"

"Well, yes, it is, but there's two schools of thought on that,

Toomer." Ike took another big gulp, and his Adam's apple leapt twice, thrice, four times. "One says that green is how it's meant to be enjoyed. The other insists that if you're drinking before it's been aged, you'll go blind or even crazy. But of course, I come down on the side of whoever's got the liquor." He smiled, a big white-lightning-fueled thing. "Hey, Toomer, listen, I've got an idea." Ike took out five of the SPOONER boaters and said, "C'mon."

He led me over to the goat pen, where he took out his pocketknife and cut two slits in each of the hats. Then he unfurled a ball of twine I'd brought to tie up the banner and secure it to the poles. In no time, he had the goats outfitted in their very own SPOONER hats. For a moment, the goats looked from one to another, blinking, as if they were thinking, What the? But soon it was business as usual, and they were back to standard goat operating procedures, as if nothing at all out of the ordinary had come to pass. Except they were now sporting SPOONER boaters.

Not long after that, I decided I *really* did need to eat. Otherwise, I was in some danger of going both blind *and* crazy. I wandered up the knoll to the serving tables, where I helped myself to a slab of ribs, a barbecued chicken leg—that's thigh *and* drumstick—a scoop of baked beans and another of potato salad, an ear of corn, some of Lorraine's spinach madeleine, and a big wedge of Willie's vinegar pie. But it was too late. Definitely a case of closing the barn doors after the cows had already stampeded through and a big cloud of dust was boiling in the air.

The quilting exhibit over, Willie and her mom came looking for me just as I was sucking the last trace of fat from the last rib bone. Without saying a word, Willie snatched my napkin and wiped some stubborn condiment or sauce from my chin. Juanita stood a few feet off, watching something in the middle distance. Well beyond

Juanita, Jerry was talking to one of the C-SPAN crew, a young man with a clipboard, a baseball cap, and a pair of bulky headphones slung around his neck.

By now, another band had taken the stage, a sort of southern rock outfit. I couldn't see them from where I sat, but I could hear what they were playing. *Move it on over, oh won't you move it on over, yeah move it on over 'cause the big dog's moving in. . . .*

By midafternoon, more than half of Mann County was present and accounted for, eating, drinking, working themselves into the proper mood—which is to say bitterly partisan and unapologetically bloodthirsty—and the C-SPAN cameras were up and ready to roll. In fact, might already have been rolling, for all I knew. The kid with the headphones and clipboard was seated on a metal folding chair, up on the scaffold, surveying the crowd, looking bored and as if he'd done this a thousand times in a thousand different towns, which he probably had. Suddenly he looked down, just below him. Jerry was back. He had his hand cupped to his mouth, shouting something up at the kid. Looking at Jerry below, the kid tipped his sunglasses onto his nose and slowly shook his head—no, no, and no, goddamnit. Then Jerry raised his open hand, palm facing the kid, and nodded, as if, yes, now he understood. No problem. It was no more than a silent movie from where I stood.

I kept finding myself alone. I had come with four other people, I was a candidate wandering amongst my presumed electorate, I was just an all-around reasonably well-liked fellow, never wanting for friends, not ever, and *yet* . . . I kept finding myself alone. I patted my pocket, checking to make sure my speech was still there. Check. Thus reassured that I was indeed doing this rather grandly responsible thing, this downright *hubristic* thing, I wandered off in the general direction of ice-cold beer—after all, I'd earned it, hadn't I?—but somewhere en route thought better of it. Coffee. Yes, in the present circumstances a much better choice. Black coffee and another big slice of vinegar pie.

But alas and alack, I was too easily distracted. First by a formation of fighter jets—part of the festivities, or mere coincidence?—that had bisected the sky and swooped down to achieve the nadir of their antiparabola directly overhead; then, in the wake of an expanding trident of jet vapor, a sonic boom sucked up all the air. Next I was distracted by none other than Tommy Cobb, who had evidently had a change of heart in his stance toward me and wanted to make it up. And who looked particularly goofy beneath his too-small SPOONER boater. Tommy Cobb and I wandered off into a stand of trees by a creek at the foot of a mountain and smoked a joint of his fine product. Spicy, distinct. Tommy Cobb asked me didn't I think it was "some bad shit," and I agreed that it was. *Very* bad. Ninety-two, he said, which I didn't understand but let pass. I would now guess that that was the dope's vintage.

And finally I was distracted by Carry Me Home, the same band that had played the Stocking Stuffers' Ball. The good ol' boys in the squared-off beards and silver shades had taken the stage and were executing their own peculiar rendition of "Can't Stop Thinking About Tomorrow," noteworthy only for its grinding lugubriousness, its total lack of promise, the unintended reversal of meaning, and what had now become the tune's implicit threat. The next thing I knew, I was holding a warm, empty beer can, swirling the foamy dregs around the bottom, belching and wiping foam from my chin, and wondering where I could get another.

I patted the notecards stacked together in my breast pocket. Check.

Then I raided Ike's truck and began passing out the straw boaters. It seemed as if it were time. SPOONER. SPOONER. SPOONER. Everywhere I looked. It was strange to look around and see my very own personal name, rendered in precise block letters, floating over so many faces.

We were well into the afternoon by now and the orations, I knew, had to begin soon.

And they did. The format for the speeches was thus: for each office, the first candidate (as it had been determined by drawing, which was Dickie in the example of mayoral candidates) rose and spoke for two minutes; his or her opponent then spoke for two; then, and this was entirely at the discretion of Judge Thackerey, each candidate might or might not be allowed an additional thirty seconds for a rebuttal.

So when the rotation came round to mayoral candidates, Dickie climbed the rostrum and spoke. He thanked the assembled politicos. He thanked the good people of Oceana and Mann County. He fairly well beamed, his teeth glistening like perfect little tiles of bathroom porcelain. A real late-twentieth-century TV politician. Panthrex, I was sure, was responsible for the transformation. When Dickie turned to the crowd, there was a smattering of applause, but it quickly subsided. Good sign.

"Thank you. Thank you very much," Dickie began, and let a silence settle over all. Goats bleated in the void, and I saw Dickie glance in their direction. Then he continued, employing the religio-sarcastic cadences of a no-nonsense preacher man. "In just a few minutes, Toomey Spooner gonna get up here and tell you all he's going to *chaaaange* the world." Dickie's voice soared on the word *change*. "Reinvent the wheel. Make a better mouse trap. That's all well and good. Of course it is. And if he wins this race, I'm going to wish him all the luck in the world." Here Dickie paused, looked down at his notes, back up and out over his audience. "'Cause he's going to need it. Let's just work our way through what all it is he says.

"Vote the Goat." Here Dickie slowly wagged his head, projecting some vague but bitter disappointment. "Now that's just charming, isn't it? But what's it mean? I know Spooner proclaims all that wonderful stuff about independence and perseverance and resourcefulness, and it all sounds pretty good. But what you've got to ask yourself is this: Is it all just talk? Vote the Goat. Really, what does it mean? I'll tell you. Walk on over there to Spooner's cute little exhibit. Lean in and smell those creatures, get a good look at them. They smell bad, they eat garbage, and they obviously don't care where they, uh, go potty." The crowd chuckled a little, just a mild pro-Fitzgerald undercurrent. "Now *that's* a model for local government." There was more laughter now, more general.

"But that's just symbols, not the substance of the Spooner campaign. So let's be fair. What is it he wants to do?" Dickie waved a Citizens for Spooner Manifesto. "First off, a 'manifesto'? Only manifesto I ever heard of was a communist manifesto. Hell, I don't know *what* to make of that." Oh boy, the crowd was coming over to his side now—you could just feel it. Willie had warned me against using the word manifesto. "Says here Spooner's first order of business will be to kick the coal, timber, and gas industries out of Oceana." Dickie paused and scratched his head. "Well, you know, *that's* interesting. But I'll come back to it. I think I'd like to save that for last.

"Lessee," Dickie continued, returning to the text, "it says here his second order of business will be to stop development. Hm. Toomey?" Dickie turned to me, where I was seated on the rostrum.

But I turned my attention to the goats, still wearing their SPOONER boaters. Meshach was again sniffing at Barbarella's sex. "That's got to be the most curious position you've yet staked out." He turned back to the crowd. "Stop development. Think about that for a minute. My dictionary says to 'develop' is to bring toward *fulfillment*; to *expand* or *enlarge*; to *improve* the quality; to bring into being; to *mature*; to *progress*. Yeah," he said, putting his best sarcastic spin on it, "I can see why we wouldn't want any of *that*. Not around *here*." Big laugh line. "But seriously, that's what he says. I'm not making this up. Read it for yourself." Here Dickie waved my "manifesto." I was kicking myself for not calling it something else. Hell, a platform. A simple checklist. Anything.

A bleating erupted, or rather a pair of bleatings, a high note and another one below it—in any mammalian species, clearly a male and a female—and to each there was an inflection of hysteria. I turned, along with everyone else. Meshach had mounted Barbarella. Both goats still wore the SPOONER boaters Ike had prepared for them. From the fringes, I saw Hunt moving in. He neared the pen. C-SPAN cameras swiveled to catch the action.

"And finally," Dickie said, trailing off. He stared for a moment at his notes on the podium. Then he looked up at the goats. His Adam's apple leapt as he swallowed. Briefly, a potent silence reigned. "And finally—uh. I'm sorry. I've lost my train of thought . . . lessee . . . OK. And finally, I wanted to point out that Spooner wants to keep jobs out of here." By now, Dickie had fully recovered. "Or to do away with the ones we've got. It says right here he wants to quote *effect our economic manumission* unquote. Well, what the hell's that? I'll tell you what it is—Spooner wants to free you from your job, liberate you from your paycheck, deliver you from your livelihood. He wants to do away with minerals and lumber!"

A pause. Time for that to sink in.

"Okay. Maybe our reliance on those industries has not served us well. Let's say I give him that. But now what? Well, new industry would be the obvious answer. New industry would be the answer in any *sane* and *sober* world, anyway. Something like a medical waste incinerator. The kind of thing Mister Vincent Bologna would like to bring to Oceana." Dickie beamed. "Vincent!" Vincent Bologna stood in the crowd, gave a little wave. The applause was not overwhelming, but it was more than simply polite, too. "Panthrex wants to move in, and become our partner in the future. Panthrex wants to bring jobs to Oceana, renewed economic spirit, independence to our people, too many of whom are already overly dependent on government for jobs or a handout. Panthrex—"

"Time!" Judge Thackerey—who was not up for reelection and was moderating—cut Dickie off when an egg timer he had cached in the speaker's lectern sounded. The hysterical bleatings of Meshach and Barbarella, which had subsided somewhat, erupted anew—and with a renewed force. Hunt was now dodging around inside the pen, trying to find some kind of purchase, some vantage from which he could arrest Meshach, but the old goat seemed powerfully determined to dodge his grasp and all the while to simultaneously maintain his penetration of Barbarella. The three of them—Hunt and the two goats—were locked in a bestial tarantella and kicked up a lot of dust. I started for the pen, but then I stopped. I knew I should do something—if only to assist Hunt—but I'd had plenty enough drinks to think it was pretty goddamn funny, too. You know, I hadn't intended it, *but.* And I'd also had plenty enough drinks to think: Fuck Dickie Fitz. I sat back down, turned, and smiled at Dickie. I think he caught my eyes for a flickering nanosecond.

"—wants to become our—"

Judge Thackerey tried again. "Time, Dickie!"

"OK, OK," Dickie said, "I heard you the first time." Dickie took his seat and I approached the lectern and microphone. I waited for some minor feedback to subside, shuffled my notecards around and then back into their original order. I had numbered them.

"How is everybody this lovely afternoon?" It was strange to hear my own voice projected over the PA system. Like the voice of God. Or perhaps simply *a* god. Some minor deity to whom one might nevertheless be well advised to pay attention.

No, as my mincing speech unfolded, it wasn't like that at all, actually. More like a bespectacled civics teacher hogging the mike at a pep rally before the big game. A snorer. After a minute, I disregarded my notes—reading them made me sound too mechanical—and more or less regurgitated, word for word, my Vote the Goat platform, which I had more or less committed to memory, and which Dickie had more or less already delivered for me, albeit casting an entirely different light on it than I hoped to. Not to mention that everybody who was interested had already read it. It was a three-yards-and-a-cloud-of-dust speech. At best. There was no Hail Mary play at the end. Blah, blah, blah. It even bored me. If the crowd was looking for red meat, I was afraid I'd given them a spinach salad instead. At least I hadn't been heckled.

Then Judge Thackerey asked Dickie if he'd like his thirty seconds for a rebuttal, though rebuttal of what was not clear. Smug and satisfied, Dickie shook his head no. Then the judge turned to me. "Toomey?" I was on my way back to my seat and had somehow not expected this upon Dickie's refusal of an additional thirty seconds. But I stopped, and thought, Yes. Thirty more seconds was just about exactly what I did need. "Yes, Judge, thank you." I could see that this surprised Dickie a little bit.

"Ladies and gentlemen, I didn't say what I really came here for this afternoon. You've listened to a lot of half-truths and nontruths, and a whole lot has been omitted. In other words, you're not really getting the whole story." Whispering and shuffling died down. It was now very quiet. "A-way back before we all grew up and got so goddamned mature, my opponent, Richard Hedley Fitzgerald, was known by those who knew him best as Dick Hed." There was some sniggering, but more than that, there were many stony faces staring back into mine. Had I already gone too far? Nevertheless. "And this Dick Hed fellow, or Dickie Fitz . . . hell's bells. Dickie Fitz, ladies and gentlemen—Jesus, *wake up*. You know that man. You know what he's like. Dickie has cheated and lied his whole life. Dickie has beat his wife and abused his child. Dickie attempted to murder a lifelong friend, his ol' buddy—"

At that moment, there was a loud thud and I felt it through the plywood on the rostrum. I looked around and Dickie was down—he'd fallen out of his seat and was curled up on the floor. He was empurpled and clutching at his chest. Les Coombs leapt to his side and began to unbutton Dickie's shirt. Alma and Dolin clambered onto the dais and knelt next to Les. Then Inky appeared from backstage. I saw Dolin say something to Jerry, who had also drawn close, and then Jerry hustled away. In a minute, an ambulance was inching through the crowd, blaring its siren in short bursts. It pulled up before the stage, idled for a few long moments, and then pulled away. Dickie, Dolin, Alma, and Inky were gone. Les rose on wobbly old knees, and stepped over to Judge Thackerey, whispering a few words into his ear. Judge Thackerey moved toward the microphone, edging me away from it.

"Y'all must be wondering what the hell that was all about," he began, blinking furiously. "Well, it seems Dickie must've ate something that didn't agree with him, that he is suffering from something like severe indigestion. That's what Les here says, and he's the doctor." The judge made a barely perceptible little motion toward Les, who nodded grimly. "But the ambulance was here, folks, and Dickie's gonna be OK. So we're going to proceed. We've got a lot of ground to cover. So . . . let's see. Where were we? I guess we're ready to begin the round for school board candidates."

I stepped forward, lighting a cigarette and donning my SPOONER boater. "Excuse me there, Judge."

"Yes, Toomey?"

"I had about ten seconds left."

Judge Thackerey looked at me with mild disbelief, but consented. "OK, Toomey. Ten seconds. Go on."

I squared myself to my audience once more. "There's one other thing here, something none of you knows. Dickie has . . . Dickie once . . ." Could I do it? The words roiled in my throat, nearly triggered a gag reflex on the back of my tongue, but, but . . . "well, to pretend that he's deserving of elective office, that's he's earned your trust, is just willful stupidity, and I, for one, am sick unto death of the charade. No, I hope it's not just a case of indigestion, as Les and the judge here suggest. I hope it's a full-blown heart attack. Hell, I hope the son of a bitch dies. Thank you."

"And something none of you knows, Dickie has . . . Dickie once . . . well, to pretend that he's deserving of elective office, that's he's earned your trust, is just willful stupidity, and I, for one, am sick unto death of the charade. No, I hope it's not just a case of indigestion, as Les and the judge here suggest. I hope it's a full-blown heart attack. Hell, I hope the son of a bitch dies. Thank you."

I watched myself descend the rostrum and disappear into the crowd. Then I hit the rewind and watched the whole thing over again, from start to finish, many times.

maturity can be defined as the ability to simultaneously entertain contradictory positions. Or something like that. *Whatever.* Anyway, the first thing is that yes, you can go after Dickie Fitz hammer and tong, all the livelong day if you want. But not after he's down. Literally down, sweating and trying to draw breath there at Lester Coombs's feet. And definitely not after he's been carted away in an ambulance. There's an etiquette here, son, that I don't believe you've caught on to. I know on the face of it, it's hypocritical, but. . . ." And he went on, more or less rambling, in great confounding loops.

But worst of all was Dickie himself, whose health seemed to have much improved overnight (to the point of qualifying as a minor miracle), and who called from his hospital bed to gloat. I was back home and screening my calls by now, but I picked up this one. My machine had already come on by the time I lifted the receiver, so it failed to stop recording and captured our brief exchange on tape.

CHAPTER SIXTEEN

In my dream the preacher Pons had reproached me for sins of omission, telling me "there are things you don't do that are ever bit as bad as the bad things you do do." Fine, fine, fine, okeydoke. But from where I now stood, the old gospelmonger's bromide had the unmistakable ring of truth. Well, almost unmistakable. But the trouble comes in trying to separate out the things you should do from the things you ought not touch with a ten-foot pole. Like General Truman Spooner's ill-advised, but personally heroic, advance on the Potomac. The epigrammatic Pons was no help whatsoever in this regard.

But in any event, I was determined to leave nothing I ought to do undone. If I failed now, it would be a failure of excess, not of timidity. With that in mind, I worked hard in the last days leading up to the election. I walked the streets, stopping anybody who'd give me the time of day. I passed out my "manifesto," now innocuously rechristened a "position paper," and took the time to explain some of the points contained therein—points which of course had been distorted by Dickie at the Fogg farm. I cruised downtown Oceana in SEWELL-2, honking and giving the goat salute to any- and everybody.

Panthrex had shelled out the money for several polls for Dickie, but somehow Jerry kept laying his hands on the results (and by now, I had to assume his agents really *were* legion, just as he'd said). The bad news was that they consistently showed Dickie with a lead over me. The good news was that his lead narrowed in each successive poll. By election day his lead was razor thin. Or, as Jerry put it, statistically insignificant.

The upshot of all this was that by the time Oceanans headed for the polls, the thing was too close to call. In a week, I seemed to have made up the ground I'd lost in the wake of the Fogg farm incident. Or Dickie seemed to have lost it. In any event, I had to wonder whether I even ought to try playing my trump card—I had to wonder if it would land me in the same deep yogurt I'd just climbed out of.

Tuesday, May 2, Election Day: well, speaking of clarity, lawdy, lawdy, lawdy, the day broke as one of those gilded, cobalt-sky mornings right out of a Maxfield Parrish painting. I felt like donning a slinky toga, placing a wreath of ivy and lavender upon my crown, and tooting a Pan flute as I skipped along the highway, all the way into Oceana. Which is to say it was beautiful and sunny across the hills, the birds were swooping and singing and happy it was finally spring, and Willie had made love to me before either of us was fully awake. Very shortly after our sweet commingling, Willie had to excuse herself. She flung the sheets away and her feet banged onto the floor.

While Willie was throwing up in the bathroom (yes, morning sickness had finally arrived), I wrapped myself in my old brocade robe and descended the stairs. I heard feet whisking over the floor and muffled voices, and I was amazed to find that Drema and Lorraine were already up and about, and had been joined by Hunt— Hunt and *Juanita*, Willie's mom. Juanita? I shoved the question aside—for now—and stumbled into the kitchen to join them. Coffee was gurgling through the pot, and steam hissed from the top as the last drops squeezed through the filter. It was evidently a second pot, as there were half-empty cups (no, half-full!, said the optimist) scattered over the counters.

"Holy smokes!" I said. "What have we here?"

Drema addressed me over her shoulder as she rolled out biscuits on the counter. Her chin and cheek and elbows were dusted with flour, and the rising sun through the kitchen window cast a golden halo around her and seemed to half-blind her as she squinted against it. "A breakfast fit for a king. Or at least for a mayor. Or a mayor-to-be. At any rate," she said, growing sardonic, "*you.*"

Hunt turned a big slab of country ham frying in a skillet, centered it just so, tugging gently at the fatty edges with a fork. "I swan, if this is not a day full of promise. To think: a Spooner will soon inherit the mantle of leadership. I just wish your daddy could be here to see it." Hunt chuckled and pulled a bottle of bourbon from his jacket pocket, tipped a little into his coffee cup, and slipped the bottle back into his pocket. Still clucking, he nudged Juanita with his elbow, and she returned his smile.

"Let's not count our chickadees just yet," I cautioned, echoing Jerry, which I regretted instantly.

Juanita was deep-frying apple fritters, adding one by one to a little pyramid of pies she was stacking on paper towels. "Is Willie up yet?"

As if to answer the question, Willie appeared from around the corner. She looked at once sweetly radiant and a little green around the gills. And at that moment I was sure that even the Virgin Mary must have thrown up in the dust behind the manger until her gut ached and she was weak in the knees. After all, it is only the conception that is supposed to have been immaculate. Go ahead, search the Holy Scriptures: for good reason, I'm sure, there's not a word about the subsequent nine months—because aesthetically speaking, all that puking wouldn't have added a thing to what is a pretty good story already, is why.

Willie said, "Good morning, all," and attempted to smile. In a very complicated way, it was hurtful to me to watch all that bravery, to see Willie so beautiful, carrying our sprout as she was. I had thought life was supposed to get simpler—man, woman, child, what could be more elemental?—but no: there was layer upon layer, now, and there were more on the way. On the upside, as surely as there was a brand-new life taking shape inside Willie, there was something new coming to life inside me, too.

After getting myself all worked up over the last couple of weeks, right then, that morning, I found I didn't give a fig about the day's election. Golden shafts of sun pouring into the kitchen. All those mouth-watering smells. The sweetly mussed hair. Blue cigarette smoke curling from ashtrays. Zero, spread belly up on the floor, watching everything, upside down, out of the corner of his eye, but especially the house shoes whisking back and forth. I felt as if I were immersed in a lovely symphony of friends and family. But Willie interrupted my reverie.

"Soon as breakfast is over, Toomey, you've got to get your smart ass out there and rassle this thing to the ground." She smiled archly and . . .well, inscrutably. Holding that pose, she leaned back in her chair, her hands wrapped around a steaming cup of coffee. My very own Mona Lisa, bathed in morning's first dewy light.

SEWELL-2 groaned and hesitated on the steep grade leading up to the National Guard Armory. Campaign signs lined the shoulder of the drive like Burma Shave non sequiturs. I parked the car and stood in the parking lot, finishing a cigarette. A wedge of geese honked overhead. They were headed north, toward ancestral waters. I wondered how purely mechanical their migrations were, or if they could have chosen differently. If, for example, they could have worked the shallows of Chesapeake Bay as easily as the inlets of the Lake of the Woods, if only they chose to do so. In other words, were they capable of defying their biological imperatives?

It was still a few minutes before eight, and the armory was mostly empty. Four or five volunteer officials huddled together, talking and smiling, sipping coffee from Styrofoam cups. Two voters—Anne and Nan McMahon, the octogenarian twins, beatific beneath pink pillbox hats—waited for one booth. I approached the sign-in table.

"Good morning, Toomey." It was Inky Fitzgerald, seated at the registry, who looked up smiling. "You just missed Dickie," she said perkily, nodding in the direction of the door—and as if she were telling me I just missed my oldest friend. She found my name in the records book and turned it 180 degrees for me to sign next to my computer-generated name. She marked the spot with a sudden X, looked at me and flashed a quick smile—nothing at all seemingly hidden there. "He got on down here right at seven so he could be the first vote, and he and Dickie Junior headed over to the North Fork Pork Farm to catch the eight o'clock shift coming on. Last minute electioneering. Now, what have you got planned for today?" For once, Inky seemed perfectly content with her lot, and genuinely curious about my plans. Which seemed as incongruous but unquestioningly right as a dream.

I leaned over the table to inscribe my John Henry. "To tell you the truth, Inky, I haven't really mapped it out. Just intended to follow my nose today." I signed with a flourish. "But I expect I'd *better* get busy and think about some last-minute electioneering myself."

As soon as I'd voted, and despite that I felt as if I were betraying poor brave Inky, I aimed SEWELL-2 in the direction of the North

Fork Pork Farm. On the way over I smoked a joint; and, with the windows rolled down and the wind whipping through the car, sang with all the lusty gusto of a Pavarotti when a corny song I liked came on the radio—I imagined myself with a huge gut and a silk scarf. *O desperado, why don't you come to your senses. . . .*

The North Fork Pork Farm was yet another industrial-social-environmental disaster, a real bad neighbor indeed. The management there was democratic in that it tended to treat its swine and its human drones with pretty much equal disregard. The human beings were paid just more than minimum wage and were by and large denied benefits—this, for laboring at the industry of death eight hours a day—while the hogs lived out their lives in tiny cages, warehoused, never feeling the sun warm their hides.

Having rounded a mountain and started down the steep grade that led to the river bottom and the so-called farm, I turned off the radio and checked my watch: quarter til eight, still fifteen minutes before the next shift commenced its eight hours of nurturing and slaughtering. As I descended farther down the shoulderless road toward the river, the new spring foliage and the mountains rising behind and before me began to crowd out the sky and the sun. The odors of holocaust rose up to meet me: sausage seasonings (mostly sage), dried blood, acrid pigshit. But most of all, the pigshit. Finally, at the bottom, the trees opened up and a gravel lot spread out around the pork dormitory, a long, low, temporary-looking metal building. I spotted Dickie's car among the others. And near the plant entrance, a knot of workers was gathered about the man himself. Dickie gesticulated with one arm, mechanically, as if he had learned the movements by rote, before a mirror. He had the other arm wrapped around the shoulders of his only child, Dickie Junior.

I parked and walked over to the plant entrance, where a large garage-like door was rolled open. Cool, putrefying effluvia wafted out of the gloom—as if from a newly excavated grave—as did muted and dispirited (and dispiriting) oinks and grunts. I could see all the way through the building to the other end, maybe a hundred yards off, where a similar door was likewise open. But between the doors, I could see nothing. Too dark inside, too light outside. With some difficulty, it seemed—his mouth was dry and his lips were sticking to his teeth—Dickie was delivering his boilerplate. It's important that you get to the polls, vote for the candidate who most nearly represents your ideals, you have a civic duty, etc. It took him a minute to notice me. But then, when he did, his face lit up with mendacious good cheer. He licked his lips and smiled. His eyes crinkled at the edges, but the disks were flat and dull. *Too-mee . . . .*

I smiled—a friendly thing—and then, without premeditation, turned and walked away, crunched back across the gravel lot toward SEWELL-2. I could feel the discomfort I was leaving in my wake, and I knew the brief episode must have seemed very strange—to Dickie, to the pork workers. So what? At that moment, I'd realized I was all out of spleen. I'd find some better way to spend my day.

As I was pulling out of the lot, away from the other cars and trucks, Dickie Junior came trotting out, coltish, wobbly, and irresolute. He didn't motion for me to stop, though, and I didn't. He glanced over at his father, and then he turned back as I was pulling past him, his thin arms and legs presenting a cubist jumble of sharp juvenile angles. And he gave me the finger. Held it, in fact, so I could marvel over this awful thing in the rearview mirror.

For the rest of the morning, I visited the various precincts. Three elementary schools, a middle school, and of course old Mann County High. But as prescribed by Kentucky revised statute, I had to remain five hundred feet from the polling place. So I loitered in the parking lots like a man with nowhere he had to be—at what I imagined was five hundred feet—like a petty criminal who might steal a Bic lighter off the front seat of your car, given half a chance. The electoral action was pretty slow, given that there weren't any national races. Mostly I just smoked cigarettes and leaned up against SEWELL-2. But I smiled and shook hands with all who passed, uttered vague, banal encouragements, tried to avoid blowing smoke directly into anybody's face.

By eleven o'clock I was pretty well bored, unable to muster enough enthusiasm to "rassle this thing to the ground"—the dope had mostly worn off, and I was hungry and ready for lunch. Besides, campaigning at Grambos' couldn't have been any less productive than loafing on school grounds like a truant, lighting up one ciggie after another, and thinking about how old everybody who passed by seemed to have gotten. Not to mention that Nick Grambos was serving those delightful lamb and ground-almond meatballs of his—his Tuesday special—which he spooned out over garlicky couscous and garnished with fresh spearmint sprigs. Plus a hot little pot of sweet, spiced tea.

Rather than head straight for Grambos', I took a meandering route and motored down narrow county roads. I finally pulled over and got out of SEWELL-2. I fingered the microcassette in my pocket, the one I'd taken from my answering machine after Dickie's imprudent call from his hospital bed. Had he really had a heart attack? Given Dickie's prevaricating nature, it's utterly impossible to say with any degree of certainty at all. Even his doctor might not have been sure.

I followed a footpath down to an old swinging bridge and walked out to the middle of it. It spanned the palisades high over the river. I stood there until the swaying stopped. Then I pulled the microcassette out and dropped it into the white water churning below. It was swallowed in the foam, surfaced two or three times, and disappeared for good. And here's what it had on it, what was magnetically etched onto that ribbon of tape:

Dickie: This heart attack business was pure genius, don't you think?

Me: Are you saying you faked it?

Dickie: All I'm saying is, there's poetry in it.

Me: Why are you telling me this?

Dickie: To increase your suffering. Besides, who're you going to tell? More important, who's going to believe you? Your animus is well documented. By the way, I caught your little performance on C-SPAN.

Me: Is Inky in on it?

Dickie: Inky. [Here, a great sigh of contempt] *No.* Inky . . . well, Inky's none of your goddamn business, is what Inky is. But I'll tell you this: she's been right here at my bedside, a regular Florence Nightingale. Because when push comes to shove, that girl's as faithful as a three-legged dog. Any other questions?

Me: No.

Dickie: Well, bye then.

It was just like Dickie to hang himself. And to count on others to be too timid, or too stupid, to do anything with it. But kindness—if that's what it was—well, I don't think he ever counted on that. Not that it made any difference at all in the result. Because in the end, he was right and would go on believing his actions had produced the desired results. But I wouldn't use my information against him. Any of it.

If I couldn't beat him in a fair fight, man to man, then I didn't deserve to be elected to office. So what if he had faked a heart attack to stanch the bloodletting I had commenced. Come what may, I was suddenly determined not to let the past exert any undue influence over the future. And at the same time I was beginning to feel mildly ennobled, I also felt as if I really ought to keep that in check. Because I knew that was *very* dangerous territory, indeed.

Bob Gregorio was seated at Grambos' counter. He was hunched over a bowl of lamb meatballs and couscous and really having at it. When I sat down next to him, I could see that he was just scooping up the last of it.

"Hey, Bob."

"Toomey. I only got here a few minutes ago. From Toronto by way of Newark." He worked hard at swallowing what he had in his mouth. It looked like he was swallowing a baseball, straining to get it past his gullet, and when it passed there was an audible *gulp.* Then he reached for the mint sprig that remained and popped it in his mouth. "But you're just the man I wanted to see. C'mon."

Bob got up from his bar stool and, putting an arm around my shoulder, led me toward the door. Outside on the sidewalk, we lit cigarettes. Then, with the ease of one who has been a lifetime resident of Oceana, Bob took me around back, where the North Fork passed behind Grambos'. We sat down on upended milk crates, and for a moment we smoked and watched the muddy water purl away.

Then he said, "I quit, Toomey."

I just looked at him. I assumed an explanation was forthcoming. He held my gaze briefly before looking away.

"For a number of reasons, really. I'd been thinking about it for a while." Bob squinted into the middle distance and drew on his cigarette. "Anyway, I was thinking that maybe your administration might have need of a very experienced corporate attorney."

"Are you sure, Bob?"

"Absolutely."

"Among other things, a job with the city of Oceana wouldn't pay a tenth, a twentieth, of what you're used to." I laughed and considered that maybe even that figure was ridiculously optimistic.

"No problem."

"Well, if I win, certainly. But you understand that's a big if. An enormous if."

"Good enough." We shook, finished our cigarettes, and went back inside and moved from the counter to a booth—before it got too crowded. I ordered up my own bowl of lamb and couscous, and Bob ordered a pistachio nest and a thimbleful of strong Greek coffee. And chewing on his sticky confection, he looked as happy as I'd ever seen him.

Nick Grambos materialized at our booth. All the vessels in his nose and eyes had burst long ago, and he always looked as if he were about to suffer a massive coronary. He was fatter than ever. But he seemed like a happy, satisfied man. "While you're waiting, Toomey, how 'bout a little Greek mystique, huh?"

"I couldn't, Nick, but thanks. Bob?"

"What the hay." This was a locution Bob had picked up in recent weeks.

Greek mystique was what Nick called his homemade liquor. It was much better than the local moonshine—like ouzo, it tasted like licorice—but like the 'shine it could knock an intemperate feller, or an unsuspecting one, on his self-indulgent ass. Nick went to the back, and returned with a bowl of couscous for me and two fingers of clear liquid in a sour glass for Bob. It had always seemed to me that Nick's Greek mystique sparkled more than mere water did; it was like liquid diamonds. Nick handed it over, and Bob knocked 'er back.

Bob shuddered and wheezed. "Holy smokes." He coughed and cleared his throat.

Nick smiled and said, "You like another?"

"OK." Bob smiled, held up his coffee cup, and tapped it with his forefinger.

"Toomey!" Jerry clamped his single strong hand onto my shoulder from behind. I turned in the booth, pulling a spoon from my mouth and dribbling some couscous over my lap. "I've been conducting an informal exit poll. Informal, but I believe fairly accurate—and I'm afraid I've spotted a trend."

"Well, give it to me straight, Jer."

"Precinct after precinct, goddamnit, Dickie Fitz seems to be edging you out. And I mean just barely. Hey, Nick," Jerry suddenly called past my shoulder, "how 'bout one of them damn, uh, whatever Toomey here's got. Thanks. Oh, Nick—*and* a draft. And Nick, a little mystique since I see you've got it out. See," he said, refocusing his attention on me, "from what I can gather, he's getting like fifty votes to your forty-nine. Of course, well, you know, that'll do 'er, certainly. *If* it keeps up like that. But what I'm thinking is that maybe, just maybe, there's something in the character of your morning voter that predisposes him to vote for Fitzgerald. You know, the anal retentive factor. And that, with any luck at all, there'll likewise be something in the character of your afternoon voter that predisposes *him* to vote for Spooner. Course, this is strictly nonscientific and could, by a more cynical man, be called no more than wishful thinking."

"Of course," I said, having a little trouble picturing a more cynical man than Jerry himself.

"But unless you get out there and work your ass off, Toomey, the afternoon's going to be rougher'n hell, too, a rout, I tell you what."

Nick passed a draft beer followed by a shot of mystique over my head into Jerry's hand, and Jerry paused and took the shot and then a long pull off the beer. His tongue appeared, and slurped away a foam mustache. "Aaaah. Not to mention the trouble Dickie's so-called Thrilla in Mann-illa might cause us."

"His what?"

"I wondered if you knew—it's been a big secret right up until this morning. Even *I* didn't know anything about it. Seems Dickie, with the help of Panthrex, is putting on an afternoon of boxing. I guess the idea is that if Dickie can bring this kind of entertainment to Oceana as a private citizen, then just imagine what he can do as mayor. They've got a crew setting up a ring in the park right now. Free hot dogs and sodas. And of course there'll be many an exhortation to vote Fitzgerald, I'm sure. But fuck 'em, because I have no doubt—"

"Toomey, sweetie!" It was Willie, with Drema, Lorraine, Hunt, and Juanita. Grambos' was beginning to fill up now, and my ad hoc campaign crew shook hands and hugged and slapped shoulders with potential voters as they made their way across the room.

"Anyways, Toom, we probably ought to head over there after lunch and get a firsthand gander at this dog and pony show. See if there ain't some way or another we can toss a goddamn monkey wrench into the works. *Spin* it."

"I agree, Jerry." What the fuck—that's how I was feeling. It wasn't mean, just neutral.

"You *do*? Hm. Well, OK then," Jerry said, moving away and raising his half-finished beer in a toast, thin, enervated foam slipping dismally down the sides of the mug, "I'll talk to you in a few, my man." Jerry smiled and dipped his armless shoulder into the throng, pushing through, using it like the prow of an icebreaker.

Bob excused himself, and my team surged into the booth around me. They chatted excitedly about the day, about what all might come to pass. Willie had scooted in close to me and slipped her hand onto my thigh, in tingling proximity to my willie. She turned and propped her chin on my shoulder.

"This morning was nice, mm," Willie was leaning in on my shoulder and smiling sweetly, "that was, I—"

"Awww," I interrupted, "me, too."

A light kiss fluttered briefly over my lips.

"He did *what?*"

"I know you heard me." I was telling Jerry about Dickie Junior's little eruption earlier that morning. We were walking down Clendenan Street—a shaded lane against which sat seventies-style ranch homes, split-foyer lodgments for many of the families who passed for eminent around Oceana—toward Teddy Wilson Park, a baseball field named after a local boy who went on to play minor league ball back in the thirties. I had played Little League ball there, and so had Dickie and Ike Chandler. But like the Sahara encroaching on the verdant veldts of southern Africa, the talcy yellow dust of the infield was making alarming inroads into the outfield, where hardly a sprig of grass now grew and where it appeared to be a case of every blade for itself. And these days, dust devils were much more likely to be spotted capering over the diamond than actual human boys. In fact, the Little League had been disbanded several years before, due to a lack of interest.

"Well, Toomey, a crab apple don't fall too goddamn far from the son-of-a-bitchin' tree."

"May be, but just to be fair, that boy's—"

"I just might puke if I hear you say it, Toomey. Just don't rationalize for them."

Then there was the thin tinny sound of a cheap public address system. I recognized the amplified voice of the laughably orotund Charlie Clayton, who was practically an idiot but was widely considered to have a most mellifluous timbre and emceed many local events. "Ladies and gentlemen, Dickie Fitzgerald, the next mayor of Oceana, and the Panthrex Corporation, which manages with care the world's waste resources today, that we may waller in a cleaner, less awful tomorrow"—I looked at Jerry, disbelieving the scope of his activities—"in association with Squared Circle Productions of Louisville, present an afternoon of boxing for your entertainment and mortification!"

A desultory cheer burbled for a moment and quickly faded.

Smiling, Jerry turned to me and held up his hand, as if to say, Hold on there, big fella. "No thanks necessary, son. Let's just say I had final edit of Charlie's script. And as you may know, he couldn't introduce his own mother without a script."

Teddy Wilson Park was actually down a short dirt road off Clendenan Street and just on the other side of a small treeless hill, which Jerry and I wound around. Shortly the diamond came into view. The Needham boys had pulled the flatbed, onto which they had mounted the PA, into the shortstop's position, between second and third, and from it were passing out what I assumed—correctly— was campaign material. The crowd that had gathered round was sparse, and restless but not unhappy. Two women, a redhead and a blond who looked as if they might be working toward their GEDs at the School of Hard Knocks, dispensed hot dogs and cold drinks from a carnival trailer with an ear of corn exploding into popcorn painted on its side. Dickie and his mother milled about, catching an ear here and there, shaking hands, now and then forcing hugs on sweet but emotionally remote men and women. Dolin was huddled with a gentleman I didn't recognize but assumed was somehow connected to Panthrex—Bob Gregorio's replacement perhaps, the company's new man in the field. Of course they wouldn't waste any time at all on something like that.

A boxing ring had been erected in the center of the diamond, over the pitcher's mound. Red, white, and blue bunting, emblazoned with "Fitzgerald," in script, was draped on all four sides. On the other side of the ring, in the vicinity of the flatbed, there were twelve or fourteen bare-chested black men, half of whom looked as if they were waiting for a bus—no, because they appeared *anxious* as well, as if they were waiting for a bus in a very *bad* neighborhood, late at night, and were beginning to suspect that the last bus had run—while the other half lightly punched their gloved paws together, snorting and shaking their heads as if emerging from a pond and clearing away the water. Oddly, all the guys waiting on buses wore green-and-gold trunks (my campaign colors, more or less) and all the other guys, the snorting swimmers, wore red, white, and blue trunks (Dickie's colors, of course). I studied what were evidently my guys more closely. Slack gray skin, bad teeth, yellow eyes. They all seemed to be recovering from something virulent and debilitating.

"So, folks, let's get this show on the road," Charlie Clayton sonorously intoned, "because we've got a full card this afternoon. First up is the Louisville Slugger, Kweisi"—Charlie leaned away from the mike and whispered something to the kid; I'm certain he was checking the pronunciation of Kweisi; the kid nodded—"the Louisville Slugger, Kweisi Johnson." Kweisi bounded into the center of the ring, arms raised. "Versus Bobby 'Night Train' Fishback!" Night Train leaned against the ropes in his corner. "*Gentlemen. . . .*" The fighters stepped toward the center of the ring, glaring at each other, and Dolin Smits, who had changed into a black-and-white-striped referee's shirt, stepped between the pugilists, whispered a word or two, and stepped away, slapping his hands together. The boxers began to circle each other, wary, tight.

"What's *this* shit?" It was Antoine Crawford, the self-styled Ethiopian. He had come up behind us. "I mean, *really* now. What the fuck are those niggers *thinking*?" Antoine didn't really seem to care whether or not anybody answered, and I didn't. Neither did Jerry, who I think fell into the aforementioned category of ofays, and who I further think was just a little bit frightened by Antoine.

I said, "Hey, Antoine." He nodded, while watching the ring.

Then he said, "This shit has always been orchestrated for the edification of the white man. It's a minstrel show. It's an insult. And this shit will not do."

At that point, the Louisville Slugger made a sudden and deadly-looking move, flattening Night Train's nose. Blood squirted over his chest. Then I heard Antoine, faintly. "Aww . . . *shee*-it." His eyes fixed on the ring, Antoine moved past us, closer, shaking his head, his dreadlocks swaying and registering his very own personal repudiation of *whatever* it was those other Ethiopians were thinking.

In a moment, the Slugger delivered another vicious blow to Night Train's schnoz, really flattening it this time, and Night Train's knees lost the power to support him, like a hydraulic system from which the fluid had been drained, and they began to ease him down, down, and Night Train looked as if he were about to sit on a nonexistent stool, and then he did, sat hard on his ass and fell back. Blood poured from his nose over either cheek and pooled on the mat. His eyes were wide open, but he looked dead nevertheless. Unaware of the idiotic redundancy of it, Dolin went to the trouble to count him out.

A couple of guys with towels around their necks dragged Night

Train away. The toes of his boxing shoes bumped together as they removed him back to his corner. There, they slapped him around a little, shot water into his face, and waved smelling salts under his nose. Finally, he regained consciousness, but only in a narrowly technical sense—there wasn't anybody there, not behind those dull yellow eyes. Antoine had made his way to Night Train's corner, where he was hanging onto the ropes and saying something to Night Train's handlers, something that required great mad emphasis. Dreadlocks flew. Antoine kept pointing at the two blood-soaked towels, one carefully draped over each of Night Train's thighs, as if they'd been hung there to dry by someone very neat and precise. And Night Train himself *still* hadn't checked back in. His head lolled, but he was otherwise motionless, his arms dangling over the ropes like dead things, like cold clammy things dragged from the bottom of the river.

Antoine had since moved on, and was now amidst the boxers. Some appeared puzzled by this passionate man, others blank, but all were unmoved. Nonetheless, Antoine continued sawing at the air and kicked at something invisible. He shadowboxed before the real boxers, exhorted them to some unknown action. Antoine soon appeared to give up whatever mad crusade he was on; clearly annoyed with the boxers, he stomped away and left the grounds entirely.

Meanwhile, Charlie Clayton had returned to the center ring and commandeered the cheap, crackling, cordless microphone. He began and stopped, banging the mike against his thigh, before he began again in earnest. "At the fifty-six-second mark of the first round"—Charlie motioned the victor to center ring—"it's Kweisi the Louisville Slugger Johnson, by KO!" Charlie seized Kweisi's gloved right hand and thrust it over their heads. The gathering crowd—men, women, and children, but mostly men—cheered the winner. For his part, though, the winner didn't look much like a champ. No, he looked as though he'd rather be anywhere else but in Oceana, putting on an exhibition of professional mayhem for the ignorant crackers now spread out before him, grinning at him, and for the ultimate benefit of one Dickie Fitz—Fitz—Fitz*motherfuckingsomething*.

Charlie announced the fighters for the second bout on the card. Raheem Rashid Washington (in Dickie's colors) and Karl "the Crusher" Crawford (in mine). This time, the opponents didn't even appear to be in the same weight class—Raheem was half again the size of Karl. But it was not until Raheem caught Karl with a vicious uppercut in the opening seconds of the fight and sent him sailing halfway across the ring—a look of utter astonishment and abject disappointment and pain stamped on his face, a blow from which Karl would spend some time recovering—that it hit me. The fix was in. All of the fights were mismatches, setups, in which Dickie's guys would annihilate mine. The event was meant as metaphor! For the audience, at least, if not for the pugilists themselves, for whom it was all quite literal, frighteningly concrete. Karl was still out, but he seemed to be at peace now. His expression was downright beatific.

"That's it," I said to Jerry. "I'm with Antoine—I'm not up for any more of *this* shit."

Now they were dragging Karl out of the ring. They stacked him like a side of beef onto the three-legged stool in his corner. His head slumped to one side. A tiny white man with a shaved head and dramatic Brezhnevian eyebrows waved smelling salts under his nose.

"I don't blame you, son. And I'll catch up with you. But you'll forgive me if I stick around awhile." Jerry smiled, patted his hip pocket, and shrugged. "I've got twenty dollars riding on this next fight, on *our* guy." Jerry tapped out a cigarette and lit it, squinting against the sun. "Couldn't help myself."

Late that afternoon, following the so-called exhibition of boxing, in which my guys (with the single interesting, and I doubt miraculous, exception of the pugilist Jerry had wagered on) got their asses whipped embarrassingly, bloodily, and after Oceana had started to wind down for the day, to depopulate and deactivate, as it did every afternoon of the world—Mrs. Stamper pulling the shades at the post office, coal trucks coming fewer and farther between, minimum-wage commuters piloting big, old, dusty, nearly broken-down American cars back up into the hills and the hollers—we all ended up back at Grambos'. Drema, Lorraine, Hunt, Juanita, Willie, me. Bob Gregorio and Ike Chandler with his pal Tommy Cobb, who seemed to have found his voice, as he commented acidly upon the commentary around him. And of course Jerry. Lastly and most devastatingly, Jerry. Because with him, he carried the word. The information. As always. And it did not add up to what a sober-minded fellow might consider particularly good news.

It was a little after six, so the polls had only just closed. But Jerry, as always, was right on top of the situation. He barreled into Grambos' projecting a strong, almost comically masculine sense of purpose, but Willie's mom, Juanita, with some help from Hunt, was right in the middle of a long, tragicomic tale—and the distraction was more than welcome—about a discredited country doctor a couple of counties over, a man who had suffered a downright biblical run of bad luck.

Everybody was laughing and Juanita was taking various oaths, swearing it was a true story. But Jerry wasn't amused. He smiled, but it was forced—he looked as if his face might splinter and fall to the floor in shards. Then he mouthed my name and nodded, toward the empty pool room. I excused myself, slipped out of the booth—Willie gave my hand a little squeeze—and followed my putative second cousin (or *whatever*) into the next room.

It was empty, the blinds drawn and parallel strips of sunlight marking the floor. A melancholic aura hovered about the unused pool tables. Jerry leaned up against one and lit two cigarettes at once, then passed me one. "Well, Toomey," he said, "here's what it's looking like. No point in sugarcoating it." Jerry drew smoke deep into his lungs, then began with what he had come to say, emitting little feathery jets of blue vapor as he spoke. "But there just ain't no easy way to put it."

With six out of seven precincts reporting—the seventh being the somewhat remote, majority African-American precinct of Davies' Bottom—Dickie was ahead in the vote 1,977 to 1,823. Adding insult to injury, the good folks of Oceana had cast their lot with Dickie quite consistently, if not overwhelmingly. Dickie Fitz had won each of the reporting precincts, by an average of just over twenty-five votes. "Dick Hed" Fitzgerald, whose well-known adult record included: breaking promises, disregarding responsibilities, betraying trusts, abusing his namesake, punching his wife, and trying to murder his buddy. But Oceanans nevertheless took a look at Dickie and me side by side, studied us, weighed us one against the other, and said, "Dickie." And although I thought I'd arrived at a point where I wasn't going to be badly stung by this eventuality, the actual dimensions of my anguish now were downright Shakespearean. All I wanted was to slay a half dozen cowards and call it a day.

But that would have been impolitic. Instead, I shook Jerry's hand and thanked him for all he'd done, excused myself, and returned to our table. I scooted in next to Willie and whispered the news. She cupped my chin in her hand and kissed me. Then I told her—although there was a sense in which I was asking permission—that I was going to drive back out to my place, spend a little time alone composing my thoughts. And she said of course, and sent me on my way with the sweetest smile since the mother of man gazed down on the baby Jesus.

Then, three miles from my place—or, in other words, about halfway between Oceana and home, or, in still other words, the middle of fucking nowhere—SEWELL-2 threw a rod. KA-BOOM. Shit! Shitfuckingfire! We—SEWELL-2 and I—sputtered to a stop and pulled to the side of the road as best we could. I slammed the heel of my hands into the steering wheel a few times for good measure, and then leaned wholly into it. I sighed. I ground my teeth. And because the road was narrow and the shoulder nonexistent, SEWELL-2 was going to be something of an obstacle for anyone trying to pass this way. But there was nothing else to do. I was going to have to walk the last three miles. Which actually turned out to be quite therapeutic. Just about exactly what I needed.

About a half mile from my place, Zero trotted out of the woods and joined me for the rest of the walk home. He'd watch the road for a second, and then glance at me, back at the road, his tongue slapping from side to side and trailing a string of saliva.

As soon as I walked in the door, the phone rang. It was Barbara McBean, the reporter for the *Oceana Shopper & Gazetteer*. She didn't exactly say so, but she was looking for a concession statement. And that was OK with me.

"I'm sorry, Toomey, but it looks like it's all over," she said, "and I was just wondering if we might get a word or two for the record."

"Well, let's see—"

"By the way, Toomey, I voted for you. All of us over here at the *Shopper* did." "All of us" amounted to Barbara and her uncle, Conrad McBean, who owned the paper, Van Dwyer, whose function was unclear to me, and old Mrs. Fincastle, who was more or less a secretary and receptionist and Conrad McBean's all around aide-de-camp.

"Thanks. I appreciate it, Barbara." What was there to say? "OK. Here goes my word or two for the record. Ready?"

"Ready."

Then I realized that I wasn't, in fact, ready to commit to anything. I *thought* I was. I thought it'd be easy. I really did. "You know what, Barbara? Can you hold for a minute?"

"Of course, Toomey, sure. Take all the time you need."

I set the receiver on the table and lit a cigarette. I smoked it about halfway down before I stubbed it out. Still, nothing was coming to me. I mean, what was there to say? *Good luck, Dickie?* I didn't believe I could wrap my mouth around those words, not in any convincing fashion. Stumped, I walked across the kitchen to the sink, lifted out a water glass from that morning and rinsed it out. Then I filled it with bourbon. I drank that standing at the sink, and then I filled it again. My eyes were full of tears, though I was not sad. A little angry, perhaps. A little nonplused. But the tears themselves were just whiskey tears.

Glass in hand, I decamped from the kitchen. From the house.

Down by the pond, I smoked a cigarette, finished my whiskey, watched the light fade behind Johnson Knob, and thought about the night I'd decided to run for mayor of Oceana. It had only been six months since then, half a year, but it seemed like a lifetime. With the sun gone, there was now a slight chill in the air. I lit another cigarette and stood on the dock, out over the water, smoking it. And it occurred to me that Deddy had been *wrong*—that only a fool himself would have mistaken Jesse James for a fool, under any circumstances at all.

Assuming that Hunt had remained in town and was probably still at Grambos'—it's true he wasn't particularly sociable, but once you got him going it was like he was making up for lost opportunities—I trudged through the woods toward his cabin. I was on autopilot, though, and couldn't have told you what I was headed there for. I walked along the high ridge that followed the North Fork, down through the stand of ginkgoes, and onto Hunt's porch. Several largish skulls were soaking in a washtub on the porch, in a bleach marinade. I went on in.

I found his whiskey and built a small fire in the woodstove. And I sat there sipping whiskey in front of the woodstove until I couldn't hardly hold my head up. Then I climbed into the loft, where Hunt had an old mattress. I lit an oil lamp and tried to make myself comfortable, but there was something hard and bulky between the blankets. It was one volume of the old journal. I turned the lamp up a notch or two, propped myself on a couple of pillows, and began to read:

April 1, 1841

Although the water has subsided a great deal, it still whorls and eddies beyond its banks, sweeping away all the dead things. Chickens, raccoons, dogs, rats, and, not infrequently, human beings. Not to mention uprooted saplings and deadwood. Enormous, gas-swollen cows bob on the current as if weightless. The sky remains leaden, as if it may yet rain again.

My fellow passengers aboard ship, most of whom were foreigners like myself and had never witnessed the havoc wrought by the spring torrent, stood at the rail, their jaws hanging wide. For me, the experience only confirmed once more my impression that everything in America is vast and awesome and perilous.

Yesterday, we arrived in Cincinnati, a city that is for the most part set against the steep hills that loom over the river. There are of course some Irishmen here, but there are almost certainly many more Germans, a goodly number of whom apply their well-known industry to the production of sausages and ale, as well as to the proprietorship of pubs, or, in the local parlance, gasthauses. Last evening, I spent many felicitous hours in one of these well-run establishments.

It was built on a wharf, out over the wide, surging Ohio River. The water, presently the color of mud due to the flooding, flows beneath the well-worn floorboards inside the place, and the foamy whorling eddies are occasionally visible through some less than flush planking. The carpenters, I guessed, were probably Irish, my countrymen being altogether less fastidious than the Teutonic races. Later, I discovered that this was indeed the case. The bustling ruddy Frau who operates the business—and who serves great steaming platters of kraut and wursts and knocks together the skulls of the deserving few—confirmed my hypothesis with evident disdain for the men who built the place, without, I should mention, casting any aspersions on me. In any event, I ate more than I had in weeks, and I drank two pails of the bitter, refreshing draught. Then I found myself at loose ends, so to speak.

Relieving myself into the river likewise with several other gentlemen, I heard the faint whistles and jeers of speculative sport—of gambling. I felt the old familiar tingle of anticipation. I shook myself dry, buttoned up, and walked alone along the riverbank until I came upon a long, low, ramshackling dockhouse, lit and raucous within. Since the building lacked any sign of being a public house, I knocked, waited a moment, and then—satisfied that it was indeed a common building— let myself in. And rich and edifying it was.

It was crowded, to such an extent that I was forced to inch sideways into the heart of the room. The air was filled with tobacco smoke, and downy feathers wafted side to side, from ceiling to floor, settling on shoulders, in hair, over the floorboards. At the center of the room there hung a lamp, and beneath the lamp two cocks fought, razored talon to razored talon and bloodied to fowly pulps. Of course with all the Germans about there was an ocean of beer, but, like a miracle or a revelation, there was good Irish whiskey to be had as well. I smoked and I drank and I bet on every glorious contest. And although my memory falters, even fails me altogether, I must surmise I lost my wagers because today I am poorer by half.

I had a dream last night, and a disturbing night fancy it was. I had fallen overboard, into the rain-swollen river, and was carried along bobbing and twisting in the current with the bloated cows and uprooted trees. Finally I was able to grasp a sapling firmly anchored to the muddy riverbank and pull myself to safety. I was wet and shivery and bereft of money and possessions, but I was alive and glad of it. The violence of the dream is what woke me.

Once I was fully awake—and convinced no danger loomed—I got out of bed, walked across the cool oak floor, and stood at the window for a long time, watching the moon arc across the velvety black sky. My eyes stung with tears as I realized it was the selfsame moon my father might've seen last night, if only he'd gone outside to have a look. But I knew he probably hadn't. Knew he certainly hadn't, for he was not given to poetry. Or to lunacy as he would have it—and pardon the pun.

He never said I would not make it to Kentucky, not out loud where I could debate him fair, but his flat iron eyes said it for him. And I very nearly came to hate him for it. He couldn't bring himself to believe in land purchased through the post, land across the sea on another continent. No, the truth is he couldn't bring himself to believe there was any more for a Spooner than what he himself had. But from where I sit, right here, right now, in my room on the second floor of this hotel on the hill, I can see Kentucky stretching away beyond the churning, muddy river, and damn me to hell for even thinking it, but I want to share it with my father.

I am almost there.

I awoke to the smell of smoky sausages frying and rich coffee brewing, but it was still dark up in the windowless loft—where it would remain gloomy throughout the sunniest day—and I was a little disoriented. Someone slept beside me, snoring very quietly, almost inaudibly, and I gently peeled away the blankets to see who it was. Willie. She seemed to be dreaming, the flat disks of her eyes circling beneath delicate lids. Someone else was downstairs, evidently preparing breakfast. That would be . . . *Hunt.* Right. *Because* . . . because I was in Hunt's cabin? Yes. Definitely.

Barbara McBean. Well, doggonit. I'd have to give her a call, first thing. Hand her an exclusive, as it were.

Lying there, I had the odd sensation of feeling cleansed, of having been distilled down to some pure, core essence. Of being more authentically, starkly, me.

I climbed out of bed, pulled on my jeans, and started down the ladder. Climbing past a window, the sun fell on my face and I sneezed.

"Toomey." Hunt was looking up from the stove, a little startled at my entrance. "Good morning. C'mon over here and sit down. I'll get you a cup of coffee." I dismounted the ladder and sat down at the table. Hunt poured a cup of strong coffee, added cream, and set it in front of me. "We looked for you all over the place last night.

her slightly swollen belly—she was just beginning to show—somehow adding to the effect.

I hadn't really thought about it before, but at some point that afternoon it occurred to me that my wife's mother would now be my aunt, and my uncle would now be my wife's stepfather. But I quit joking about how down-home and Kentucky this was when I saw how uncomfortable it was making everybody—some may have been overly sensitive to the stereotypes perpetuated by popular culture and the media, and some may in fact have been only a couple of generations removed from similarly cozy arrangements. I was just joking, and I'm pretty sure everybody knew it, but that didn't seem to make much difference, so pretty soon I just shut up.

Ronald Coleman Pons (aka Ronnie the Reverend), the old gospelmonger's boy—who was, by now, well along into middle age himself—was all set to officiate, but he was getting fidgety. He had another wedding in town at 4:30, which I had earlier promised him wouldn't be a problem. But Ronnie was by nature an anxious fellow—I always suspected it was all those gloomy hellfire sermons he'd had to endure as a boy—and I saw that I was going to have to get this show on the road, despite that everybody seemed to be having such an informal good time just the way it was.

So we took our positions in the coffee tree arbor. Juanita and Eugenia hustled around, arms waving, hands coaxing and shooing, arranging the guests and the members of the wedding. Swift Camp Creek provided not only an ambient burbling—which announced its passing, like a train whistle dopplering away into the distance—but a silvery reflection that danced over everybody and on the pale undersides of the leaves above. And from everywhere, it seemed, I could hear the sound of Barbara's shutter repeatedly snapping.

Then we were ready. And then there's a long blank, because I evidently suffered something like a traumatic blackout and don't remember any of it—not until I kissed Willie, and that was like coming to out of a deep sleep. Or a trance. But when I asked, everybody said I'd done fine, hadn't behaved in any way at all that reminded them of a zombie. I figured they would've said that no matter what, though.

"Now, if you two lovebirds could just step over here to one side, please?" Willie and I were still locked in an embrace, and Ronnie Pons had placed his hand on my shoulder, as if to remove us to one side so he could proceed. And he did. Before Willie and I were really through with our part of the ceremony, before we had achieved any satisfactory closure on the most momentous single moment in our lives, Ronnie brought forward Hunt and Juanita to join *them* in holy matrimony.

"OK . . . Hunt?"

Hunt had been flitting his gaze left and right, nervous, but now he snapped to, projecting an odd martial countenance. "Yes, sir!"

"Do you, Hunt Spooner, take Juanita Rains to be your lawfully wedded wife, to have and to hold, for better or for worse, for richer or for poorer, in sickness and in health? Will you love, comfort, honor, and respect her? Will you share all life has to offer with Juanita from this day forward?"

"Goddamn right, I will, Ronnie." Hunt grinned like an idiot at his bride. Ronnie sighed, looked to Heaven for strength, and said, "That ain't the way it goes, Hunt." Then Hunt smiled even more broadly and said, simply, "I do."

"And do you, Juanita Rains, take Hunt Spooner to be your lawfully wedded husband, to have and to hold, for better or for worse, for richer or for poorer, in sickness and in health? Will you love, comfort, honor, and respect him? Will you share all life has to offer with Hunt from this day forward?"

"I will."

"Then with the power vested in me—"

"Ronnie?" Hunt had removed a sheet of paper from his jacket and was now unfolding it.

"Right. I'm sorry, Hunt." Even here, Ronnie, Jr., did not abandon his abstracted monotone. "Hunt Spooner, ladies and gentlemen, has something he wants to say. Go ahead, Hunt."

"It's just a poem I'd like to read." Hunt held up the paper, as if to demonstrate to those assembled that there was indeed a poem. "But I didn't write it." And then he began, summoning a clear, most sonorous elocution.

Let us feast to your shapely figure
—swift, mighty—side by side,
Accept my best poems and songs
bright-languid, noble, decorous one.
No woman but you in my home
its mistress may you be,
False women and all the wealth I see
none of mine will pay them heed.
Turn toward me your sole and palm
and your brown hair in beauty,
Your keen green young round eye
—may I fall in feast on your moist locks!

Clearly a little discomforted, Ronnie Pons pulled himself together enough to utter the words "With the power vested in me by the Commonwealth of Kentucky, I pronounce you husband and wife. Hunt, you may kiss the bride." And with that, Hunt fell to feasting on Juanita's moist locks. She gasped and reached for her yellow turban as it tumbled to the grass.

I thanked Ronnie and apologized for any delay. We wandered away from the bower of coffee trees and toward his old Cadillac El Dorado, and I discreetly slipped him a one-hundred-dollar bill, twice his actual fee. Then, before the congregated celebrants could begin disassembling, I called for their attention. This part of the program had gone unannounced. "Ladies and gentleman, the Right Reverend Mark Smith, who's come all the way up from Nashville to be here with us this afternoon."

The "Reverend" Smith, or Mark, as he asked me to call him, was a friend of a friend of a friend. He wore crazily mismatched, brightly patterned clothes including a T-shirt that read "Elvis Hitler"—he told me that was a band in Nashville—along with black high-top Converses, and his longish, salt-and-pepper hair was pushed back on his head, in a sort of modified Sun Records pompadour. He was young, or at least no older than I. And despite that his ecclesiastical credentials were mail-ordered from the back of a magazine, as far as I could determine he was ordained to perform legally binding ceremonies. Which was symbolically important to me. The Reverend Smith advanced up through the middle of the audience—smiling left and right, intensely, as if he intended to merge with his new and temporary parishioners—and took his place at the front. He carried no Bible, no prepared text.

Then the Reverend Smith, Mark, said, "Will the intendeds please come before me." He motioned gently, fluidly—physically, he was an extraordinarily graceful man—to his left and to his right, and Drema and Lorraine appeared before him from opposite directions, sailing across the grass in their Surinamese ceremonial robes. Diamonds of sunlight pouring through the leaves danced over the ground, over smiling friends, over everything. And it struck me that *this* was what ought to be meant by perfect, holy communion.

This, where the sickening aroma of carnations and roses and lilies—of death—did not roar up around me, unbidden. *This*, an utterly clear affirmation of life, for the living, who, by god, need it every now and then (I don't think that's asking too much). *This*, simply one of the best ideas we terribly flawed human beings ever came up with.

The Reverend Smith smiled serenely and said, "Good afternoon, Drema. Good afternoon, Lorraine. Here." He reached between them, joining Drema's right hand to Lorraine's left. Then he stretched wide his arms, and placed his right hand on Drema's left shoulder, and his left hand on Lorraine's right shoulder. "That's better, isn't it?"

Then a pair of blue jays began to squawk, in the tall, broad coffee tree behind the Reverend Smith, who turned to see what all the commotion was about. Drema and Lorraine craned their necks to see around the reverend. From the dire and insistent sound of it, I wondered if maybe a cat hadn't got up in the tree. But then the blue jays flitted away, taking turns at mugging a panicked cardinal, nipping at his tailfeathers, as all three shot through the trees and disappeared.

At this point, the Reverend Smith dipped into his jacket pocket, fished around for a moment, and then deposited something into his mouth. He swallowed hard, as if taking pills dry. And a look of satisfaction spread over his face.

"OK, where were we?" The Reverend Smith rejoined Drema's and Lorraine's hands, replaced his own hands upon their shoulders. He cleared his throat. Sand-colored Surinamese robes rippled like summertime curtains in a soft window breeze. "Lorraine Basile, seeker, wayfarer in the universe, child of God and of man, do you approach this union with a solemnity of heart and lightness of soul? And do you intend to be fair and faithful, forsaking all others?"

Before Lorraine could affirm her betrothal, a commotion arose behind the temporary dais, from the same coffee tree the blue jays had come screaming out of. What seemed like a thousand—or ten thousand!—blackbirds suddenly lifted out of the tree as one, turned in the sky like dark water rising from a drain, and soared east. A long, low groaning issued from the tree itself, followed by what sounded like a small-caliber pistol shot. Then there was a series of crashes. Drema, Lorraine, and the Reverend all ducked and moved away from the tree, in an impulsive, lizard-brain reaction. Riding a large, rotten limb like it was a bucking bronc, Odel, descendent, emerged from the dense bower and hit the ground with an awful thud. He hit facing down. A silver pistol squirted out, ending up several yards from him. Odel tried to lift himself, with a sort of modified push-up, and collapsed on his right arm. Jerry and Lester jumped over to him. Jerry grabbed the pistol. Lester tried to roll his patient over onto his back, but the patient resisted, if weakly, being the contrary sort. Jerry pocketed the pistol and returned to his folding chair as if nothing at all had happened. And I knew that the pistol was going to end up either in a pawnshop or in Jerry's private collection.

Odel rose partially and looked at us over his shoulder, his face twisted with pain. "Forsake all others? *My ass!*" Then he collapsed again. Lester managed to get Odel up and maneuver him into an empty chair.

"He's got a busted flipper," Lester pronounced wryly, "but this SOB'll be just fine." You could see that Odel thought the "SOB" business gratuitous and a little mean, and that it hurt his feelings. Odel cradled the broken arm with his good hand, cutting his eyes left and right before directing his gaze to his lap.

The Reverend Smith reorganized, and looked at Lorraine. "I do?"

"I do."

"And Drema Spooner, seeker, wayfarer in the universe, child of God and of man, do you approach this union with a solemnity of heart and lightness of soul? And do you intend to be fair and faithful, forsaking all others?"

"I do."

"Well, good. Insofar as Kentucky revised statute allows it—and I only regret that this is not a ceremony sanctioned by law, but I promise if that ever changes we'll get together and do it again, gratis—I pronounce you wife and wife. Drema, Lorraine, you may kiss one another."

Then, one by one, the six of us descended the green bank and let the Reverend Smith baptize us in the cool clean waters of Swift Camp Creek. He had insisted on it as his payment, saying he couldn't accept money for the holy work he did. And I agreed, despite that it was not clear to me exactly what it was we were being baptized into. Mark, after all, was strictly nondenominational. But it didn't matter, and I was glad I'd agreed to it. When it was my turn, the reverend held my nose and placed his hand in the center of my back, then lowered me for a moment into the water. When I emerged—my hair slick on my head and water running down across my neck and eyes, and blinking it away—I felt as much like me, as much like the person I *imagined* myself to be, as at any moment of my entire life. Cleansed and new, ready for my new roles, loaded for bear or whatever else the vast Unknown Unknowable—what with its well-known penchant for infinite variety—cared to throw at me.

Following the ceremonies, and after we the six newly betrothed had changed into dry and less formal attire, we all drove back out to my place for the reception. Drema, Lorraine, Willie, and I were in SEWELL-2, and Hunt and Juanita were in my pickup, which Merle

Cooke had finally repaired and returned to me. But happy to be driving SEWELL-2, I'd more or less turned the truck over to Hunt, who'd not had a vehicle of his own in years. Or ever, as far as I knew—not even in the days when he was collecting radiator hose. He used to trundle the stuff back to his shack on a bicycle with a basket on the front.

Juanita and Willie had planned the reception, then left its execution up to Jeanie and Janine Earle, thirtysomething sisters who shared a little house in town and catered locally, though there was not enough demand for their services to constitute what could reasonably be called "making a living." But it was more than a hobby, too, and the Earle girls carried it off beautifully. They cleaned out the barn, and erected a stage at one end—or, rather, hired the Needham boys to do it—where the sliding barn doors opened against the night. They reproduced the menu Juanita and Willie had decided on, which featured, among other delicacies, wild mushroom empanadas, smoked salmon fingers with cucumber sauce, paper-thin curried potato pancakes, and a fantastically rococo melon basket. And, at my insistence, baby smoked oysters on toast points with a dab of French's mustard and a coffee pot full of hot Dr Pepper. They erected a champagne fountain beneath a twirling disco mirror ball. Then they tried to get out of the way once the reception began, but I persuaded them to stay, enjoy like everybody else the fruits—so to speak—of their labor.

Right at six the barn began to fill up. We had invited twice as many guests to the reception as to the wedding, including, among others, Odel Dent, who had convincingly sworn that his vendetta had reached its logical terminus, and who admitted he'd be a fool to continue it—especially now that he was carrying around his "busted flipper" in a sling. We also extended invitations to the Smitses and the Fitzgeralds. It just seemed like it was now time to come back together. We were all Oceanans and we had to live together, one way or another. So did our children and our children's children. And you can't think about a thing like that too soon.

Hunt cut in and danced a dance with Willie. So I cut in on Dolin and danced a dance with Naomi Smits. Which started a chain reaction of cutting in, and soon everyone was dancing with someone other than the one they were used to dancing with. We all twirled beneath the disco ball. Carry Me Home sawed its way through several accommodating slow ones. Then they cut loose with a real rocker—"Family Tradition"—and broke the spell.

Alma and Inky Fitzgerald had arrived with Dickie Junior not long after the reception started, but big Dickie had not. Willie and I made a point of making them feel welcome. We showed them to the hors d'oeuvres and the champagne fountain, shared a toast with them. I poured Dickie Junior a Roy Rogers.

He began to stammer an apology for giving me the finger that day, but I cut him off and told him I'd never think of it again.

Finally, around nine, Dickie himself wandered into the barn. Still, twenty years later, he stood taller than all the others. He looked around, searching, his gaze swiveling left and right. Then he spotted me, and started across the barn. My sense of déjà vu was acute. He pulled up before me. He looked uncomfortable, like a skeptical nonbeliever arriving for his first session of group therapy.

"Toomey." He stuck out his hand and we shook. "I still feel cheated out the thing—I'm not gonna lie about it—but I wanted you to know I've withdrawn my demand for a recount. It's over far as I'm concerned. So, congratulations. I know it's a little belated, but it's the best I can do."

"I appreciate it nonetheless, Dickie." We shook again. "I'm going to step over here for a smoke," I said, nodding in the direction of the barn door. Dickie followed. Out in the open, I lit a cigarette, and Dickie asked if he could bum one. Dickie Junior and Zero were running in circles around each other—Dickie flapping his arms and Zero barking—and then around Ike Chandler, who was kneeling in the field and preparing fireworks. The sun was setting, and the sky was streaked with purple and orange.

Watching his son and my dog, Dickie Senior leaned his back into the barn door's frame, cocked one leg against it, and crossed his arms. Exhaling smoke, he said, "This is the only cigarette I've had since my heart attack." I looked at him. "Yeah, it really was a heart attack, Toomey. Not a bad one, but it was a wake-up call. You know my dad had one when he was young, too. It killed him."

"I wish you well with it, Dickie."

"Sure you do, Toomey." Dickie took several puffs of his cigarette and held it at arm's length, examining it. "Consider this something like a peace pipe. And maybe . . . I don't know 'maybe' what. Just that things look a little different to me now." He stubbed out what was left of his cigarette and dropped it into his shirt pocket. "Well." Dickie stuck his hands in his pockets and looked around back inside the barn. Then he brought his attention back to me. "I didn't really intend to stick around. I just wanted to, you know, congratulate you. So."

He turned and headed for the open door. I didn't try to stop him. He walked over to Drema and said something, smiling and rubbing a spot on the side of his head, and she nodded and said something back. Then, on his way out, he bent to the buffet to snatch a cupful of melon balls. I watched him walk through the high grass and climb into his pickup. And as he drove away, I watched a cloud of pale dust form over the road in the gathering night.

Just after dark, Ike Chandler assembled a pile of fireworks outside the barn. It was a new moon—a total blackout—and there was a brilliant lather of stars against the soft black sky, like crushed diamonds dusted over velvet. The old Milky Way spiraling quietly and imperceptibly through space and time, just as it has for 15 billion years. But then, kneeling in the adjacent pasture, Ike—with the "help" of Odel and Dickie Junior and Zero, who circled the production, dipping his head, smiling, wagging his tail—lit a Screaming Rebel Rocket, and, lo and behold, announced the presence of man a-way up there. The rocket sputtered and spat for a moment, throwing off sparks, before it roared into the night above and exploded into a holy icon, a replication in miniature of the big bang, the beginning of time itself.

Close to midnight, Carry Me Home wrapped up their Lynyrd Skynyrd medley and launched into an extended—and remarkably spirited—version of "These Foolish Things," as per my request, made several weeks in advance so the band could learn the old tune. Carry Me Home had now dimmed the multicolored lights over the makeshift stage, and the boys swayed romantically behind their instruments, behind squared-off beards and silver shades. Their sax player had taken center stage. This was to be the evening's finale. Every now and then a firecracker still popped softly in the distance.

> *O will you never let me be?*
> *O will you never set me free?*
> *The ties that bound us*
> *Are still around us,*

There's no escape that I can see.
And still those little things remain
That bring me happiness or pain . . .

Willie and I held each other close, turning in the dust, cheek to cheek.

A tinkling piano in the next apartment,
Those stumbling words that told you what my heart meant,
A fairground's painted swings,
These foolish things remind me of you . . .

Drema dipped Lorraine, and then they spun like marionettes, connected only by each other's hand.

Gardenia perfume lingering on a pillow,
Wild strawberries only seven francs a kilo,
And still my heart has wings,
These foolish things remind me of you . . .

Hunt and Juanita had taken a seat on a bale of hay, and were engrossed in one another, though not speaking at all as far as I could tell.

The winds of March that made my heart a dancer,
A telephone that rings, but who's to answer?
Oh, how the ghost of you clings,
These foolish things remind me of you. . . .

And on and on and on, just like that, in a long slow fade toward dawn. . . .

But I suppose all of that still begs the enduring aboriginal question: Now what?

Well, I've sworn an oath obliging me to "defend the constitution of the commonwealth and uphold the laws and ordinances of the municipality," i.e., Oceana—and I intend to do so. But enlarging upon my sworn duty—which, taken by itself, leaves a lot of room for personal interpretation—I propose to govern with a steady and benevolent hand. Of course that's the relatively easy part. So, other than that? It probably won't come as much of a surprise, but I've been making a list.

Resolved:

I will bathe every morning and floss every night. I will quit smoking—soon. I will take up jogging, and perhaps in a year, maybe two, run in a marathon. I will get my total dietary fat down to 20 percent or less. I will become a temperate fellow, a man of moderation, which is not to say a dark thunderhead over the parade grounds, either. I will live one day and then the next, because there's no other way. And, most important, I will humor, encourage, and protect Willie and the sprout—the sprout!—who I've about decided to hope is a girl, a girl in the image of sweet Wilhelmina Rains herself, a girl who cartwheels among the flowering apple trees in the spring and tans the color of honey and tosses her wild black hair against the blue, blue sky. . . .

Plus:

I might even learn a trade!

Take up Japanese!

Skydive with the Mann O' War Fly-Devils!

And when it's all said and done, they'll swear that I was in the thick of it, that I was *engagé*, that there's no denying I was there.

There there!

ACKNOWLEDGMENTS

Since writing this book turned out to be more of a collaborative effort than I ever imagined it would, there are a few people I must thank for their indispensable assistance: Robert Olen Butler, writer and teacher extraordinaire, for support and guidance every step of the way; Staige Blackford, the editor of *Virginia Quarterly Review*, for giving me a chance; the Kentucky Arts Council, one of the Bluegrass State's most essential agencies, for a well-timed and much needed Al Smith Fellowship; Maria Massie, my agent, for efforts above and beyond the call of duty; Moira Crone, my editor, for suggestions that proved invaluable; Tom Marksbury and Frank Schaap, my excellent friends, for their very kind permission to use their heart-rending tune, "One of Our Weaker Moments"; Will Herrick, a weird but lovable genius, for indefatigable computer assistance; Mark Smith, an inestimable preacher pal of mine who lives in Nashville, for obvious reasons; and my mother and father, especially, for years and years of forgiving indulgence.